HATCHET GIRLS

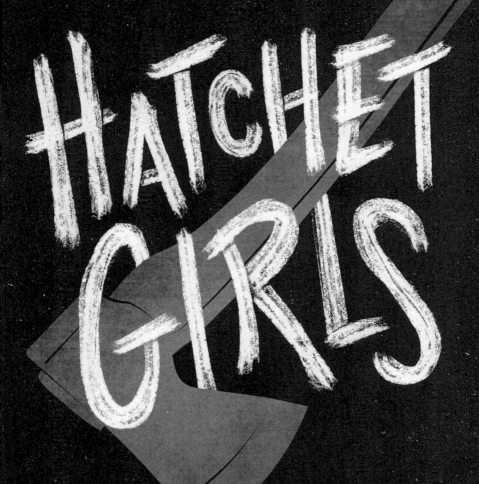

HATCHET GIRLS

DIANA RODRIGUEZ WALLACH

DELACORTE PRESS

Text copyright © 2023 by Diana Rodriguez Wallach
Jacket art used under license from Shutterstock.com
Lettering by Stephanie Gafron and Liz Dresner

All rights reserved. Published in the United States by Delacorte Press, an imprint of Random House Children's Books, a division of Penguin Random House LLC, New York.

Delacorte Press is a registered trademark and the colophon is a trademark of Penguin Random House LLC.

GetUnderlined.com

Educators and librarians, for a variety of teaching tools, visit us at RHTeachersLibrarians.com

Library of Congress Cataloging-in-Publication Data is available upon request.
ISBN 978-0-593-64341-9 (hardcover) — ISBN 978-0-593-64342-6 (lib. bdg.) —
ISBN 978-0-593-64343-3 (ebook)

The text of this book is set in 11.5-point Adobe Garamond Pro.
Interior design by Cathy Bobak

Printed in the United States of America
10 9 8 7 6 5 4 3 2 1
First Edition

In memory of Esther Clinton,
scholar, writer, teacher, and tamer of dragons.
May all who read this say her name.

All ye, who in future days
Walk by Nunckatessett stream
Love not him who hummed his lay
Cheerful to the parting beam,
But the Beauty that he wooed
In this quiet solitude

This inscription was carved in the year 1862 into a rock in the Bridgewater Triangle. Still visible today, the rock has been dubbed Solitude Stone because a missing person's body was once discovered nearby.

CHAPTER ONE

TESSA

When your life changes forever—fundamentally tumbles off an already-dark cliff into a holy-hell-bottomless pit of destruction—you shouldn't be wearing a fuzzy bathrobe.

Tessa Gomez snuggled into the plush white fabric, tightening the wrap's belt as peppermint tea wafted from the mug beside her. It was October, that limbo period when it was too early in the season for her mother to turn on the heat but too cold in the apartment for them not to. Massachusetts was chillier than Philadelphia, somewhat, but that wasn't the issue; what took getting used to was the length of the cold. Here winter started weeks earlier than it had back home.

Home.

It had been a little over a year since they'd moved to Fall River, and still Tessa had unpacked only her clothes. There was nothing tacked onto her beige bedroom walls, and no photos were shoved into the crease of the mirror above her desk. She hadn't gone on a single date. And most of the people she hung out with were actually her brother Vik's friends.

Tessa's cell phone pinged, and her eyes flicked from the rom-com on her laptop to the photo in the group text. Kids from school were huddled around a bonfire, red Solo cups in hand. *Party at Izzy's!*

She ignored it.

Her brother disapproved of the New and Improved Tessa—the girl who stayed home on Friday nights to finish articles for the school newspaper, who deleted her entire social media presence without regret, and who legitimately saw chilling with a movie as a personal reward. It was as if every evening she spent huddled under her down comforter only increased Vik's worry that he was losing the Tessa he grew up with—only she didn't know who that was anymore. Or maybe she didn't want to remember.

Vik would graduate high school this spring. Tessa next spring. And until then, she had to power through.

Tessa focused on the movie as she heard Tía Dolores pull the cork on a bottle of wine in the kitchen. Their apartment, which sat above a laundromat painted obnoxiously pink, had only six rooms—four bedrooms, one bathroom, and a combo living room–kitchen. Tía Dolores and her girlfriend, Frankie, leased the place three years ago, after Frankie graduated from law school. Tía Dolores was Tessa's godmother, and her mom's sister, and she had insisted her door was always open—especially after the funeral. It was Tessa who had convinced her mom and her brother that they needed a change, somewhere devoid of memories painfully erupting in twisted masks every time they turned a city block.

Tessa's cell phone pinged again, and she set her jaw, not even glancing at the screen. *Vik,* she thought, *I already told you I'm not coming.*

She and her brother grieved differently. Vik seized onto life, falling in love within weeks of crossing their new high school's threshold—and not with just any teenage girl. Like many towns in America that had *one* family who seemed to own everything, Fall River had theirs, and the name was Morse. Their wealth stretched beyond a successful clothing boutique or catering business; no, the Morses owned historic textile mills converted into swanky loft apartments and hip office space. In an otherwise blue-collar town, their mansion took up an entire block.

So it was quite the high school scandal when Mariella ditched her longtime boyfriend, who drove a BMW and played golf with her father, for Tessa's brother. And with Mariella came a collection of okay acquaintances. Well, maybe one was a little more than okay.

Another ping.

Omigod, I said no! Tessa groaned, eyes stubbornly locked on the YA adaptation she was watching. The book was better.

Another ping. Then another. And another.

Reluctantly, she gave her phone a sideways glance and spied a firework display of bright-blue bubbles.

Text. Text. Text.

Tessa shifted her laptop, its slick surface swishing against her comforter as she reached for her phone.

Text. Text.

Her stomach tightened, bracing for another kick from life.

Text. Text.

She closed her eyes and plucked the device with quivering fingers. She had been here before. Bad news carried a weight that could sink into your gut before your brain fully knew what was happening.

She filled her lungs; then she opened her eyes and took in the words now trembling on her smudged screen.

Is this YOUR Vik?

Did he do it?

Do you know where your brother is?

OMG, poor Mariella!

Seriously, an AXE????

These weren't messages from the usual group chat. These were texts from random classmates, dozens of them, ones she hardly knew, people she didn't even think had her number.

Then her eyes caught on a few lines from Phil, her focus sharpening on information from someone she trusted: *Did u see the news? There are reporters on Mariella's lawn. She's not answering. This has gotta be a mistake. Call me.*

There was no link. No details. *The news?* Tessa flicked on her tiny flat-screen TV. She switched to a local channel. It was midnight, not a news hour, yet as Phil had indicated, the station showed a reporter in a gumball-pink skirt suit standing in front of the iron fence that edged the Morse family home. She was holding a microphone.

Sapphire and ruby lights swirled from cop cars in the background. An ambulance from South Coast Memorial idled in the circular driveway, its back doors swung open, ready to be loaded with whatever newsworthy emergency was about to make itself known. Someone inside that renovated two-hundred-year-old mansion was injured so badly it warranted a TV crew. Lots of them.

Vik had picked up Mariella earlier that night. He had said they were going out, and Tessa figured they'd end up at the party eventually. But what if they'd stayed home? Vik could be in that house. Right now.

"Mom! MOM!" Tessa screeched, her body flinging forward.

Her mother had already said good night; she was likely nestled in bed, directly on the other side of their paper-thin wall. She could probably hear the din of the television. Maybe even Tessa's breathing.

Still, Tessa screamed until her throat strained. "Ma! Come now! It's Vik!"

Her pulse chattered her teeth, and her spine shot ramrod straight. Her arm stretched out, pressing the volume up, up, up. Air sputtered from Tessa's lungs as her eyes caught on the chyron: "Axe Murders in Fall River."

Murders. Plural.

No, no, no. Tessa blinked, faster and faster, as if she could mentally push the reporter back to the beginning to explain why she was stationed there. Where was Vik?

He can't be hurt. There was no way. Tessa couldn't lose him too.

Mom tripped into the doorjamb, a floral robe frayed at the edges covering her baby-blue nightgown. Then Tía Dolores slid in behind her wearing gray fuzzy slippers and a Nirvana T-shirt, a glass of white wine in hand.

"¿Qué pasó?" her mother asked, her voice frantic.

Tessa couldn't answer. She couldn't rip her gaze away from the screen. Instead, she pointed.

Show Vik. Show us he's alive. Tessa desperately prayed, her hands clasped so hard her white knuckles threatened to burst through her skin.

Then her prayer was answered.

The carved wooden double doors to the Morse estate swung open, and the camera pivoted. A shadowy figure emerged in the half-light of the front porch, the silhouette easily recognizable—tall, solid, with wide shoulders and floppy black hair in need of a trim.

Her mother smacked a palm to her chest and stumbled back a step. "¡Ay, Dios mío! He's okay."

Tessa's shoulders relaxed down her back. Her stomach uncoiled, for a moment, maybe not even that. It was just enough time for her eyes to catch on the handcuffs.

Her brother was being steered off the front porch, through the ornately painted Victorian columns belonging to the town's largest home and its richest family, and his wrists were bound together. A police officer wrenched Vik's arm, and camera flashes popped, bright bursts that competed with the stars speckling the inky sky. A crescent moon hung low, right above Vik's head, and below him was a news chyron that read "Suspected Axe Murderer, Victor Gomez, Now in Custody."

"What is happening?" yelped her mother. Or maybe Tessa. Or her aunt. Or maybe they all said it in unison.

"Why do they have Vik?"

"Is he okay?"

"Who got killed?"

"What is going on?"

Questions slid on top of each other, piling higher and higher as her mom and Tía Dolores dropped onto Tessa's mattress, one clutching her arm and the other her thigh. That was how Tessa knew she was awake. She could feel them. This was real.

"As we've been reporting, local business moguls Catherine and Winthrop Morse were found dead in their home this evening. According to police, the couple were killed by an axe while asleep in their bed. A person of interest has been taken into custody, eighteen-year-old Victor Gomez. He is a Fall River High School senior and reportedly dating the victims' teenage daughter. She is said to be unharmed. Motive is still unclear. Local residents are likely aware of the town's dark history, as tonight marks the first axe murders in Fall River since 1892, when Lizzie Borden was charged with murdering her parents."

The camera panned to her brother, who stepped into the beam of a blazing floodlight, and they all gasped. His dark eyes were wild, darting skittishly, as crimson gore dripped down every speck of his tan skin.

Her mother collapsed, her thin frame slumping against Tessa's shoulder as though her bones had melted beneath her skin.

"Ma! Ma!" Tessa guided her onto the mattress.

"Rosie!" yelled Tessa's aunt. "She's fainted. Omigod! I'll get some water." Her aunt raced from the room, her black wavy shag wrapped in a rainbow sleep scarf that seemed too colorful given the circumstances.

Her mom's eyes fluttered, then gradually cracked open. "A dream," she murmured. "Dios mío, a nightmare. Just a nightmare."

Tessa didn't have the heart to tell her otherwise, so she let her mother bask in a moment of oblivion.

On the tiny screen, the image of her brother stared back, his white T-shirt so saturated in scarlet, it looked as though he'd used it to sop up a spilled can of paint with a cheesy name like Sangria or Ferrari. His hair was soaked, streaking crimson rivulets down his high cheeks.

"The sensational trial of Lizzie Borden, in which she was acquitted, secured one of Fall River's most notorious residents a place in both infamy and nursery rhymes," said the white female reporter, with a somber look so forced it edged on gleeful. "Seems like Fall River may have just seen history repeat itself."

Tessa shook her head, her wavy hair tugging from beneath her bathrobe, her teeth clenched so tight her jaw ached.

Mom pulled herself to a seated position, and Tessa softly rubbed her hunched back. Tía Dolores stumbled into the room, a glass of water in hand.

"Drink, drink," her aunt ordered, shoving the plastic cup their way.

"That's not my Victor. Not my Victor. Not my Victor," Mom sputtered. Again and again.

Over and over.

The words sang. They skipped.

They hummed in rhythmic harmony.

> *Lizzie Borden took an axe,*
> *And gave her mother forty whacks,*
> *And when she saw what she had done,*
> *She gave her father forty-one.*

It had been over a century since the last axe murders in Fall River, Massachusetts, and kids still sang rhymes about it on the playground.

Tessa didn't know what had happened earlier that night, but she was certain of one thing—she was not going to let them sing about her brother.

CHAPTER TWO

The day of the murders . . .

MARIELLA

Mariella Morse's hatred for her father was so ingrained in who she was, it should've been listed on her driver's license: seventeen years old, blond hair, blue eyes, organ donor, despises father.

To be clear, this wasn't a dramatic-teenage-girl-overreacting type of thing. Her father deserved the flares of revulsion that burned in Mariella's chest for every swing he took at her mother, every dish he threw at a wall, and every fake smile he beamed at swanky parties. *Hey, pal, let's go smoke a cigar.*

For a while, she thought all she needed was to make it to age eighteen. Adulthood. She'd leave Fall River, buy her mom's freedom, and not glance once in the rearview mirror. New York City was top of her list. Start spreading the news. Then her father changed the parameters of her trust fund, limiting her access until she hit the wrinkle-cream age of thirty. Mariella might as well be dead.

She felt dead already.

No, she just needed to sleep, a full night, without nightmares. Or what she hoped were nightmares, though she was pretty sure dreams weren't supposed to leave bruises.

"Mari, how do you look this good after a crappy morning of school?" Vik plopped down next to her on a square chunk of granite outside the school's north entrance. Crudely cut stone benches dotted the perimeter of the newly constructed building, contrasting with walls of shiny glass windows and classic white columns. A paper-bag lunch sat in his lap.

"I always look good." She forced the smile he expected, and Vik swung a long arm around her shoulders, black hair dripping into his dark eyes.

Mariella rolled the cough drop on her tongue, trying to hit every drip of saliva, the menthol flavor so intense, it cleared her sinuses. But not her mouth. The foul taste of raw sludge still lingered with every breath and swallow.

Outwardly, Mariella Morse looked exactly as she always did. Her lip gloss was perfect—Rose Berry, which she'd reapplied after homeroom, half expecting to see dirt packed between her teeth, matching the taste she couldn't shake. But when she gazed into the mirror, her smile was as bright as it had ever been. Concealer hid the indigo circles beneath her lashes. Foundation, blush, eyeliner, and mascara made her blue-gray eyes pop and her fair complexion look flawless. She was a walking airbrushed ad for a

SoCal cosmetics line. But inside, her soul was at the mercy of a shadow that had teeth.

"Your hair smells so good." Vik flashed the seductive look he wore well—his grin a little crooked and a twinkle in his eyes that sent a heaviness down low in her belly.

She knew the whispers would be here soon. They always came when he was around.

Vik pressed his lips to hers, not just a peck or a polite PDA. No, Victor Gomez knew how to kiss, for real. And he never held back. Neither did she.

Mariella swallowed the remnants of her lozenge as her mouth tangled with his. How was he not gagging? It had been weeks since she'd ingested *whatever* that was, and ever since, her nights were long, her skin was itchy, and no amount of toothpaste or Listerine could wash the corrosion from her tongue. But Vik never seemed to notice.

He pulled away, thumb tracing her bottom lip. "Cough drop?"

She examined his eyes. That was really all he tasted, menthol. *How could that be?*

"Allergies." She waved at the dead leaves shriveling on their branches awaiting a breeze that would send them spiraling to a decaying pile of mulch.

Kiss him again, a whisper hissed. Inside her ears. Inside her brain.

Ah, there they were, just a little late.

Mariella followed the command, as always, angling her face and pressing her chest against Vik's. Her lips moved with his, and her fingers wandered down his back, a slow tickly drag.

Vik abruptly stopped, his breath nearly a pant. "Later," he whispered, steam in his voice suggesting exactly what he meant.

And she would be seeing him later, but for circumstances far graver. Vik just didn't realize why.

Guilt slid from her heart to her gut, and she shoved another lozenge into her mouth. The menthol traveled down her throat, healing the fireplace poker blistering her esophagus. Lately, her nights were not only sleepless but painful. It was as though during the few hours she'd manage to doze, her jaw was unhinged and hung wide open.

Or it was held open.

She shivered, tucking her hands into her chunky sweater, a frost creeping up her skin in the brittle October air. Vik wrapped his arm tighter around her.

"Want my sweatshirt?" He reached for the hem of his Philadelphia Eagles hoodie, prepared to tug it off. He'd freeze for her. He'd sit in a T-shirt with his teeth chattering, and she wouldn't even have to ask.

Meanwhile, Zane, her last boyfriend, wouldn't even lend her his suit jacket after homecoming, because he didn't want Mariella's perfume to infect it (his words, not hers). If the whispers plotted against Zane, Mariella would hand him over with an extra scoop of not giving a shit. But that wasn't the plan.

"I'm good." Mariella shook off Vik's gesture.

"I'll keep you warm." He pulled her in to his chest and rested his chin atop her head.

She sank into his solid frame, his muscles gained from work, not working out. Vik fixed cars to help his mother pay the bills, which was one of the many reasons Mariella's father *should've* respected him, if not liked him. But he didn't, of course. Because that would require Winthrop Morse to accept that his daughter had a life beyond their home, one that he couldn't control.

Tell him you love him, a whisper commanded; then a force tugged her fingers from her sweater cuff and raked them down Vik's chiseled jaw. Something, some power that felt outside herself, held her icy hand against his high cheek. She couldn't resist.

"Love you," she whispered. Then the compulsion abruptly dissipated, and her hand dropped to her lap.

No. She shook her shoulders. She loved touching Vik. She wanted to do that.

"Love ya too, babe." Vik kissed her again, and the Sprite on his tongue was so deliciously sweet that Mariella groaned. Vik mistook her response, drawing her closer.

Yesss, a whisper cooed, tingles springing down her arms, only she wasn't sure if the prickles surged from her own feelings or from somewhere else. *Something* else.

It had been weeks.

All she'd done was drink a cup of tea. It was supposed to solve everything—make her powerful and give her answers.

But she never expected *this.*

That first night, in a depthless sleep, Mariella had found herself standing in her bedroom, outside of her own body. The air smelled of a freshly dug grave. Her home was silent, the dull hum of a motor (a bike?) roaring somewhere in the distance. She hovered, floating, and watched a thing, a shadow, with eyes crackling like crimson coals, peer at her exposed flesh. Its forked tongue slurped curiously as it drifted closer with elongated limbs. Her body lay slack on a fluffy queen bed, in a pale-blush nightgown, completely immobile and unable to scream. Or fight. Or run.

The real her, the ethereal her, swatted frantically. She slapped at her sleeping figure, snatching for the body that belonged to her, desperate to wake it, but her ghostly hand slipped through her own skin and bone. Then Mariella drifted, farther and farther, helplessly watching as a thing crawled up her limbs and pressed its fingers—talons?—into her milky thighs with a sadistic, satisfied snarl. Pleasure. Its rows of shark teeth glinted as an oily tongue stretched for her ear. It licked her freckled skin.

Mariella screamed—or tried to scream. Her mouth cranked open and her lungs pushed, but the air only rippled with a drowning silence.

Then she'd bolted upright. Mariella sat in her bed. She'd returned to herself. Sweat slicked her nightgown to her chest and her hair to her neck. Her lashes fluttered with the wings of a wasp. "It was a dream," she'd told herself. Again and again.

Then she'd looked down at the plum welts marring her thighs; they were shaped like handprints, with tiny puncture wounds left by pointed nails. Hers were chewed. She reached for her neck and her skin was filmy. Gritty.

The next morning, the whispers began.

The words, the plans, they sang in her skull. Promising, promising. *You want him dead, Mariella. We can help. Yes, we can help with that . . .*

Vik sniffed her hair. "Is it weird I think it's cute you get your hair done by my mom?"

"Is it weird your hair smells exactly the same as mine?" She inhaled the citrusy aroma of their locks mingled together, potent and welcoming against the decay of her breath—her mouth, the air, and the season. It all stunk of death.

Vik pecked her neck.

"Ugh, the love birds," Phil said as he dropped onto a chunky granite bench beside them, a boxed grilled cheese sandwich in his lap.

"Don't mind us." Mariella grinned, her cheeks aching from the constant smiling. Did men smile this much?

No one noticed the difference within her. Not even Phil. If anyone should've sensed something, it should have been her best friend. But he asked barely any questions.

"You're kinda hard to miss." Phil rolled his eyes at their PDA.

Mariella chucked a Cheez-It, taunting, but Phil caught it with a backhand and tossed it in his mouth.

"It's gonna suck when it's no longer warm enough to sit outside," said Vik's sister, Tessa, as she strolled over to the group.

She carried a paper-bag lunch, just like her brother's, packed with a yogurt, grapes, hummus, and crackers. Mariella knew this because Vik ate the same thing. Every day. He and his sister were annoyingly bonded.

Tell her she looks pretty, the whispers instructed, always urging her to keep Tessa close.

"I like your shirt," Mariella said obligingly, gesturing with her eyes.

Tessa was wearing a beige peasant blouse with a rosy floral

pattern that was kind of okay. She probably bought it off a sale rack from one of those discount stores that sell reject designer fashion and offer shopping carts to hold your merchandise. Mariella used to obsess about details like this, and maybe she would again, when it was all over. Soon.

Tessa's face lit up at the compliment, then she smoothed her top. "Thanks."

Vik nudged Mariella's shoulder in a thank-you gesture. He really loved his sister, which was sweet. And he loved Mariella. He told her all the time. He texted Mariella back within seconds, he helped her with AP English (remembering all kinds of Biblical allusions from his Sunday school days), he drove her anywhere she wanted to go, and, quite simply, the boy made her sweat. Mariella didn't want to hurt him. And she wouldn't.

It'll all work out, the whispers insisted.

"You guys hangin' out tonight?" Phil asked, then crunched a baby carrot drenched in ranch dressing. The question was aimed toward Mariella, but his eyes were predictably set on Tessa. Tessa's cheeks flushed with the hint of a smile, and she averted her gaze in that flirtatious way girls sometimes do.

"Yup." Vik winked at Mariella.

"We've got *big* plans." Her words held hidden meaning.

Their Friday night dates had taken a twist recently. They couldn't hang out at Mariella's house, because her father ran their ten-thousand-square-foot home like a private prison. *No guests allowed!* And they couldn't hang out at Vik's, because he lived above a pink laundromat, in an apartment with zero personal space and walls thinner than Kleenex. So, they'd been going into the woods. *The* woods. To be alone. To be together. To breathe. To prepare.

And tonight would be the last time.

"Damn, I was hoping you'd be at the shop after school," said Zane as he joined the group. "My engine light came on."

Vik nodded, but his jaw tightened.

Zane was the only boyfriend Mariella's father had ever approved of, because Zane's mom was a lawyer, and his dad owned the construction-management firm that had built their new high school. Zane's family also oversaw renovations to some of the textile mills owned and rehabbed by Mariella's father, which sort of made her dad Zane's dad's boss. Winthrop Morse, of course, loved that—total control, not just of his daughter but of her boyfriend *and* his parents. *Whatever happened to that nice boy you used to date?*

Never mind that Zane acted like the world existed just to serve him. *Your mom's a hairdresser? Great, will she cut my hair for free? You work at an auto-body? Awesome, can you fix my car off the books? Hey, Mariella, could you pick up the check at dinner tonight?* Zane was the cheapest rich person she had ever met.

He lowered himself onto a corduroy jacket, not letting his ironed jeans touch the chalky granite.

"I'll be at the shop this weekend," Vik said, forcing an agreeable tone. "You can bring it by tomorrow."

"I'm playing golf. Sure you can't do it tonight?" Zane pressed.

Tell him you have plans, the whispers ordered. Mariella sat up straighter. Vik's family needed money; everyone knew that.

Vik might actually agree to meet Zane tonight, just for the cash, which would ruin everything she'd arranged.

"Sorry, Zane. No work tonight," Mariella said, wrapping her hands around Vik's biceps and nuzzling his shoulder. Vik leaned in, gazing down at her with a look that screamed, *Damn.*

She might truly love Vik. She said it all the time, but it was hard to know for sure, given that her home didn't exactly set a good example for what love should look like. But Mariella knew she didn't want to hurt him. And she wouldn't, right? If everything went according to plan, no one should suspect a thing.

Vik kissed her hair, and Zane coughed with annoyance, a nasty grimace on his face.

Vik smirked back.

"What about you, Tessa? What are ya doin' tonight?" Phil asked, shooting Mariella a look that said, *Maybe don't have these boys fight over you on school grounds?*

Mariella tossed him a look in return: *Maybe finally ask that girl out?*

Phil bit back a laugh.

They had been reading each other's eyes since they'd shared paste in kindergarten. Mariella didn't have siblings, but she had Phil, and he was the only person who really knew what her life was like. Vik was too sweet for the truth. If he saw her mom get shoved against a wall, he'd go straight to the cops and sincerely think that they'd help. But between her dad's businesses, the country club, the fundraisers, the political donations, and his goddamn high school football team, there wasn't an adult in this city not willing to look the other way at a domestic issue involving Winthrop Morse.

An arrest would never happen. And a "wellness check" would not go well for her mother the next day.

"I'm not doing anything." Tessa sucked on a spoonful of yogurt. "Just some newspaper stuff and a movie."

"Alone?" Phil asked.

Tessa nodded. "Unless you count my mom."

Tessa hadn't dated—not once—since she'd come to Fall River. Vik claimed she was too hung up on an ex-boyfriend back in Philly. Mariella of course pressed for details. *What's his name? Why'd they break up?* But Vik stayed loyal to his sister. "Tess will tell you if she wants." Tessa never did. Nor did she ever tell Phil that she wasn't interested, at least not flat out. Instead, Tessa and Phil waffled somewhere in between. *Are we friends? Are we more than that?* It had been months, and still Mariella watched her best friend awkwardly squirm.

"I heard Izzy's having a party, a big bonfire in the woods behind her house," Zane said, eyes on Tessa. "Why don't you come? I'll drive."

Phil cleared his throat, hazel eyes stretched with panic at the thought of Tessa and Zane alone. In a car. Mariella didn't need to read his mind to know that.

"I dunno." Tessa wiggled.

"I thought you were staying in." Phil leaned toward her, trying to draw back Tessa's attention.

"She can change her mind." Zane gave Tessa a flirtatious look.

Stop her, the whispers commanded. *Vik will want to protect his sister. He'll go to the party with her. It'll ruin everything. He'll choose her. You know that . . .*

A sudden swarm of ants raced beneath Mariella's skin, in all directions, clawing paths up into her chest and down through her forearms. She glared at her fingers, expecting tiny black insects to burst from her nail beds; instead the sensation moved to her ears. A buzzing roared in her head.

Mariella! Now! The plan is tonight. It must be tonight!

"Zane, have you met Tessa?" Mariella blurted, hugging herself to keep from scraping the itchy bugs beneath her flesh. "Stop being weird. Let her do her thing."

"She's right. I have to finish an article for the paper." Tessa stared at the granite bench. "Besides, I'm more of a rom-com and peppermint tea kind of person."

"You weren't always." Vik gave his sister a look. He made comments like this a lot, little hints about the Old Tessa, as if she had been awesome in a different life. Mariella almost hoped that was true, because in this life, the girl was the personification of boring.

Tessa glared at her brother. "It's the new me."

"Well, the new you acts like she's eighty," Zane teased.

"Hey, Tessa's got better plans than me," Phil cut in. "I gotta work. Ya know, you still gotta come by and see the place."

Hope dripped from his voice, and Tessa smiled, neither confirming nor denying.

"I'll give ya a private tour," Phil persisted.

Vik nudged his sister. "The Lizzie Borden House is, like, the *only* tourist attraction in town. Even *I've* seen it."

"Because your girlfriend owns it," Tessa griped.

"My *parents* own it," Mariella corrected.

"Yeah. We're just the lowly fools who run it." Phil's self-deprecating words had been said before, because they held an uncomfortable truth. Money was the unavoidable wedge rammed into their friendship. Mariella's family had it. Phil's didn't.

The Lizzie Borden House, now a bed-and-breakfast, had been in the Morse family for generations. Phil's parents had managed it for as long as Mariella could remember. That meant Phil's parents were her parents' employees. Even worse—the Barkers paid rent on an apartment that Mariella's father owned, which was also physically *on* the Lizzie Borden property. Mariella and Phil practically grew up in that haunted house. There were pictures of them toddling around the parlor where the body of Lizzie's father was discovered. Phil was the one who taught Mariella how to use a Ouija board. They held séances in middle school. They checked out books on ghosts and witches from the library as soon as they'd learned to read. It was a unique start to a friendship that had lasted for seventeen years.

"You're much more than that." Mariella looked at Phil. "You know that."

"I do." Phil blew her a kiss.

"You know, my cousin claims she's psychic, and she won't step foot in the Lizzie Borden House," Zane said, eyes still on Tessa. "So are you too freaked out? Or do you not believe in ghosts?"

"Oh, I think the place is creepy, but not because of ghosts. People *died* there." Tessa didn't want to be insulting, but to an out-of-towner, it was more than a little weird that the town's biggest tourist attraction was a real-life murder house.

"It *is* creepy," Phil said. "That's why I like workin' there. I like tryin' to understand the unexplainable."

"And do you?" Tessa gave Phil her full attention.

He ran a hand through his styled blond hair, Tessa's stare clearly making him flustered. "I, uh . . . I'm workin' on it. Ya can't live in Fall Rivah and not believe in somethin'." Mariella knew that whenever Phil got worked up, his Massachusetts accent came out thicker than usual, which was pretty much every time he talked to Tessa.

"Ugh, you guys and your Bridgewater Triangle garbage." Vik groaned. "Just go see it, Tess. It's a house. Nothing more."

"Oh really? Then stay overnight," Phil challenged.

"Maybe I will." Vik shrugged. "I'm just not a ghosts and goblins kind of person. That crap doesn't exist."

"Yeah, well, I've seen some wicked weird stuff," said Phil.

"You're not exactly selling me on a tour," said Tessa.

"Don't worry, I'll keep ya safe. Besides, you love history. Come on . . . stop by?" It was the closest Mariella had ever seen Phil get to genuinely asking Tessa out. His eyes widened, the look of a puppy at a shelter desperately wanting not to be passed over.

Tessa tucked a lock of wavy hair behind her ear, gaze twinkling. Mariella held her breath, thinking the girl might actually say yes—finally.

Then Tessa shook her head. "Not tonight. But soon."

If she weren't Vik's sister, Mariella would have told her to find somewhere else to sit at lunch.

"Okay, I'll hold ya to it." Phil's voice concealed his disappointment, but his eyes didn't.

A lull fell over the conversation, and they all watched Phil watching Tessa.

Vik leaned toward Mariella and whispered, "Have I mentioned how glad I am to not have to awkwardly flirt anymore?"

Mariella stifled a chuckle, her mouth filling with mulch as Vik trailed his hand down her arm and entwined his fingers with hers.

She could still back out of her plans. There could be another way, something less dangerous, or less permanent. Something that didn't involve Vik. If Mariella took some more time—

You know what you need to do. You know what you need to do. You know what you need to do. You know what you need to do, the whispers repeated, louder and louder, cramming against her brain, pushing against her eyeballs, and burning hot tracks down the inside of her nose. She squinted, teeth grinding, pressure building until her head felt ready to pop. God, the buzzing. She tightened her fingers in Vik's, using all her energy not to pound on her skull.

The whispers were right.

The timing would not be this perfect again.

Winthrop Morse was going to die.

Tonight.

And Victor Gomez was going to kill him.

He just didn't know it yet.

CHAPTER THREE

After the murders . . .

TESSA

Tessa sat in the back of a car, staring at chaotic flashes bursting in the distance. She'd never before given a second's thought to the celebrities on TV suffering public meltdowns that involved cameras and outstretched microphones. She'd figured they'd probably deserved it.

Her opinion had now radically shifted.

"Look, ladies, I think this is as fah as I can go," said the driver, his accent thick. He slowed the decently clean yet significantly dented Lincoln Town Car about a block from the police station.

Tessa peered at her aunt.

"No way." Tía Dolores pushed upright, straining against her seat belt and banging on the driver's headrest. "We are not doing a walk of shame through *that*." She gestured to the seething crowd.

"Whaddya friggin' want me to do?"

"Drive into 'em. Run 'em over. I don't care." Her aunt flopped back, her voice lacking a speck of sarcasm.

Tessa stuck her head between the headrests—forever the youngest, she was seated in the middle between her mom and her aunt. Frankie, Tía Dolores's girlfriend, was already inside the station, and had been all night. She was now Vik's lawyer.

God, my brother has a lawyer.

"Please, you gotta help us," Tessa pleaded in a you-catch-more-flies-with-honey tone. She even smiled, a gesture so painfully inappropriate for the situation, it actually hurt her cheeks.

The driver blew a stale puff through his bulbous nostrils dotted with broken capillaries, then reluctantly pressed on the gas.

Tessa sat back, resting one hand on her mom's knee; her other touched an old black gum stain now smooth and hardened on the seat cushion.

"It's gonna be okay," Tessa whispered the lie.

This was all her fault. If Tessa hadn't forced her family to move, Vik wouldn't have met Mariella; if he hadn't met her, then he wouldn't be in a jail cell right now. Somehow, Tessa had found a way to pack even more trauma into her mother's already overflowing baggage.

When the news broke last night, she, her aunt, and her mother separated to their individual bedrooms. Tessa listened to her mother cry. Then she tossed and texted to drown out the pain.

Tessa: I don't know how I'm supposed to sleep

Phil: It's 3am and I'M up bc I can't stop thinking about it. I'm so sorry

Tessa: Vik didn't do it. People know that, right?

Phil: I know you and your mom don't deserve to be going through this

Tessa: Neither does Vik

Phil: Neither does Mariella

Mangled emotions ballooned in Tessa's throat, because of course he was right. Mariella's mom and dad had been murdered, violently, only hours ago. Tessa couldn't begin to imagine the hell Mariella was in. Well, Tessa could imagine the devastation of losing a parent—but not both of them, and not like that.

But Vik was Tessa's priority, and he wasn't a killer. Vik was the kid who set out bowls of milk for the stray cats in their Philly neighborhood. He was a summer camp counselor for their old church. He used to carry in groceries for their elderly neighbor. Vik helped his mother pay the rent. What they were accusing him of was impossible.

Tessa: I'm so sorry for Mariella. I really am. But Vik is my brother

Phil: And you're my friend

Phil: No, you're a lot more than that

Tessa stared at his last text, full of meaning. She knew that on the other end, Phil was watching three little dots flash, awaiting her response. But she didn't know what to say. Not right now. Not with all this. Were they more than friends? Yesterday, she probably would have said . . . maybe. But right now she was so confused, she could barely spell her own name. She should have gone out with Phil weeks ago, she should have gone to the Lizzie Borden House last night, or she should have gone to that party.

Maybe if she had, Vik would have gone with her and he wouldn't have been with Mariella, or anywhere near her parents. What if, what if, what if.

Tessa: I'm going to try to sleep

Phil: Okay. You can call me anytime. Really. I can't stop thinking about you

Tessa: I know. Thank you

Phil: You're stronger than you realize

Tessa stared at his words, a response immediately forming in her brain, though she wasn't sure if she should send it. She wasn't sure how Phil would take it, or even how she wanted him to take it. But then her thumbs were moving before her brain could tell them to stop.

Tessa: I received 3 million texts tonight, and you're the only person I texted back

Three little dots blinked.

Then a response.

Phil: 🖤

She turned off her phone. Tessa wasn't alone. Technically, yes, she was by herself, in her bedroom, staring at her miniblinds, waiting for sunbeams to slip through the plastic seams, but she knew her mom and her aunt were doing the same thing.

Eventually, a teaspoon swirled against a mug in the kitchen, and Tessa got up. They regrouped, staring silently at cups of milky coffee.

Then Frankie called. She'd pulled some strings.

Frankie had grown up in Fall River, part of the huge Portuguese community. She couldn't walk into a bar without knowing

the hostess was Tommy's kid and *how was his sciatica doing?*
Frankie had strolled the same public school halls as most of the
cops on the force. And Vik, while eighteen, was still a high school
kid who needed his mother. So after Vik was questioned, scraped,
swabbed, clipped, and questioned some more, Frankie was able
to arrange a family visit.

The car inched forward, and cameras flashed against their
tinted windows. Tessa wrapped her body around her mom's, and
Tía Dolores wrapped her body around Tessa's—a pile of protec-
tion.

"Let's pretend they're not here," Tessa whispered. Denial can
be a great comfort when used properly.

Eventually, the car screeched, wheels grinding to a halt on
the asphalt, and their tangle of hair and limbs was thrust forward
against their seat belts.

"This is it," barked the driver. "Can't go any fahther. Christ,
I'm never getting outta heah."

Tía Dolores peeled her weight from Tessa, then Tessa peeled
herself from her mother, and they stared through the windshield
like specimens gazing up at the microscope lens—eyes were on
them. Cameras with network logos pointed their way, balancing
on the hulking shoulders of men in baseball caps, while arms in
tailored suits clutched microphones. Voices rose, crescendoing as
one, screaming a barrage of questions. But Tessa wasn't worried
about the reporters; there was another crowd. Slightly to the left
and behind a barricade of easily movable temporary metal fences
was a violent storm of picketers, spewing spit and hoisting signs
that formed a sailor's knot in Tessa's stomach.

AXE Murderer, Go Back to Philly!
Give HIM 40 Whacks!
Justice for the Morse Family!
Victor Gomez Is a Coward!

They were mostly middle-aged, entirely white, and ferociously angry.

Tessa swallowed the watery lump in her throat and twisted her neck toward her mother. "We got you."

Tía Dolores clutched her sister's hand. "Everyone, dry your eyes. For Vik."

Tessa wiped her lashes. Mom stifled a sob, a rumpled tissue pressed to her face, but it was the best she could do. The door flung open. A police officer, dressed in standard blues and looking barely older than Tessa, stood outside with his lanky arms spread wide as a crossing guard's.

"Give 'em room! Back up! Now!" he hollered with the force of a gym teacher who didn't need a whistle.

Tessa crept out first, squeezing her mom's hand with all her might; her aunt held the other. It was hard to tell which one of them was shaking the hardest. But each woman was dry-eyed for the cameras. If her brother had access to a TV somewhere, they wanted him to see their chins up and their expressions defiant.

It was their turn to do this for *him*.

Almost a year and a half ago, Tessa and Vik had lost their father. At the time, Tessa had assumed it was the worst thing that would ever happen to her. She thought they'd never recover from the tangible sadness that roped an anvil around their home and weighed down their souls. She and Vik talked about it, all the time—how when they left their city row house, shoulders slouched with despair, they would step onto the curb and find the strength to straighten up. They would take a deep breath, the air lighter beyond their den of grief. The world was shockingly still alive. Life continued to move forward out there. But when the school day ended, and they recrossed the threshold, the atmosphere inside wasn't just hotter, stickier, and dustier, it was *heavier*. It was as though their father's death had created an additional gravitational pull on their four walls and a roof.

But Vik never collapsed under the weight. He didn't curl under the covers in the middle of the day. He didn't let his grades slip or his attendance lag. He got a job after school to bring home extra cash. He figured out his dad's passwords and helped his mom pay the bills. At night, when Vik heard Tessa sobbing into her pillow, he'd come in and sleep uncomfortably sprawled on her beanbag chair. Vik didn't offer advice. He didn't tell her it would be okay. He'd just say, "I'm here." And those two little words gave Tessa solace.

Now it was her turn to be *here* for her *him*.

Tessa inched from the car. The air pulsed with revulsion so thick that it slipped through her pores, slithered into her gut, and sucked up all the oxygen so completely that her mom stumbled a step. Tessa squeezed her hand tighter.

"Ms. Gomez, follow me," said a voice. Female. Authoritative.

Tessa's eyes shot up and spied a pale woman in a dark suit, probably six feet tall, with the frame of a professional soccer player. She extended an arm.

"I'm Detective Ertz," the woman explained.

Tessa latched on to her forearm with her free hand and followed the lifeline through the belligerent mob.

"Step! Back!" the woman shouted.

Everyone listened, shuffling obediently in reverse.

Tessa turned her eyes down, long black wavy hair covering her face, her teeth clenched to bite back the complex web of fear and helplessness weaving through her soul.

"Did your son do it?"

"Has Victor always been violent?"

"Is it true he has a record?"

"Do you have an axe at your home?"

"Are you and your brother romantically involved?"

Tessa jolted upright, eyes sparking fire as a flash blinded her vision.

"Do not answer," ordered Detective Ertz, tugging Tessa forward. "They just want a reaction shot."

They're allowed to say that? About our family?

The last article Tessa had written for the school newspaper (which she submitted just *last night*) was about how the district's dress code policy banning "distracting" clothing almost exclusively targeted girls. Tessa was required to get two named sources on the record, both girls who were forced to change attire because of exposed midriffs or bra straps, before the *Fall River HS Gazette* would publish it. Yet countless professional media outlets will post misleading pictures with headlines and articles full of disinformation and receive no repercussions.

It was the first time the magnitude of the situation truly hit Tessa—these events could not be undone. No matter what happened next, even if Vik was justifiably proved innocent, this moment, this crime, these accusations would follow them forever. Online. At job interviews. On college applications.

This was who they were now. The Gomezes. The Morses. The axe murderer. The victims. And the complicit family members. They *were* this story.

Then a set of glass doors was flung open, and Tessa, her mother, and her aunt were thrust, staggering, into a wall of blue.

"I want to prepare you. He's upset, obviously, but he's also very confused," explained Frankie, though in this setting, she was known as Francisca Abreu, counsel for the defense.

She'd been a defense attorney in Fall River for the past three years, and she hoped to eventually transition to the Innocence Project in Boston. No one, absolutely no one, thought she'd ever be working for their family.

"I don't know what to say." Mom threw herself at Frankie, a fresh sob breaking out. "Thank you for getting us in to see him."

Frankie gave Tessa's mother a "there, there" pat on the back. "Don't thank me yet." Her voice was weary. "It can be just you and Tessa." Frankie's look screamed apologies at Tía Dolores. "I had to *fight* to get Tessa in."

"Of course. I understand. I'll wait out here." Tía Dolores nodded supportively.

A year ago, her aunt and Frankie had taken the family into their apartment. Frankie showed them around her hometown.

She ate their Puerto Rican plantains and rice, then served them Portuguese grilled sardines and salted cod. Frankie brought them to her Catholic church, she helped them enroll in school, she got Vik a part-time job at an auto-body shop, and now she was defending him for murder. This had to be embarrassing, if not reputation damaging, for Frankie. This was the biggest case the town had seen in decades, and Vik was practically her nephew.

Tessa tugged her mother's arm. "Come on, Ma, let Frankie breathe."

Her mother nodded, shoving the same sodden tissue at her nose, her red-rimmed eyes swollen like a boxer's in the final round.

"Is he hurt?" Tessa asked, her stomach bracing.

Frankie shook her head. "Physically, he's okay. Some bumps and bruises, which is to be expected given . . . the scene. But no maltreatment by the police. Trust me, I've known most of these guys since our first Holy Communion; they wouldn't dare."

"Good, good." Tía Dolores nodded.

Frankie's eyes flicked to Tessa and her mom. "You ready? Follow me."

Frankie led them through a brightly lit hallway. Fluorescent bulbs crackled and cast a sickly glow on the facial complexions of the passing officers, each cop nodding a greeting to Frankie. She flipped her long dark hair behind her shoulder, catching the wide lapel of her black leather jacket. Her posture exuded confidence.

She stopped at a door with a small square window. "It's not much."

They entered a glorified walk-in closet—there was no other

way to describe it. The space lacked the intimidating conference table set in a spacious gray room with a two-way mirror, like you see in the movies. In fact, if Tessa spread her arms, she could likely touch both walls, not that she wanted to. A slender tabletop was shoved to one side, against beige cinder blocks. They crowded beside it. There were a few metal chairs, and a cop standing guard near the now closed—and likely locked—door. Their collective body heat would fill this space in seconds.

Tessa guided her mother to a seat, supporting her fragile five-foot frame so she wouldn't collapse on the linoleum. And just as Tessa and Frankie sat, the door slammed opened once more. Her brother appeared, or someone who was wearing an elaborate Vik costume and getting the details all wrong; the body was too slumped and the skin too sallow.

For their entire lives, Vik was picked first on the playground, not because he was the best athlete—he was okay—but because if he was on your team, you'd have the most fun. Vik played pranks and told jokes, he stole the ball and messed around, he laughed *all the time,* and he never seemed to care if his team won; because of that, they always won. For seventeen years, Tessa had been fairly jealous of her brother's spark—it couldn't be taught, and it couldn't be copied. It simply *was* Vik.

Now Vik's head was bowed, and he dragged his feet, shoved into laceless loafers, dirty and preworn, matching his rumpled crimson prison uniform. His wrists and ankles were cuffed and shackled. *Shackled.* He clattered with every movement, and a gasp escaped her mother's lips. Tessa nudged her elbow into her mom's side, and Mom straightened her posture.

Reflexively, Tessa stood, extending her arms to hug her brother, but instantly, the cop at the door thrust a hairy finger her way. "Sit down! No touching." Spittle sprayed from his mouth.

"Dial it back, Jimmy," Frankie snapped, then turned to Tessa, her gray eyes soft. "You're not allowed to touch each other, for obvious reasons."

The cops thought Vik might hurt them. They saw *him* as the dangerous weapon, even in shackles, and despite their guns.

Tessa gulped, then sat with obedience.

A different cop gripped Vik by the shoulders and lowered him into a chair at the far end of the skinny table.

"Okay, boys, attorney-client privilege." Frankie gestured between herself and Vik, eyeing the cops. "Give us some privacy."

The officers silently left the room but stayed just outside the door, the back of one buzzed head clearly visible.

Tessa took in her brother, his spine curved and his hair purposely covering his eyes. He kept his gaze on the scratched floor tiles.

"Vik?" Her voice came out like a question, as though she wasn't sure it was him. Or maybe she wasn't sure this was real.

He lifted his chin so slowly, Tessa wondered if he'd been drugged. Then she spied the indigo bruise on his cheek and the dried blood caking one corner of his lips. She shot a look at Frankie, who made a sympathetic face as though this was as "unharmed" as they could expect.

She turned back to Vik, his glare locked on the far wall, unable to meet her gaze.

"Are you okay?" Tessa asked meekly, knowing it was a stupid

question but needing to put it out there, because it was the only thing the women who'd come here today cared about. Him. How was *he*?

Vik swallowed, chewing his lips, but no words emerged. Tessa recognized the look—Vik had worn it at their father's funeral, neck tendons taut and jaw clenched as he helped carry their dad's casket past the pews. Vik looked that way now, as if he were afraid to open his mouth, because he didn't know what sound would escape. He nodded stiffly.

"We're gonna get you out of here, okay?" Tessa squeaked. "Frankie's all over this. Aren't you?"

Frankie nodded, but for the first time, there was doubt in her eyes. "Of course."

Tessa's brow furrowed, but she pushed away the warning signs. "You see? It'll all be over soon. Just close your eyes and think about next year. You'll be a freshman at Temple, and I'll come visit." Tessa forced a smile. "We'll go to football games and tailgate. Then I'll join you in a year, just like we planned. We'll get an apartment. Maybe we'll take a class together. And this will all be over, a crappy, horrible memory. We won't even talk about it."

Vik cocked his head, eyes screaming, *You know that's bullshit.*

"We *know* you didn't do this." Tessa leaned toward him, hand outstretched.

Vik lifted his own arm in response, then he seemed to realize once again that his wrists were shackled to his ankles by a clanking chain. He stared at the cracked skin on his knuckles and the chafed pink skin beneath the metal cuffs. It was as though he didn't recognize himself. His body. His smell.

What *was* that smell? Tessa's nose crinkled.

The space was so cramped that Tessa could detect her mother's deodorant and Frankie's hair spray. But there was another, fouler stench, one that had entered with Vik. It wasn't his sweat, his feet, or even his breath; those were each a familiar fog in Tessa's life. No, Vik currently reeked of mulch freshly dumped in the garden, heavily enough to trigger a gag reflex. It could be the soap. He had clearly showered recently, because the Jackson Pollock of blood splatter he'd been covered in last night had been erased, but soap wasn't supposed to make you smell dirtier. Or maybe in here it was.

Or maybe when you were in a prison cell, you weren't supposed to care.

Tessa forced back a wave of raw emotion, not letting her mouth turn down. She could do this—fake voice, fake calm.

"I don't remember anything," Vik whispered, his hands dropping with a metallic clatter. "I don't know what Frankie told you, but I don't remember what happened."

"I'm looking into it." Frankie's eyes flipped between Tessa and her mom. "It might be some form of amnesia, his mind protecting itself. Or it could be a foreign substance. I've ordered a tox screen."

"He may have been drugged?" Tessa asked, almost hopefully. It was the first thought she'd had when Vik walked in; this person didn't look like her brother.

"It's possible. I'm also gonna get a psych eval. A trauma specialist. I know some good people," said Frankie.

Vik clucked his tongue, and at first Tessa thought it was in response to the mention of a shrink, but then his eyes squinted and his lips puckered. It was as though he were tasting something rotten, and Tessa couldn't tell if it was from the situation or an actual rank flavor on his tongue. Who knew what he'd eaten for breakfast, or if he'd eaten at all. They hadn't.

"Vik, listen." Tessa stared at her brother with as much love as she could express, forcing him to look her way and meet her eyes. He did. "We know you. It doesn't matter how confused you are, we *know* you didn't do this."

"Tess . . ." That single word stuck in his throat, water welling on his lower lashes. He gulped hard to keep the tears back, keep everything back, and an ice pick slid into Tessa's heart, piercing whatever resolve she held on to. Her chin wobbled. "Nothing makes sense." He croaked. "We were in the woods, hooking up, like normal, it was our regular spot, then . . ." Vik's voice drifted, his eyes milky with confusion. Her brother had a built-in GPS, his memory so sharp he could direct you anywhere if he had been there only once. He taught himself how to fix cars. He could recite NBA stats like he played for a team. "Then I'm suddenly standing in her parents' bedroom. I'm not even allowed in her house. Her father hates me. But I was in their *room,* covered in blood, with an axe at my feet."

"Maybe you walked Mariella inside? Or she called you after she found them? Maybe it was all so traumatic, you have PTSD and the cops have this whole thing jumbled up?" Tessa turned to Frankie.

"There's no phone record of that. And the blood wasn't just on his hands and feet," Frankie replied. "You saw the news footage. There was too much . . . residue . . . to be consistent with someone just trying to help."

"You don't know that. We can't possibly know anything! It hasn't even been a day! Vik doesn't remember shit. You're his lawyer. He didn't do this. Defend him!" Tessa snapped.

Frankie's eyes narrowed. "I know we're all emotional." Her tone was firm. "But remember who's on your side."

Tessa dug her teeth into her cheek, hard, to shift the focus to a pain she could control. "I'm sorry," she whispered, her mouth full of bloody desperation.

"It's okay," Frankie said. "We're all still processing. And we *will* piece this together. It'll just take time."

Time that Vik would spend behind bars, on a mattress covered with vomit and urine stains, pooping in front of strangers on a seatless metal toilet and showering in a crowd of possible criminals.

This can't be happening . . .

Vik scratched at his skull, a metallic rattle as he shook his ear like a swimmer who couldn't clear a clog of water. "It's so loud," he rasped, both fists banging his head.

The room fell silent, heavy, as he pounded his skull with meaty thunks.

"Easy there. This is *a lot.*" Frankie's voice held concern. "The police can keep you here for forty-eight hours before charging you. This is a high-profile case, and it's getting a lot of attention. They're crossing their Ts. I could get loud, I could force an arraignment now, but this is a *double homicide.* If it doesn't go our way, they'll move you to a much worse facility. Our best chance is to find out the truth, and sort this out, before you're formally charged. I have the full support of my firm."

"Okay, good. Then that's what we'll do." Tessa nodded way too quickly.

"I'm trying to remember, I am, but . . . I keep hearing . . . I mean, I keep seeing . . ." Vik's face crumpled in pain, his fists thudding his temples once more.

Tessa's vision clouded with tears she refused to let fall as she wrung her hands under the table. If their painful seats were flipped, what would Vik do for her? She knew he wouldn't placate her or waste time with obvious lies. No, he'd act, just like he had when he'd paid their overdue credit card bills and boxed up their father's dresser drawers.

"Vik, what you're hearing and seeing—maybe they're memories?" She leaned forward. "Describe them. Tell us. What is it?"

"No!" Vik dropped his hands with a clank, his heated gaze on Tessa. "You should go home."

"Huh? No. Let us help you. What's happening?"

"I don't know! Don't you get that?" He slapped the table so hard, all the women in the room jerked back. Then Vik covered his face in shame, hands quivering. "I'm sorry. I didn't sleep."

"That goes for all of us," Frankie said.

"Victor . . ." Mom finally spoke, her voice was so soft Tessa barely heard it, even in a space this small.

Vik hadn't glanced at their mom since he'd slunk in, and Tessa knew this was an act of self-preservation. He'd sooner set his eyeballs on fire than confront the raw pain etched in every crease on her face.

"Victor, look at me." Mom's voice was insistent. "You didn't do this, right?"

Achingly, Vik's glassy eyes turned toward her and his lower lip shook.

"You couldn't do this. I know you couldn't," Mom went on. Her hands reached for him, and there was no cop to stop her. But Vik pulled away.

He collapsed—for maybe the first time, ever, in front of his family. His chest caved, his head hung, and he convulsed, tears splashing onto the table.

It's impossible to hide your true feelings from a mother who loves you.

"Ma, I'm so sorry. I'm so sorry I'm putting you through this," Vik sobbed, curled into his lap. "I don't know what happened. I don't!"

Tessa hugged herself, arms wrapped across her chest to hold the pieces of her fractured family together. For the past year, Vik kept pushing Tessa, saying that he didn't understand her anymore and that she wasn't the same. Now, it was Tessa who feared she might never recognize her brother again.

"Victor, you need to think." Mom's voice was stern. "You need to remember. You need to tell them."

"Have . . . have you seen Mari?" Vik creaked, anguish contorting his face as he looked at Tessa. "Is she okay? God, her screaming." He smacked his lips like he wanted to spit, like he wanted to expel the bad taste, the bad memories. "That's what I remember. Afterward. I can't stop hearing her screaming . . ."

Tessa opened her mouth, but nothing came out. She couldn't tell him the truth—that when they sat in the kitchen this morning, pretending to eat, they'd made the mistake of flicking on the TV. "Fall River Axe Murders" was on every channel, even the national broadcasts. The image of her brother's face doused in blood, his eyes feral, and his wrists handcuffed was now newsroom wallpaper. The chyrons read: "Is the Next Lizzie Borden a Man?" and "Wealthy Business Leaders Axed to Death by Daughter's Boyfriend" and "Victor Gomez Took an Axe." Vik was still being questioned, yet he'd already been found guilty by most of America.

Then it got worse.

Footage of Mariella Morse, "the victims' daughter," began to play, over and over, in a loop next to the talking heads. She was standing in her massive driveway, while twin black bags holding her parents' corpses were wheeled into blinking ambulances.

"Mariella, do you have a statement? Did your boyfriend do it?"

Vik's girlfriend, who'd eaten lunch with Tessa just yesterday, stared straight into the cameras, her bleary gaze more lifeless than Vik's was right now. *"My parents are dead. Both of them. My mom never hurt anyone. Ever. And he butchered her with an axe. My life . . . everything . . . is over. Vik Gomez is a murderer."*

"Vik, don't worry about Mariella." Tessa swallowed back the words she couldn't say. "She's got a lot of people around her."

"No, she doesn't!" Vik cried, grabbing fistfuls of hair by his ears. Then he gagged on the taste of his own saliva, his breath a rancid gust. "She's all alone in that house. And I . . ."

"We don't know what happened," Tessa interrupted, "but we know you are *not* capable of murder. So stop worrying about Mariella and start worrying about yourself."

"Tessa's right." Frankie clapped once with authority. "From this point on, you have no contact with Mariella Morse. Any of you." She looked directly at Tessa.

Like I'm supposed to do nothing? Tessa tried not to roll her eyes. She might not be a lawyer, a cop, or a detective, but she was a sister. And Frankie had already said that they *needed* to prove Vik innocent before the wheels of justice took over. There had to be something Tessa could do.

"Victor," Mom spoke up. "Look at me. Right now. I need you to hear me."

A velvet curtain lifted, and silence fell heavy in the tiny room. No one twitched a muscle or blinked an eyelash. Her mom was center stage, holding the audience captive. Victor shifted toward her, eyes still leaking down both cheeks.

"I love you," Mom said with all the affection in the universe. "Nothing can change that. Ever. You hear me? You are my son."

And with that, tears sprang from Tessa's eyes. Tears she'd promised she wouldn't let Vik see, but now she couldn't stop.

Her brother deflated, sniffling, shoulders trembling. "But I'm *his* son too."

They all took a collective gasp.

Vik continued, rattling his shackles. "We don't talk about it, but look at me. I'm in jail, just like *him*."

"You are nothing like him." Mom's voice was strong.

"And he is *not* your father," Tessa cut in. "*We're* your family. We know who you are."

"And we will get you out of this," Frankie confirmed.

Never underestimate the power of a group of determined women.

Vik blinked at them, then wiped at his nose with the back of his exposed forearm. He sat straighter. "I've never been able to win an argument against any of you."

"And you won't today. I'm here." Tessa repeated the words he'd said to her when she was in her lowest moments of grief, and she hoped, from the depth of her soul, that it brought him even the tiniest flicker of the solace he always brought her.

The door to the room buzzed open once again, and the female detective from the crowd stood in the entry, the one who'd ushered them from the car to the door.

"Time's up." The detective looked at Frankie as she spoke. "And before they leave, I'd like a word with his sister."

CHAPTER FOUR

The day of the murders . . .

MARIELLA

Vik dropped off Mariella at the Lizzie Borden House after school. Her father had asked (read: ordered) her to retrieve some paper-work requiring his signature—as if his multiple cars didn't run, and as if he weren't the reason she had no driver's license. She told Vik she'd walk home afterward. She needed to think.

You've got this. You've come this far. Just see it through . . . The whispers filled her head.

Car exhaust overpowered the stink of wet leaves as she scuffled past the gray, boxy facade of the district courthouse, her heel catching on a seam in the sidewalk. She turned onto Main Street, its rectangular sienna brick buildings adorned with hunter-green awnings and faded gold-lettered signs. There was no Prada or Gucci. Not even a Gap. Just law firms, insurance companies, a senior center, and a mortgage broker.

Like every teenager in America, Mariella was certain her town suffered from all-we-do-is-watch-paint-dry syndrome. The difference being—her family didn't *have* to live here. Winthrop Morse was rich. Their little trio had the means to pack up for Boston or Providence. They could join the socialites at swanky black-tie galas featured in the backs of glossy city magazines. Mom could play tennis with women named Buffy and Kiki. Mariella could go to private school and wear a cute little plaid skirt. But no, out in the big wide world, Dad would be just another low-rent real estate developer trying to suppress his Masshole accent. Those Beacon Hill aristocrats, who could trace their gold coins back to the days of King James, would smile to his face, then whisper behind his back, *What's his name again? Wally? You know, forget it, I don't even care.*

No, her family stayed put so Winthrop Morse could be the big fish in a dried-up pond. It didn't take a degree in psychology to figure out what that meant.

Mariella paused at the light, then crossed the busy boulevard near city hall, which was built atop a highway overpass and looked like an in-need-of-a-power-wash DMV. Not that Mariella had ever been inside a DMV, because, again, her father wouldn't let her drive. And why do you think that was? Because he knew the second her fingers touched a set of car keys, the first place she'd go would be *away*. Anywhere far, far away.

Mariella crunched forward, the grinding asphalt mixing with the buzz in her head, that constant buzz. A pea-soup-green 4x4 truck whizzed toward her, its bed holding grimy equipment—construction or plumbing, she wasn't sure. The driver, who was white and at least thirty, though it was hard to tell with his burly black beard and mirrored sunglasses, stared through his rolled-down window. She could feel his eyes creeping on her, and the truck slowed (the better to see you with). The man pursed his lips, tongue on his teeth, and let out a high whistle. Then he honked the horn. A peppy *beep beep*. Flirty. Perverted. Mariella tugged her striped gray-and-white sweater tighter and glanced away, a move she'd been forced to perfect ever since she was eleven years old.

That was when it had started. Fully grown men, probably with depressed wives sitting at home chugging chardonnay, would catcall, whistle, and honk. They'd lick their lips and wink. Some would grab their crotch. *Hey there.* Honestly, how did they expect her to respond? Did they hope she'd wave down their car at the next red light and hop in the passenger seat? They knew she was a teenager, because a) they had eyes, and b) she was walking and not in a car of her own. No, these ogling slimeballs wanted to be disgusting. They wanted to make *her* feel gross. They wanted her to know she wasn't safe. She never would be, not in her own house and not out in the world.

But you will *be safe,* a whisper promised inside her skull.

Mariella released her arms, shoving her palms into the pockets of her jeans. Sometimes, and this was strange to say, the whispers felt like her closest friends. They'd been in her brain 24-7 for the past two months. And despite *everything* that came with them—prickling skin, maddening thoughts, and a nightmarish shadow . . . They. Were. There. They talked to her during the moments her life was at its worst. They saw the cracks and

Spackle in the faux finish of the Morse family facade, and they helped, albeit in a we'll-show-you-how-to-murder-your-father kind of way. But the whispers gave her a plan, and the plan was going to fix everything.

You're ready. It will work out, the whispers hummed.

Mariella yanked on the waistband of the jeans sliding down her hips. She was losing weight. Her bra straps kept slipping. Her whole closet was either ill-fitting or itchy lately, and everything made her sweat. Nothing felt right.

She trudged past the children's museum, a Romanesque-style castle built of gray stones, with an actual tower and green copper spires. It was almost as old as Mariella's Victorian estate, housing a majestic toy wonderland built for fairy princesses. Though Mariella had been inside only for field trips and fundraisers. Obviously, her father was a benefactor (there were pictures in the paper to prove it), and he'd trot her out in a velvet dress and patent leather shoes for every annual holiday party. *"Your daughter is so precious! You must love coming here with your daddy!"* Even in grade school, Mariella knew to keep her mouth shut. As if Winthrop Morse would ever set foot in a "Lego room."

Mariella turned at the corner past the museum, hiking up the steep hill in her high-heeled boots, her legs barely straining. She'd done a lot of hiking with the hope of inhaling some inner peace with the cold air. She couldn't wait for every last leaf to plummet to the streets of Fall River. No one was expected to be happy during the gray skies of winter.

Mariella kicked past a block of churches, one on every corner, from Baptist to Catholic (lots and lots of Catholics). Then she spied the staggering exterior of her home ahead. Even *she,* who put this address on her school forms, knew the property was ostentatious. Fall River was known for modest homes with siding and shutters. Yards had chain-link fences, sidewalks were cracked, and most larger buildings were divided into apartments, many with air conditioners dripping from outdated windows.

But once you crossed Maple or Walnut Streets, you reached a tiny pocket of haves in a city of have-nots. It was called the Highlands.

It was where the Morses lived, and even where Lizzie Borden had lived, after she was acquitted.

It was also where Mariella's father would die.

A muddy taste surged in Mariella's mouth once more as she gazed upon the elegant structure that had forever contained her. The doors were closed, with rarely a guest invited inside. There was no entertaining—no fancy shindigs or high-end fundraisers.

This was a fortress with a low iron gate comprised of black metal vines curving and twisting, ready to rip from the posts, claw up the walls and through the sealed windows. The main entrance, around the corner, had a semicircular drive and a stately front porch where her father entered. It was also where the drivers took them.

But Mariella preferred the side door. It stood directly beneath her second-story-bedroom windows, which overlooked a tiny triangle park. She stepped onto the grassy island, which divided the road, and rested her hand on a warped, knotty tree. Her fingers skimmed the bark, covered in a thick layer of limey lichen. Its branches sloped low and hovered above the mossy ground. Mariella had spent so many childhood hours climbing the branches in this park. She and Phil would pretend to be wizards with magical wands and secret powers. They'd collect tiny sticks to craft voodoo dolls of her father. They'd recite spells that rhymed and imagine having the power to fly, far, far away.

Mariella stared at her house, the manicured grounds and the classic gazebo. The architecture was stunning, a work of art, a pointillist painting that was idyllic from a distance, but the closer you stepped, the messier it got. No dot was taken seriously—not as an individual.

Then a familiar squeak arose, a cheerful yapping, and Mariella shifted toward her neighbor's house. A burnt-red shih tzu danced on hind legs, paws up and waving, its bangs in a ponytail. It weighed less than Mariella's cat.

"Hey, Rocky." Mariella stepped into the yard, the pup penned by an electric collar and a barrier no one could see. *I feel you, Rocky. I've got an invisible fence too.* She sighed, scratching his ears.

The raspberry-red Victorian home on High Street was nearly as old and as well maintained as the Morse property. It had sulfur-yellow molding and perky pink accents, with a distinct glass cupola rising from its roof. Not a speck of paint was chipped, because Adelaide Churchill wouldn't stand for that.

"Hi, dear," Mrs. Churchill greeted as she clipped a wilting hydrangea. The flowers had been a wedding-dress ivory this summer; now they were rotted and morphing into the color of coffee-stained teeth.

Death is everywhere, a whisper hissed.

"Hi, Mrs. Churchill." Mariella waved. "Thanks for feeding Fancy last week."

Mariella and her parents had vacationed at a beach house in Roaring Creek, Connecticut. It was only for three days, but Mariella could have pulled the duvet over her head and moved in. The seaside town was somehow even darker than Fall River. Or was everything dark to her lately?

"Anytime, dear." The woman grunted as she rose on creaky knees, tucking a gray lock of hair behind her ear. She wore dangling pearl earrings and a white blouse that buttoned up to her neck. To garden. "I was just returning the favor." She nodded to her pup trying to lick Mariella's face. She let him. Human beings might suck, but Mariella adored animals.

Every time Mrs. Churchill visited her sister in Boston, which was fairly often, Mariella fed and walked Rocky. It got Mariella out of the house, with a look-at-what-a-kind-neighbor-I-am excuse, while also providing Mariella with exactly what she needed—old people held on to a lot of interesting things in their homes that could be surprisingly useful.

"You visiting your sister again next week?" Mariella asked, rubbing the dog's belly.

"I am."

"Well, I'll be here."

At least, Mariella hoped she would. By then, she and her mom would be living alone. They'd have the grand estate to themselves. They could sell it. Maybe the town would buy it, turn it into a historical museum. Then she and Mom could use the money to flee somewhere with a seaside breeze, somewhere so distant no one would be able to place their accents. Vik could come with them; he could open an auto-body shop. Though he wouldn't have to work. None of them would. They'd inherit all the money and all the businesses. Maybe Mariella could write a novel? Or a socialite's memoir? She wondered what her mom's dreams were, if she'd ever had any, before she'd met him. Winthrop Morse would forever be reduced to a name on a few city plaques. Real life would finally begin. For both of them.

"Say hi to your parents for me," Mrs. Churchill called as Mariella turned on her heel, waving goodbye.

"Of course," Mariella said, neglecting to tell her that she might want to deliver that hello herself, at least to her father.

Because it would be the last one.

Mariella lounged on her pillow-top queen bed, her fingers buried in Fancy's long white fur. Everyone assumed her cat was a Persian because of course the Morses would have a purebred pet. But Fancy was a mutt. Mariella insisted on adopting from Fall River's animal rescue, partially funded by Lizzie Borden herself. But that wasn't why Mariella had gone there. She simply wanted to save something, to have a living creature's life be better because of her. Mariella wanted something to love that she knew would love her back.

The cat purred, her claws kneading and fluffing Mariella's thighs before plopping down, her warm heft better than any weighted blanket. Then Fancy's green eyes gave a slow I-love-you blink, and the cat began to doze just as an acoustic pop song poured from Mariella's speaker. The female singer-songwriter crooned lyrics that were melancholy and emotional, because how else were young girls supposed to feel? Boys rage on the drums, and girls cry on guitars. Maybe if men stopped raging, then girls would stop crying. Anyone ever think of that?

Her phone buzzed.

Zane: Let's stop playing games. Come over

It had been almost a year.

Mariella texted back a cryptic smiley emoji.

The whispers liked to keep Zane close—actually, they liked to keep all her friends close. You never knew who might be useful.

Zane returned emojis of his own, much more vulgar.

Zane: Tonight

Mariella stared, the cursor blinking. Zane was right. Everything would change tonight.

She didn't respond.

Instead, she rested her head on her pillow, her eyelids growing heavy, mascara-coated lashes batting her cheeks. She hadn't slept more than two hours straight in so long. She had time for a nap, and she'd need her strength for later. Her limbs sank down, her breath slowed, and darkness fell behind her eyes.

She drifted into a heavy abyss until she was abruptly standing in the corner of her bedroom. Her soul hovered near her walk-in closet, weightless and floating above the polished wood floors.

She stared at her sleeping frame resting on a mound of pillows so high, she was practically sitting up. Fancy was curled tightly on her lap in a way that made it hard to determine her head from her tail, just a fluffy lump.

It was coming.

Mariella could sense it, but she couldn't stop it and she wasn't even sure if she should try. She was so close. The whispers were getting rid of her father. All she had to do was obey. This was no different from what she'd been doing her entire life—following the orders of those more powerful.

A wind blew in her bedroom; she couldn't feel it in her ghostly form, but she watched the breeze lift the highlighted blond hairs from her sleeping face. Her window was closed.

Then the shadow appeared.

There was a shift in the corner, dark and insidious. The figure slithered, amorphous, with hellish fire sizzling in eyes that studied her every inhale. It had no knobby wrists, knees, or elbows. Instead, it slunk, rubbery limbs clawing up her legs, then her slender arms. Demonic fingers wrapped around her wrists until its talons touched on the opposite sides and squeezed her freckled flesh. The bones of her forearm ached. How could she still feel her bones?

This wasn't real.

It bared its rows of glinting fangs, its slimy tongue dangling. It was taking its time. If it weren't a shadow, if it were truly alive (it wasn't, right? This was a nightmare), she'd say it was enjoying itself.

A scream rose in her throat and fought to escape. It was pointless; she knew that. But it was licking her face! A thick dark tea dripped in ribbons from its tongue and into her body's gaping mouth. Mariella tried to wail, lungs heaving, straining, but nothing emerged. Silence. A foul stink rolled through the room, wafting from its inky secretion. Decaying roses, moldy strawberries, and squishy onions. How did the stench not wake her?

Why couldn't she stop this?

Silent shrieks roared from her ethereal lips. Her lungs ached, desperate to slice through the gummy air.

Then the shadow lifted its tongue from her sleeping form. Its crimson eyes turned toward her floating figure, and if a shark could smile, this was what it would look like—its lips lifted at the corners with rows of pointed teeth exposed and ready to bite.

Until . . .

Mariella sat up in bed and gulped at the air, choking, her esophagus flaming. Her body lurched forward, weakened, as she ran her fingers down the slime on her neck. Scraping. Smearing. How could she feel it?

It wasn't real. It wasn't real.

But Fancy was no longer on her lap; instead, her green eyes glowed from the closet. Mariella rubbed harder at her neck, and she winced from the movement. She yanked up her sleeves and spied red welts encircling her wrists.

Vomit rose in her throat, and she forced it back, breathing long and slow until her stomach unclenched. The smell of rotting earth sat on her tongue, every night, every nap—it was the taste of horror.

Two months ago, when Mariella first took a sip of whatever that was, she had just found her mother curled on the bathroom floor, shaking and bruised. The two of them had sobbed with a collective sense of powerlessness. Then there was the tea. It was magic. (*Please let there be magic!*) It promised to tap into ancestral powers that would miraculously stop her father from inflicting more damage. Mariella thought she might inexplicably find a way to get her father locked up in prison, maybe for some white-collar crime. Or she might find the perfect glaring loophole in her mom's prenup, so she could finally divorce her abuser and not be left on the street. The tea was derived from her relatives' ancient recipe, and it overflowed with unexplainable solutions and mystical hope.

But if Mariella had known that she would go on to taste perpetual sludge, that a shadowy creature would stalk her nightmares, and that buzzing whispers would invade her brain, she never would have . . . Wait, come on, was that really true?

Mariella hated what was happening to her. She hated the lack of control.

But she also hated her father.

More. *Be honest.* She hated him more.

And the whispers were about to follow through on their magical promise of help.

Her phone vibrated on the nightstand beside her, and Mariella swiftly snatched it.

Phil: Heads up—your dad just left the B&B. He's on the warpath

Mariella's stomach rolled. Dear God, what now?

Mariella: But I picked up the stupid paperwork!

Phil: I don't think it's about that. He was screaming at my ma over nothing

Mariella: I'm sorry

Phil: Stop apologizing for him

Mariella: This is the last thing we need

Phil: Want me to pick you up?

Mariella: No, I'll call Vik

Phil: Okay. I'm here when you need me

Mariella: I know

Phil: 🌕 *You got this*

Before she could respond again, a door slammed open downstairs, the sound booming. In a house this massive, you'd be surprised at how much an echo traveled. A crash. A break. A cry.

Mariella shifted toward her doorway, noticing the rich smells drifting beneath the seam. Her mother was cooking. She was downstairs, alone, making soup. Something autumnal and comforting.

And before the door smacked shut, Dad shot words like bullets.

Mariella threw her legs off the bed, angry bruises blooming on her thighs. She pushed down her pain and the nightmare. She texted Vik: *Can you pick me up? Now?*

Vik: Of course. Be there in 5

Mariella: I'll be on the corner

She snatched her leather backpack; not the one she took to school, but the one she took for travel. The one that held more and was always ready. She slung it over her shoulder, tied her boots at the ankles, and crept toward the carpeted hallway.

"You sit in this house, all day, doing nothing! And you can't even have dinner ready?" Her father's insults bellowed up the winding stairs.

Mariella paused, unsure whether to take the next step and risk the creak of a floorboard. Dusty air caught in her raw throat as she eyeballed the wall lined with family photos going back generations. To the other Morses. Including Lizzie Borden and her sister Emma. Mariella had to wonder if their parents had deserved it.

Mom's voice hovered purposely beneath the whir of the vents pushing out heated air. She didn't want Mariella to hear, her way of protecting her. And it made Mariella's heart twist even more.

She crept toward the landing.

"I don't know how you can be this lazy." Dad hurled his abuse. "Aren't you embarrassed? You do nothing all day."

Oh, really, Dad? You want to know what Mom does all day? She cries. Then she forces herself to push open the bedroom curtains so she can make your meals, and iron your shirts, so as not to have more reasons to cry that night.

"Shh, I don't want Mariella to hear," Mom whispered.

They weren't in the kitchen. They were much closer than that, maybe near the entryway. Mom had probably come to take her father's coat, because of course she'd be expected to hang it for him. And he started in on her before she even got the hanger set on the rod.

"Who the hell cares? Let her hear." Dad's husky voice was packed with threats.

Mariella stomped, her hiking boots slamming step after step.

She was not going to give him the satisfaction of her fear anymore. She charged down the mahogany staircase, and as soon as she cleared the first-floor ceiling, Mariella peered in the direction of where she'd heard the voices.

Her parents stood in front of the double-doored closet. Her mom's head was bowed, her gaze on her designer slippers, unable to meet her daughter's stare.

Her father, however, had no such problem.

"So you *are* home," Dad spat.

"Leave Mom alone." Mariella breathed as much fire as possible into those three little words.

"You don't tell me what to do. In my own house."

"Mariella, leave." Mom's voice was measured as she pointed at the door with her eyes.

"We don't have to live like this," Mariella pleaded. There was still time. They could run. Start over. Figure it out.

"What are you gonna do?" Dad took a step, snarl on his lips.

"She's just being a teenager," Mom deflected. "Mariella, I'm fine. I'll see you later." Her words were clipped and controlled.

"Listen to your mother."

Mariella took in her father's twitching cheek and her mother's painfully calm face. Winthrop Morse hadn't actually hit his daughter. Yet. He'd swatted a few times. Pushed her twice. But he hadn't left a mark. Sometimes, in the most toxic part of her soul, Mariella wished he would, so that she could have physical proof of his cruelty, and so that she could stop fearing that the abuse inflicted on her mother included blows really meant for *her*.

Mom placed a manicured hand carefully on her husband's

arm. "We got a letter from your fraternity today. They want to honor you at the reunion. Isn't that nice?" She guided him away, creating distance between him and his daughter. He surprisingly followed.

"Took 'em long enough," Dad grumbled.

We'll help you. The whispers were almost gentle. *We'll help her. You can do this. For both of you.*

Mariella swallowed her guilt and shame—at leaving the house and at leaving her mom. With him. He could kill her.

That's why it has to be tonight. There's no more time, the whispers insisted.

They were right.

Mariella turned for the door, and she did as she was told.

CHAPTER FIVE

TESSA

The detective standing in front of Tessa was wearing pink lipstick. Actually, it was more of a rosy nude, paired with a slick blond bun, blushed cheeks, and impressively long eyelashes.

According to the plaque on her desk, her name was Detective Julia Ertz. Though Tessa heard a fellow cop call her Jules.

"So, all you know is that your brother left the house at six last night to pick up his girlfriend, Mariella Morse. You thought they were either hanging out together or going to a party. But they never arrived at the party. And Vik's state of mind was"— she flipped the page of her skinny spiral notebook in annoyingly dramatic fashion—" 'good, normal.' "

"Yes." Tessa nodded in the affirmative. Then Frankie tugged her arm like it was time to go.

"If you have no further questions, I think we're done here." Frankie rose.

"Of course, you've been so helpful." The sarcasm was thick in the detective's voice.

But Tessa wasn't trying to be unhelpful. She honestly knew nothing. Vik didn't share the details of his dates with Mariella; that would be gross. Whatever they did—or didn't do—when they got together was their business. Well, until it made the news and landed him in jail. Tessa wished she had more information. She wished she could do anything to help.

The detective stood, her six-foot frame towering over Tessa, who was scraping five two-and-a-half. The half was important. Tessa felt it made her technically not short.

"Teresa, one more question." The cop used her full name, which only her abuela ever used and always with a Puerto Rican accent. It sounded just plain wrong from this woman's lips. "Do you *like* Mariella Morse?"

"What?" Tessa lifted her eyebrows in surprise.

This wasn't a question she was expecting.

"Do you like your brother's girlfriend? Do you think she's a good person?"

Tessa looked helplessly at Frankie, unsure if she should answer. Was it perjury to lie to a cop about her feelings?

"How is this relevant?" Frankie asked, sensing Tessa's unease.

"Because the news is painting Ms. Morse as a damsel in distress and her parents as martyrs. But from what I hear, a lot of people didn't like the Morse family," the cop explained.

"Then, you'll have to ask them." Frankie sounded definitive.

The detective kept her eyes trained on Tessa. "I'm sure you

heard Mariella's statement to the press. She's saying your brother butchered her parents with an axe, in her home, while she was there, and she wasn't able to stop him."

"What are you saying?" Frankie tilted her head, black hair cascading over her shoulder as she read the spaces between the officer's words.

"We're still waiting for the final report from the medical examiner. Autopsies aren't complete, but I can tell you this, it takes a while to swing an axe that many times. And Mariella didn't call the police until *after* both her parents were dead. Let's just say that scene, the whole night . . . I have some questions."

Frankie's mouth fell open, and Tessa could sense what she was thinking, what Detective Ertz was implying. "I'd like to hear those questions," Frankie said.

"And I'd like your client to remember some details," Ertz countered.

Frankie narrowed her eyes, a retort on her lips, when a uniformed officer from across the room shot up and called her name, arm flapping. "Hey, Frankie, we got paperwork, about your kid. The axe guy," he shouted. "I need ya to sign this!"

"You mean the kid who's presumed innocent," Frankie yelled back.

"Yeah, yeah. Just get ovah heah." The cop waved.

"I'll be right back." Frankie looked at Tessa. "Don't say anything."

As soon as Frankie walked away, Detective Ertz snatched a yellow Post-it pad from her desk and began scribbling with a red pen.

"Does your brother believe in ghosts?" the cop blurted.

"What?" Tessa's forehead crumpled. Where the heck did that come from?

"Ghosts? Witches? The supernatural?" The detective talked quickly, still writing. "Did Vik want to be a ghost-hunting YouTube star? Was he into that stuff?"

Tessa thought back to their conversation at lunch—God, was that just yesterday? It was as if time had sped up since then and dropped her family off in a future dystopian hellmouth. But what had Vik said about the Lizzie Borden House? He wasn't a "ghosts and goblins type of person." Tessa eyed the cop cautiously, the answer on her tongue, but Frankie had told her not to talk, so Tessa pressed her lips firmly shut.

"Fine." The detective took the hint, then she handed over the Post-it. The note read "Julia Ertz" and was followed by a phone number.

"That's my cell." The detective's eyes lasered on Tessa. "I've lived in this town my entire life. Believe me when I say, *I have some questions.*"

There was an intensity to her words and a flicker of hope to her actions, but before Tessa could break her vow of silence, Ertz shifted her sight line. Frankie was moving their way. Ertz peered back at Tessa with hidden meaning; she didn't want Frankie to know she'd just handed over her private phone number. Tessa folded the Post-it and slid it into her back pocket.

Ertz nodded with a grin. "If you think of anything, Teresa, call me. Anytime. Okay?"

Tessa nodded. She wasn't delusional enough to think this cop was on her side. It was clear the detective thought her brother was guilty, but it also seemed she thought there was a lot more to the story. What ghosts and witches had to do with her theories, Tessa had no clue, but having a cop thinking outside the box was a lot better than believing all the cops had already slammed the box shut.

🦅

Frankie led Tessa, her mom, and her tía Dolores to a side exit partially blocked by a dumpster and hidden from cameras and crowds. A car was already idling.

"It was awful." That was all Tessa said to her aunt, who was desperate for details. But Tessa and her mom were unable to speak about the unrecognizable slump to Vik's spirit. Not yet. The entire drive, Mom rested her weary head on her fist, her body angled toward the window, and her mind in silent contemplation. That was until the pink laundromat came into view, and they all spied the crowd flocked on the sidewalk, blocking the plate glass window with the whirling machines inside.

"Vultures," Tía Dolores hissed at the cameras.

"Please go around back, to the alley, behind the pizza place," Tessa instructed the driver as she leaned forward in her seat.

Vik was friends with Angelo, who worked the register at the pizza shop, which shared a wall with the laundromat. Vik changed the oil on Angelo's ten-year-old junker for free, almost every month, in exchange for free slices. Tessa knew there was a basement entrance, connecting the pizza parlor to their building. It was out of sight of the reporters.

The SUV crunched down the dark alley, which was bordered by a chain-link fence topped with barbed wire. The three women crept out by the basement door and rushed safely inside, their shadows unnoticed by the hungry crowd.

"What do they want from us?" Tía Dolores griped as they stomped down a few concrete stairs.

"To profit from our pain," Tessa replied.

Her phone buzzed.

Phil: I saw you on the news. At the station. Were you able to see Vik?

Tessa's thumbs moved swiftly as the group navigated between metal shelving units in the dimly lit cellar, scents shifting from marinara sauce to laundry exhaust as they inched closer to their destination.

Tessa: Yeah, he looked like a stranger
Phil: I'm sorry
Tessa: You didn't do anything
Phil: I know, but I wish I could help
Tessa: I wish you could too
Phil: Wanna come over? Watch a movie? Take your mind off it?

As if that were possible. Her mind couldn't think of anything else. Tessa led her mom and her aunt toward a metal door with a sign showing a stick figure hiking upstairs.

Tessa: I don't think I can leave my mom
Phil: I get it. Whenever you're ready

Phil: I'm thinking about you
Tessa: I know. Thanks

Tessa tugged open the heavy door, steel scraping the cement floor. Fluorescent lights flickered, casting an eerie green glow.

"I don't feel right leaving Victor." Mom spoke for the first time since they'd left the station, leaning heavily on the banister as she climbed the steep steps.

"I know. But Frankie's with him. She's amazing." Tessa turned to look at her aunt. "I'm so glad we have her."

"She *is* perfección. And if there were something we could do for Vik, she'd tell us. We'll see him at the arraignment," said Tía Dolores.

Tessa couldn't shake Frankie's expression when she'd talked about the bail hearing, emphasizing the *double* homicide. The case was gaining national attention. Pressure was mounting.

But Vik didn't do it. He'd never done anything illegal in his life. Ever. That had to count for something.

They pounded toward the first floor, all of them huffing from exhaustion and sleeplessness. They lived on the second story, and the last thing her mother needed was to climb an extra flight of stairs.

"He's all alone." Tears clogged her mom's voice. "This is so wrong."

"I know," Tessa agreed. Vik should be at the garage working today. He should be complaining about Zane trying to get free engine maintenance or a discounted tire. He should be fighting with Mom about the laundry on his bedroom floor and begging

Tessa to leave the house. He shouldn't be trying to remember how he ended up at a murder scene.

Tessa tugged open the door that led to the apartments, and immediately thumping beats of reggaeton reverberated into her chest. There were three apartments above Laundry World, but this staircase led only to their unit, which should be empty.

Tessa swung toward Tía Dolores, eyes accusatory.

"What?" Her aunt shrugged as if Tessa should have expected this. And she should have. "Did you really think they wouldn't come?"

Mom gripped Tía Dolores's biceps with a fresh jolt of life, then she accelerated up the stairs in time with the bass line of the latest Bad Bunny hit. The garlicky scent of mofongo wafted all the way down the steps, reminding Tessa's stomach that she hadn't taken a bite of food since sometime yesterday. She trailed her mom, the sudden bounce in her step more reassuring than the sounds of life, normal life, up ahead.

Tía Dolores yanked open their front door, which of course was unlocked, because she must've told them where to find the spare key. "Ay, you made it! ¡Bienvenidos!"

A rush of Puerto Rican relatives paraded to the entry, groping for hugs, shoulders, kisses, empathy.

"¡Ay, bendito!"

"¡Como esta Victor?"

"¡Todo se fue al garete!"

"¡Es mierde!"

Tessa didn't speak much Spanish. Or any, really. She could

understand it, from being around her relatives so much, but she only spoke in English.

"We just saw him. He's okay," Tessa lied, slapping on a strained half smile as her tía Gloria gripped her in a way that demonstrated why the term *bear hug* existed.

"¡Mentiras!" Tía Gloria continued squeezing, rocking them side to side. "All lies. *We* know Victor."

"I know." Tessa nodded against her aunt's shoulder, her eyes growing damp. But inside that hug, the tears weren't just from sorrow; she felt love and gratitude. Tessa hadn't realized how isolated she'd been ever since she left Philly. These people, her people, had traveled here without a single question or a word of explanation. Because they all knew, down in their very bone marrow, that Vik would never do this. They didn't care what the news said, what the evidence said—this wasn't Vik.

Tessa spied her abuela hugging her mother, fingers tangled in her hair.

"Shhhh, shhhh," Abuela whispered as Mom sobbed on her shoulder. A mother needing her mother.

Tessa gulped the tears building in her own throat from an amalgam of colliding emotions ranging from fear to love. She stepped back, twisting her head toward Tía Dolores, who was rapidly speaking Spanish to her tío Ricardo, detailing everything they knew of the case so far. Their eyes met, and Tessa smiled in appreciation. If it weren't for Tía Dolores's girlfriend, Vik wouldn't have a lawyer. And if it weren't for her kindness, they wouldn't have this support right now.

They needed this.

"Ay, the plátanos!" Tía Gloria rushed toward a sizzling frying pan with a batch of sliced bananas spitting oil.

Bad Bunny blared from the kitchen radio, relatives chatted too fast to follow any one conversation, and coffee was brewed, pot after pot, mixing with the scent of pork, garlic, and saffron steaming in the air. For the first time since the news had broken, Tessa's shoulders slid down her back. She smoothed her black-and-white flannel shirt, and she imagined she'd traveled through time and was back in her kitchen in Fishtown, before it all fell apart.

"Hey," said a voice from behind her. Deep, masculine, familiar.

Tessa's hands froze on her hips, fingers tight.

She should have known he would come.

If she had been more clearheaded, she probably would have texted him. Not just because he was one of Vik's best friends but because he was a lot more than that.

At least, he had been once.

Tessa turned, body stiff, and just the sight of those chocolate eyes sucked the wind from her chest so forcefully, she rocked back a step.

Oscar Jenkins was smiling, as always, because he was the happiest person Tessa had ever met. He held a spark in those dimples that could rival even her brother's.

"Hey." She grinned, from her heart to her eyes. Just the sight of him.

Had she really forgotten? *No,* her heart thumped in response, pounding against her ribs in a way it hadn't in over a year.

"I hope it's okay I came. My mom's here, obviously." He pointed a finger at Toni Jenkins, Mom's best friend. Oscar was her son, and Tessa's ex-boyfriend—she broke up with him the day before they left Philly.

Tessa took two big steps in her low-top sneakers and wrapped herself around him. His solid arms locked on her waist, where they'd always fit, and she pressed her forehead against the brown skin at the crook of his neck, her fingers scratching at the familiar feel of his fade.

Everything she'd been holding in, the crushing fear pressing her spine, the tears rising behind fake smiles, it all flowed onto Oscar's chest. So naturally. She sniffled, dampening his black T-shirt.

Oscar hugged her closer.

Someone was there to take care of *her*.

They sat on the fire escape that extended from Tessa's bedroom window, hovering above the back alley and chain-link fence she'd rushed by only moments ago. The reporters were clustered on the front sidewalk, mercifully out of view.

Tessa picked at the rusted metal railing, the thick white paint chipped and cracked, as she stared down the dim alley that ended in a barren parking lot. She might never get over how much parking there was in Fall River. Open outdoor lots sat everywhere, most with barely a car or two in the spaces. You could just pull over and park on the side of the road, and there wasn't even a meter.

In addition to the pizza parlor, Laundry World sat adjacent to a restaurant-supply store. The front boulevard was wide and busy, with a Dunkin' nestled kitty-corner to keep reporters fueled. Apparently, Dunkin' was the WaWa of Massachusetts. The chain was everywhere, and walks for morning coffee had become a ritual on the weekends. With Vik. He drank his black; she got hers flavored, iced, sweetened, and full of milk.

Was Fall River going to become just like Philly? Where she couldn't stroll down a street without being haunted by memories of a life she no longer had?

Her knee bopped anxiously, shaking the rickety metal stairs, which were anchored to the wall by screws likely older than she was. Oscar gripped her knee, stopping her jitters. They were hip-to-hip on a fire escape that felt like home to the city kids they were. Plus, it was the only place they could find privacy in an apartment full of talkative relatives.

"Damn, he really doesn't remember anything?" Oscar shook his head.

"Nope." Tessa folded forward, the hood of her black sweatshirt flopping onto her head, shoving her wavy, dark hair into her face. She tugged the zipper higher, the air just a few degrees shy of needing a winter coat. "He was so confused and so . . . God, I don't even know. He *sobbed*."

"Shit."

Oscar had been at their father's funeral. Vik gave a eulogy

without shedding a tear. He actually made people laugh, even with a mahogany casket in front of him.

"How are they explaining the memory thing?"

"They're not." Tessa sat up, yanking her hoodie strings tighter. "They're gonna get a shrink, and check for drugs and stuff, but you know Vik."

"It's definitely not *that*." Oscar tsked. "Hell, remember the roller-skating thing? I thought Vik was gonna kill me."

It was spring, about a year and a half ago, pre–her world collapsing. *Before Times,* as Tessa called it. Spruce Street Harbor Park had just opened for the season on the Delaware River. Colorful striped hammocks swung between trees, alongside gourmet food trucks and beachy Adirondack chairs that looked across the muddy water from Philly to Jersey. The outdoor ice-skating rink had been converted to roller-skating for the warmer months, and Tessa and Oscar were supposed to meet Vik and his new girlfriend.

"What was that chick's name?" Oscar asked. "Libby?"

"Lexi," Tessa corrected. "Man, Vik was *sooo* pissed."

It was the first time Tessa had ever drunk a beer. Oscar had snagged some from his cousin's birthday party, and they chugged them before walking down to the rink, tripping over their feet the whole way. Tessa had never roller-skated in her life, and she was so hysterical at even attempting to lace the four-wheeled boots, she nearly fell off the metal bench she sat on. That was when Vik smelled the Coors Light on her breath.

"You got my sister drunk!" Vik hollered, shoving Oscar's shoulders, hard. Oscar was as new to alcohol as she was, and he started to topple at merely the sound of Vik's booming voice.

"We're just having fun!" Oscar collapsed beside her, the two of them giggling and holding each other up.

Then her stomach started to churn, bubbling and twisting. The world spun, and the clouds in the blue sky zipped faster than they should. Sweat broke out under her arms and down her cheeks. Maybe it was the convulsions of the giggles or maybe it was the smell of Old Bay seasoning on the crab fries nearby, but Tessa barely made it to the bathroom in time. She puked in a public restroom with puddles on the ground that she really doubted were water.

Eventually, Vik's date, Lexi Wheeler, awkwardly peeled Tessa off the cruddy blue tiles, and as soon as they emerged, Vik marched Tessa to his Jeep. He said nothing as she rolled down the window, the air smacking her clammy face as they drove. Vik snuck her past their parents, who were watching a movie in the finished basement, completely oblivious.

The next day, Tessa awoke to a combination of a drum solo and a piercing sword in her skull. When she looked down, she saw that she'd managed to wash her face and put on her pj's, but she couldn't remember. Chunks of the night were missing.

"Don't ever do that again," Vik said, the look of disappointment on his face worse than any her mother could give.

"Well, we know Vik doesn't drink." Oscar pulled her from the memory. "And if it's drugs, then his girlfriend's a psycho who slipped him something."

"I'm not ruling that out." There was a reason Tessa didn't

want to answer questions about Mariella Morse with Detective Ertz—Tessa honestly didn't know her. And definitely not well enough to immediately absolve the girl of harming her brother. "Frankie's looking into everything. Seriously, I can't believe this is real life. What are we gonna do?"

"There's nothing you *can* do." Oscar touched her arm. "You got him a lawyer. A good one."

"I know, but my mom . . ."

"Is a grown woman," Oscar interjected. "Let her handle this."

"But I can't just sit here!"

"Maybe sittin' here is what you need. Give yourself a minute before you go off and do something." There was an undercurrent to his words, and they both knew it.

The last time tragedy struck, Tessa convinced her family to run away before the wound could heal. She left behind Oscar, her life, and everything she knew.

Tessa curled into her lap, hair tumbling in front of her face.

Oscar pulled back his hand from her arm. "Hey, I'm not trying to kick you while you're down or nothing, but it's been a year and you haven't called, or texted, or visited. You're not on social media. It's like you up and disappeared. Did that really help?"

"No. Maybe. I don't know." Tessa dug her fingers into her wavy locks.

Tessa had been with Oscar, in his car, when her father took his last breath.

Dad had asked her to run an errand after school. They had her abuela's birthday dinner the next evening, and Dad wanted

Tessa to pick up a card and cupcakes. But by the time Tessa remembered, she was wrapped up in Oscar, with locked doors and steamed windows. *Whatever,* she thought; she could get the cupcakes tomorrow. They stayed blissfully entangled, their phones turned off so no parent could track their location to a dark parking spot along the Schuylkill River.

Eventually, they got dressed and flicked on their phones, finally seeing a barrage of messages. Bubble after bubble. Not as many as followed Vik's arrest, but somehow unfathomably worse.

Vik: Tess come quick. Something's happened to dad

Vik: Where are you? There was an accident

Vik: I think you're with Oscar. I'm gonna try him

Vik: Whenever you get this just go straight to Temple Hospital

Vik: Tess OMG! You have to call me

Vik: I can't believe this is happening. Where are you?

Vik: Don't call mom. Whatever you do, don't call mom

Vik: It's bad really bad

Vik: We're still in the ER but you've gotta get here!

Then she saw a voice mail alert, and she hit play: "Teresa, it's Pop. I don't see the card or the cupcakes on the counter. I think you forgot. I'm gonna run out and get them. The bakery's still open. I just need to hurry. So if you get this, don't pick up the cupcakes. I'm doing it now. And we're gonna talk about you being more responsible."

Those were his final words to her.

Minutes later, her father was T-boned by a suburbanite texting and driving right through a red light. Dad was rushed to the hospital, and by the time Tessa and Oscar raced through the emergency room doors, he was gone. Tessa never got to say goodbye, and she never got to say she was sorry.

Tessa went out the next day and bought her abuela those cupcakes. And she'd been trying to be responsible ever since. She owed it to her father. She had to prove she could be a better person, a New Tessa.

But she couldn't do it in Philly.

That intersection—her dad was hit only three blocks from their house. Their family couldn't walk past that corner anymore. Tessa couldn't see Federal Donuts and not think of her dad picking up a dozen on Sundays after church. She cried at the sight of the bodega where he would grab cheap ten-dollar roses for her mother, and she swore the cheesesteaks from his favorite place were now overcooked on stale bread. The memories were everywhere.

And especially with Oscar. If she had just gotten those cupcakes . . .

So Tessa convinced her mom and brother to put the hovering dark memories in the rearview mirror; only, the storm clouds seemed to follow them up I-95 and raise them another thunderbolt of catastrophe.

Tessa clasped her hands behind her head, tugging on her neck, stretching her knotted muscles. "Oscar, my mom's been through so much already."

"So have *you*." He nudged her shoulder. "And Vik."

"He can't go to prison." The words physically hurt to say.

"I know." Oscar leaned in, his warmth spreading against her

skin. He smelled exactly the same—cinnamon gum and woodsy deodorant. Tessa closed her eyes, her head swimming with emotions too tight to unravel.

"But, girl, I gotta keep it real." Oscar's voice was gentle. "What happens next, it's not up to you. Ask any mom in North Philly—you can't control the legal system. And right now, you've got a brown kid accused of killing two rich white people."

"That's why we've gotta do something!" Tessa bolted upright.

"We will. We'll come *at* them, but I don't want you to put this all on yourself. You got that one detective. She sounds all right, might not play straight by the book. And I like what she said about *Mariella*." Oscar's nose crinkled, like her name tasted bad. Tessa appreciated that. Of course, Tessa knew Mariella was a victim—her parents were dead and that was tragic. But it didn't stop Tessa from blaming the girl who was last seen with her brother, the one who called Vik a murderer. Tessa was grateful not to have to explain her feelings to Oscar. "A rich white girl is at home and doesn't call the cops till after *both* her parents are dead. And Vik remembers nothing. That's sketchy as hell."

"Thank you!" Tessa swung toward him, not realizing how close he was. Her nose almost bumped into his.

Oscar didn't pull back. Instead, they stayed there, two people who always seemed capable of creating an electric charge.

It had been over a year, and her heart was acting like she'd been in his car yesterday. Whatever had been between them in Philly—love, it had been love—was still there. They hadn't broken up because they stopped caring for each other. Instead, Tessa had packed up her feelings with the knickknacks in her room and pretended she could go the rest of her life without opening that box in her soul.

. Then the box showed up on her doorstep.

"I know Vik didn't do it," she whispered.

"You don't gotta convince me," Oscar said, eyes on her lips with that look he always had, the one that sent a sizzle burning through her. "I'm on your side. You know that."

Tessa rested her forehead against his; then he reached for her hand, lacing their fingers. It was so familiar, so "back in the day," the smell of him, the feel of him.

But time *had* passed. Shit *had* happened. Bad shit.

"Tessa! Tessa, where are you?" Tía Dolores shrieked from inside the apartment.

Tessa jerked back, awkwardly clearing her throat as Oscar smacked his hands against his thighs and straightened his posture.

Tessa bent toward the window, peering inside. "What it is? What's wrong?"

Her aunt stood in the doorway, her curly black shag shaking in a way that meant more bad news, which didn't seem possible. When you hit rock bottom, you aren't supposed to find another charred layer buried deeper below the crust.

"It's the news." Tía Dolores's tone was grave. "They found out about Vik's bio dad."

CHAPTER SIX

The day of the murders . . .

MARIELLA

Mariella sat next to Vik in the Jeep, the sleeves of her oversized sweater pulled into her clenched fists. The wool was fuzzy and chunky, with wide stripes, the sweater hiding the bruises blossoming on her wrists. From *it*. They matched the welts on her legs but in no way compared to the internal lesions ripped open by her father's words.

She'd left her mother there.

Not for long, the whispers reminded her.

Mariella swallowed her tears with a throat raw from poor attempts at screaming. Shame coursed through her veins. She'd let this happen. The shadow. Her father. Mariella could have fought harder. But here she sat, in this car, doing exactly what she was told.

No one cares about a sad little rich girl who doesn't make the right choices.

"You okay?" Vik took his hand off the leather wheel, still shiny and uncracked. He'd bought the Jeep used, back in Philly, and it had a million miles on it, but it was immaculate, cared for as if it were a Porsche straight off the assembly line. Vik was a kid who'd lost two dads, had a single mother, and grew up with virtually no spare money. Yet he was driving his own car, paid for with the money he'd earned.

Mariella wasn't allowed to work. Neither was her mother. A driver's license was out of the question for Winthrop Morse's daughter, and Mom couldn't have a car in her own name. Dad controlled their credit cards, bank accounts, and trust funds. Mariella wasn't supposed to date Vik (or anyone else, really), and Mom was no longer given access to her friends. Her mother could barely leave the house.

So of course, Mariella had drunk the tea. The shadows, the whispers, all of it—was any of that actually worse than her father? At least the tea offered hope.

It's almost over, the voices insisted. Her constant mantra. *It's almost over. It's almost over. It's almost over.*

Vik reached for her arm, as he often did when they drove together. The Taunton River skirted beside them, flowing beneath a dense white fog. Its nut-brown water rippled against the gray warships lining Battleship Cove. Fall River had the world's largest collection of World War II battleships, which every public school kid in the area could tell you, thanks to their Massachusetts State History class. Even the mile-long truss bridge connecting them to Providence and Somerset was named after a WWII soldier—Charles Braga, a local Portuguese immigrant who died in Pearl Harbor. Mariella knew that, yet she couldn't properly pronounce the name of the Native American tribe that was slaughtered here after the Pilgrims landed, creating the Bridgewater Triangle's earliest legends. People have a way of selecting whose history is worth remembering.

Mariella wondered what the future residents of Fall River might remember about her father, and she doubted it would be her mother's bruises.

Vik's fingers brushed her skin, clasping around her wrist, and she flinched with a shock of pain, a yelp escaping her lips before she could stop it.

"What's wrong?"

"Nothing," she sputtered, her thin voice betraying her. She pushed her blond waves in front of her face.

They slowed at a red light, the dark-blue bridge stretching in the distance, the postcard symbol of the city, its steel beams crossing in the triangular patterns of a cage. Welcome to Fall River.

Vik's eyes bore into her profile, but she couldn't shift his way. The truth about what went on inside the Morse home was a secret guarded by painfully clenched teeth. Damn, she wasn't sure her father even understood how abusive he was. He was too busy being honored by the town (and apparently, his college fraternity). *Winthrop Morse, Local Son, Revitalizes Fall River.*

Mariella didn't have any siblings. Her grandparents were dead. Her mom had a sister who she had been cut off from decades ago and who Mariella had never met. And her dad's only brother had died of cancer when Mariella was five years old. Phil was the one person who had been in Mariella's life long enough to catch on to the family's painful reality, and he was also born and bred here, with a deep understanding of how far her father's connections stretched.

Mariella peered out the car window, at the textile mills dotting the waterfront, once crumbling and abandoned, now converted into trendy real estate—owned by her father. Everywhere Mariella looked, she saw Winthrop Morse. She couldn't escape him.

Vik leaned over, tucking a lock of hair behind her ear so he could clearly see her face. She felt exposed, but also comforted; she leaned into him.

"You're in knots." He massaged her shoulder.

"Crappy day."

"Wanna talk about it?"

She shook her head no. "Let's just go to our spot."

"You sure? The sun'll set soon." His eyes flicked between her, the digital dashboard clock, and the traffic light. It switched to green, and he returned both hands to the wheel, pressing on the gas.

"Yeah, I just want to be with you, someplace quiet, and away from here." Mariella allowed her head to rest against his shoulder, exhausted from the nightmare that haunted her sleep and the one that trampled her halls.

She smelled the lemony blend of his shampoo, mixed with the dryer-sheet scent that always clung to his clothes. She tried to let the aroma of Vik fill her nostrils and erase the stink of dead plants that constantly filled her mouth. She rolled a cough drop over her tongue, sucking the menthol.

It wasn't enough. Nothing was ever enough.

"We can go somewhere else. Someplace closer?" Vik said. "It could get cold tonight."

"You keep me warm." She wrapped her hands around his biceps as he drove, repeating his words from earlier today.

"Always," he said.

Always, the whispers repeated.

"Always," said Mariella.

And she would have said it anyway, even if the whispers hadn't told her to. At least she thought she would have.

Vik treated hiking like a stroll on a white sandy beach. He wore slippery soles that couldn't possibly grip the gravel, his easy smile conveyed "no place to be," and he swaggered, his fingers threaded through hers. The tall pines stretched toward graphite clouds as Mariella's boots crunched along a wide path lined with dried brittle needles in a washed-out orange hue. He rubbed his thumb against her wrist in what he meant to be an affectionate gesture, but her bruise pulsed. She contracted.

Vik stopped, his sneakers skidding. He dropped the backpack he was carrying, for her, full of supplies that made a splashing sound. "What's going on?"

"Nothing." She gave a rehearsed *What do you mean?* look.

His eyes sharpened. "Let me see your wrist."

She tucked her fingers into her knitted sweater sleeves, forming fists he couldn't see.

A bird, something gray and speckled—a pigeon? What was that doing here?—flapped overhead, the wind of its wings whipping her hair. In all the times she'd hiked the Freetown–Fall River State Forest, she'd never spotted a bird. Or heard a tweet. Not a single one. These woods held a hollow silence, the bubbling movement of water on rock the only occasional sound. And there were no smells, no pungent pollen or floral blossoms.

At first, the nothingness was confounding, even frightening—but now it made sense. Something *was* alive in here, horribly alive. She could feel it now.

"You can tell me what's wrong." Vik reached for her.

Mariella didn't look his way. Her eyes scanned the thick tree trunks marred with chartreuse lichen and choked with invasive vines, twisting and knotting. Skinny saplings sprouted around them, one after another after another, all fighting for light. There were no birds, but there were bugs. Yes, insects swarmed and crawled in this ominous place. Mariella swore she could hear them breathing. She could feel their eyes, all those eyes, watching her, tracking her.

"I'm just tired," she said, her body feeling . . . off. Edgy. Cold.

These woods could sap your sanity. She knew that all too well.

Vik touched her biceps, then pushed up her baggy sleeve so abruptly that she stumbled. Her hiking boot caught on a rock, and Vik held her, restoring her balance, her sleeve shoved up to her elbow.

The bruise he exposed was practically magenta. It formed a

circle around her wrist, swelling the creases where her forearm kissed her hand. The shadow's talons had met along the two bulging tendons below her palm. One wrong move and slice—she would have been opened up. In her nightmares.

Because it *was* a nightmare. She was hurting herself in her sleep. Her mind was so exhausted, she was so worried about tonight, that she was causing herself physical harm. A sheet must have accidentally wrapped too tightly around her joint, while her fists thrashed her thighs in bed. It made sense.

"What is this?" Vik spat. "*Who* did this?"

Mariella tugged away, sliding her sleeves down and wrapping her arms around her chest, hands shoved into her armpits.

Say it's rope burn. From gym class, the whispers fed a lie.

A sickly wave of heat burned toward her belly as she pictured the shadow's oily tongue. Dripping. No, it couldn't be real. *Nightmare, nightmare, nightmare.*

"We had to climb the rope in PE today. I guess I grabbed it wrong."

"You don't have gym on Friday." Vik stepped closer, his mind sharp.

"I meant yesterday." The deceit piled high in her throat, and she swallowed it down with the vile taste of her saliva mixed with menthol.

Vik paused, controlling his breathing, trying to calm himself. He was finally seeing the truth.

Mariella prepared to explain, but a sudden pull of air stopped her. The gush was audible and cool. It came from behind her. Or above her. Was it the wind? Only it felt rhythmic. In and out, the air pushed, soft and subtle, matching her breath. *We're here. We see you . . .*

It wasn't the whispers. It wasn't inside her. It was the woods; it was out there.

A chill raced over her skin as the temperature dropped several degrees. Mariella shivered, rubbing her biceps.

"Mari, I love you. You know that. So I'm just gonna ask—is there something going on? At home?" Vik's words plunked into Mariella's gut, and she was shaking her head no before he could even finish his thought.

Don't let him know, the whispers instructed. *You know what he'll do. It'll ruin everything.*

"I'm fine." Mariella tried to smile, but it felt like a grimace.

"I've met your dad *once* . . . In a year." Vik placed his hands protectively on her shoulders, his palms so warm. He leaned his head toward hers and let out a long sigh. "Is he hurting you?"

Mariella was supposed to say no. There was no way Vik could possibly help (not legally, anyway), and she had to safeguard the family name. The money. If somehow the news of what her father was really like spread beyond Fall River, Mariella and her mom would be left with nothing. Her dad had threatened her with this more than once. If Winthrop Morse got #MeToo'd, he swore he'd use all their finances (which were in his name, and his name only) to fight the charges in court. It would smear all of them, and the story would follow her and her mom forever, with bank accounts bled dry. And that, of course, was only *if* her dad got arrested, which was highly unlikely. Do you know how hard it is to prosecute domestic violence? Without a dead body? And in a town where everyone would be on *his* side because he signed their paychecks, or funded their charities, or got them elected?

No, Mariella had to end this her way. At least, she thought it was her way.

A low rustle shuffled from a nearby bush. Her senses felt heightened. She cocked her ear, trying to pick out the vibration, but only caught the continued breaths from Vik's chest and the sound of the hairs lifting on her arms. Can you hear your hairs rising? A rush of sludge filled her cheeks, and she fought the urge to spit, eyes skittering about. She could feel the bugs again, breathing and watching—from the trees, in the branches, and burrowed into the moldy logs. Something in these woods was alive and aware of Mariella's presence.

Stick to the plan, the whispers ordered, but Mariella squinted, trying to force the invasive voice away. This was *her* mind. Her choice. She was in control. Tears blurred her vision as she shook her head, and Vik's arms were instantly on her, wrapping around her shoulders, misinterpreting her emotions. One hand cradled her head. "It's okay. Shhhh. It's gonna be okay."

She nodded against his shoulder, because she wanted it to be true. She really did. But *okay* felt like a fairy tale. Tears soaked his sweatshirt.

"We'll figure this out," he whispered.

Maybe he could fix this? Maybe there was a way to stop her father, permanently, with no one else getting physically hurt. Without *Vik* getting involved. Didn't she owe it to Vik to try? She wanted to try.

This opportunity will never arise again. It must be now. Do it. Do it. Do it. The shouts collided against her cranium, slamming into gray matter, crashing against her eye sockets. A buzzing, buzzing, buzzing reverberated through her body, a fiery itch spreading beneath her pores. She stepped back, scratching at her arms, her bruises, her soul. A wind gushed by, carrying the stench of motor exhaust, sharp and biting. A rev of an engine echoed in the distance. A dirt bike. The woods were full of them. They weren't alone.

You know what to do. You know what to do.

Her hands clapped to her ears, her gaze frantically searching. Those eyes, where were those eyes? She could feel them, fighting with the whispers. Or they were part of the whispers. Or was her mind too far gone? Maybe all of it, all of it at once.

"Mari, are you okay? What's going on?" Vik sounded panicked.

"Let's get to the Ledge," she blurted, dropping her arms. Then she marched, feet clomping. She had to go.

"Are you sure? It's getting late." Vik trotted behind.

"I don't care." She continued forward, soft gravel smashing underfoot.

Liquid gargled in the backpack as Vik stomped behind her. "Mari, we have to tell someone. About your dad." He reached for her shoulder, but she shrugged him off.

"There's nothing to tell." She didn't slow her stride.

She wouldn't let Vik stop her. The whispers were right. She had a plan, and she would see it through before the window of opportunity closed. It was the only way. Her way.

"He's hurting you. Is he hurting your mom too?"

"I never said any of that." She huffed with conviction. "Stop pushing your daddy issues off on me." It was a nasty card to pull from the deck, but she slapped it on the virtual table.

"What?" Vik skidded to a halt, his high-tops sliding on the sandy path.

"You heard me." She didn't stop. She knew he'd follow her. He'd never let her hike in this forest alone; he'd fear the woods were far too dangerous for a girl. It was almost laughable. Mariella didn't have a single female friend afraid of a stranger in the bushes. No. The men in hockey masks could stay in the horror movies. In the real world, the vulnerable were far too busy dreading the men they saw on the street, in their homes, or in their schools, every day.

Vik resumed his stride, as expected. Danger, danger.

"You don't mean that," he said.

"I do. I'm sorry that your stepdad died, and that the other one is, well, *not available,* but leave my dad out of this." Vik never spoke of his bio dad. In fact, he'd only mentioned it to Mariella once—that he and Tessa had different fathers. Mariella was now hoping it was a subject sore enough to completely divert the current conversation.

Good. The whispers approved.

"Mari, that was mean." Vik's long legs stretched, keeping pace, step for step. "I know you're hurting, but I'm only trying to help."

She spun around. "Can we just *not* right now?" Her arm

flung at their surroundings. "I come out here to breathe, not be interrogated. If you can't do that—"

"Of course I can do that." He clasped his hands, begging her to let him in. "Whatever you need."

"Well, right now, I need to get to the Ledge, away from everything. I want to see the sunset and be *us*." She reached for his hand, knowing exactly what he liked. Mariella tilted her head, wavy blond locks falling over her shoulder, then she batted her lashes and looked deep into his espresso eyes.

Vik immediately responded, stepping closer, then he placed both hands gently on either side of her face. "I love you. You know that, right?"

She nodded. Because she did. And she loved him right back. He'd see that soon. When this was all over, they'd run off together. She could give his family money, make their lives easier. Everyone would be better off.

Mariella sucked a long pull of air, feeling the woods, the trees, her ancestors seep into her organs. She didn't need to worry; everything would go according to plan.

Yes, exactly, the whispers agreed.

"I love you so much," she said. Then she kissed him. Hard. Her lips smashed against his, and she tugged him closer, pressing firmer.

Her arms bumped the backpack that hung on his shoulders. He didn't even know what was in it. He never asked. Because Vik trusted her.

And she would keep him safe.

Mariella's tongue brushed against his, and she knew the rank flavor corroding her insides would soon be within Vik. He'd be a part of it. And then forever would start.

The backpack sloshed.

Yes, it was time.

CHAPTER SEVEN

TESSA

Vik's biological father wasn't a secret. But he was the reason Vik didn't drink.

José Cortez was an alcoholic, a mean one.

Tessa's mom, Rosie, spent years trying to force his sobriety, taking insult after insult every time he staggered through the door. She eventually gave up when he cheated on her with a bartender, which Tessa only knew because she overheard Mom and Tía Dolores discussing it once. By the time Rosie left, she was already pregnant with Vik. She leased a new apartment and serendipitously met a kind, gentle, and handsome next-door neighbor—Raúl Gomez. Rosie was in a relationship with Raúl by the time Vik was born. The two got married, Raúl adopted Vik, and they had Tessa.

Vik's bio dad was rarely mentioned; not because of any seething resentment, but because José sought no relationship with his son. Also, José was arrested so often for misdemeanors that the courts likely wouldn't have let him see Vik very much even if the man had pressed the issue—which he didn't. After his third DUI, José was sent to jail for six months. But it was his fourth DUI that put him behind bars for a decade. Vik's biological father killed a four-year-old on her bike while he was intoxicated behind the wheel, at noon on a Sunday, without even a valid driver's license.

Vik was nine years old at the time. Tessa was eight. And that was the end of that.

They all did the math. Vik would be an adult by the time José got out. If they wanted to form some sort of once-a-year-phone-call relationship after that, it would be Vik's choice. Regardless, Vik would always and forever call the man who raised him Dad. Because he *was* Raúl Gomez's son. He *was* Tessa's brother. Full stop.

Only every news station in America, and maybe beyond, was now saying otherwise.

Is there a murder gene? News at eleven.

"They're acting like that jailbird has anything to do with Victor." Tía Gloria threw a backhand at the TV.

"Just turn it off," Tessa insisted, marching into the room.

Tía Dolores and Abuela flanked her mother on the sofa, whispering in Spanish everything from "It's not your fault" to "We always knew that man was a [insert a lot of Spanish cursing here]."

"He saw Victor twice in his life!" Tía Gloria paced the shag area rug.

"Pendejo doesn't make one phone call to Victor in ten years, send one child support payment to your mama *ever,* but he's going to give a statement to the newspaper?" Tío Ricardo's voice boomed through the apartment.

Tessa unzipped her sweatshirt, the air suddenly stifling. Was someone baking now? She thought she smelled cake. She tossed her hoodie on a kitchen chair as a newscaster read the statement again. Thankfully it was a written message, and it was brief: *"I am always here for my son, Victor. Whatever happens next, it is in God's hands."*

Really? The man found Jesus in prison? Tessa stomped toward her uncle, snatched the remote, and pounded the off button. It would have been nice if Vik's sperm donor had had this awakening before he'd killed a kid, and before the worldwide media could contort his toxic choices into a murder gene running through her brother's blood.

Tessa's fingers clenched. *Goddamn that piece of . . . ugh!* She exhaled through gritted teeth, glaring at the ceiling. It was as though the news enjoyed purposely getting everything wrong. Tessa shook out her wrists, trying to toss the tension from her body. *No.* José Cortez may have spiraled around her family like a booze-filled tornado, threatening to destroy everything in his path, but he wasn't known for physical violence. Not like that. His pattern was to drink himself into a blind oblivion and crush her mother psychologically. Then one day, he managed to get his hands on car keys, despite them being repeatedly confiscated, and he turned those two tons on wheels into a weapon. It was alcohol that fueled his horrific choices that led to deadly consequences.

But Vik wasn't a drunk. Nor was he anything like his biological father.

"Tessa, you're a writer." Tía Gloria looked at her. "Why don't you write the truth."

"I'm on the high school newspaper," Tessa told them. "We don't cover murders."

Omigod, school. Can I even go back there now?

Oscar put a comforting hand on her shoulder.

"You two could put something on the internet, something viral," Ms. Jenkins suggested.

"Ma, that's not how the internet works." Oscar looked at his mother. "You can't *make* something go viral."

"And even if I wanted to post something, no one would believe me. I'm his sister. Of course I'll say he's innocent. We need *evidence.*"

Her mind suddenly stilled.

Tessa needed evidence.

She knew Vik was being framed. Obviously. If any drug, drink, or toxin was found to be wiping Vik's memory, he hadn't voluntarily taken it.

That meant there had to be evidence pointing to someone else.

It sounded like Detective Ertz thought Mariella might be involved. Of course, Ertz also seemed to imply that a ghost or a goblin could be to blame. At the very least, the detective had questions. She had doubts. Tessa pulled out the Post-it note from her denim pocket and snapped a picture. *If you think of anything, Teresa, call me . . .*

Everyone in this room knew Vik was innocent because they *knew him.* Well, someone *knew* Mariella that well too, had known her since birth.

And he'd been texting Tessa nonstop.

Oscar's tires crunched over the loose gravel in the dark alley as Tessa stood on the fire escape, gripping the rusted railing. It was finally time to visit the Lizzie Borden House. Phil was at work.

It was hard to explain why she had been so reluctant to take Phil up on his repeated offers—but to her, a "private tour" implied much more. Tessa liked Phil, only she wasn't sure how much, and she feared she wouldn't be given the time to explore those feelings. One date would launch them into an instant relationship with no low-key buildup or get-to-know-you period. Expectations and exclusivity would begin immediately. Labels would be assigned: boyfriend, girlfriend. *You love him, right?* And if Tessa and Phil broke up, the drama would ripple through the entire group, especially between Vik and Mariella. *How could your sister do that to Phil? He's my best friend!* So Tessa stayed home and forced herself to learn from her past mistakes. She was making better choices in Fall River. She was being responsible.

But tragedy struck anyway.

Tessa stared at Oscar's black early 2000s Chevy SUV, bought with money Oscar earned while making tacos at a fast-food joint. The vehicle should be unfamiliar to any nosy reporter, but to

Tessa, it was anything but. In fact, at one point in her life, they'd spent so much time inside those four scratched and nicked doors, she thought they could live there.

Until the night they'd spent *too much* time in that interior.

Tessa lowered herself onto the fire escape's ladder, pulling down the brim of a maroon Phillies baseball cap, borrowed from Tío Ricardo. Her black hoodie was shoved over that, very back-alley chic. She stretched her legs onto the metal slats, dryer exhaust blasting as she climbed down. She reached the last rung and hung a moment before dropping onto the asphalt.

"I feel like I should go with you." Oscar stepped from the SUV.

"You gotta trust me. Phil's more likely to talk if you're not there," Tessa said, shuffling toward him and the memories. Visions of them entangled in the back seat flashed, tickling her skin.

"That's because he's into you."

"We're friends," she said, still gazing at the car.

"He's asked you out."

"Sort of. But I've never said yes." She finally turned her eyes to Oscar. "Maybe if I had, I would have kicked off an alternate chain of events where none of this would have happened."

"Of course. Because you control the universe now." Oscar cocked his head.

"It's possible." She smirked.

How did he do that? How could he make her smile at a time like this?

"It's not just Phil." Oscar took her hand. "I'm not cool with you going *anywhere* alone right now. What if the press chases you? Or those lunatic protesters find you?"

It was sweet he was worried, but it was even better that he wasn't stopping her. Oscar knew she had to do this, and he was not only accepting it but he was lending her his car.

"I'll be careful." She took the keys. "And Phil's a good guy. He's got a whole plan to sneak me inside. I'll be okay."

"You better be. Or I'm comin' after him."

Oscar engulfed Tessa in a hug, the keys jingling in her fingers as she wrapped her arms around his neck. He'd gone to the barber before he'd come here, she could tell. "Vik would do this for me."

"I know. And if you need me, I'll be out the door in two seconds."

"I know. I'll text you as soon as I get inside."

She pulled back, and Oscar's eyes hovered on her lips, his intentions clear. He wanted to kiss her. And part of her wanted him to—maybe she always would—but she had too much swimming in her head to add the cannonball that was her feelings for Oscar. She had to focus on Vik, not on what *she* wanted, or *who* she wanted. *Be more responsible.*

Tessa turned toward the car and abruptly yanked open the door. Then she gripped the leather wheel, and her fingers stiffened. That smell, that chemically vanilla air freshener mixing with the aroma of Oscar. The scent used to linger on her clothes. Sometimes she wouldn't wash her sweaters for weeks because she liked the scent of him wrapped around her.

Memories flashed—his hands, his lips . . . the ER, the tears, then the doctor's solemn face: *We did everything we could.* The visions wove together, forming a liquid lump in her throat. She swallowed it down, shifting the car into drive.

Then she waved at Oscar and pulled out of the alley alone.

Wearing Oscar's black Ray-Bans, a flannel button-down beneath a dark hoodie, and a baseball cap from a World Series that played not long after her birth, Tessa felt safe in her anonymity, which she needed. Because instead of going straight to the Lizzie Borden B&B, Tessa made a detour.

She hovered in Oscar's SUV across from the towering Morse mansion. Despite its opulence, the estate was shockingly old in a way that reminded Tessa of the historic homes back in Philadelphia's Fairmount Park. Only it had been updated with a modern paint job using contemporary shades of black, gray, and white.

News vans with satellite dishes now lined the property on three sides, with journalists gathered in the triangular park in front of her. Their powdered faces fought for light between the crooked arms of tree branches, while wing-tipped shoes collected mud and high heels sunk into moss. The WELCOME TO THE HISTORIC HIGHLANDS sign was framed in every shot. Still cameras, however, were focused on the house, desperate to catch a revealing shot of the tragic victim. Only, the curtains were drawn, and a light fog dulled the view.

Tessa had needed to come, even if just for a moment; she needed to see the crime scene linked to her brother. She pictured that night. Handcuffs. Police officers. Body bags.

Her eyes landed on a bronze plaque, secured near a cornerstone; it read: THE BRAYTON ESTATE, 1843. In the past twenty-four hours, Fall River history was all over TV and social media. Tessa had learned that the Braytons once owned many of the textile mills in town—if you wanted a herringbone jacket in the 1800s, this was the place to get it. Then the manufacturing jobs were shipped overseas, the mills were closed, and the city fell on very dark times. That was, until Winthrop Morse was born, entered the real estate industry, and single-handedly saved the community.

Tessa wasn't overstating. The news was making Winthrop out to be the Patron Saint of Fall River, the man who'd bought up the dilapidated textile mills and converted the ailing structures into hip waterfront lofts, condos, brewpubs, and office space. Adding to his legacy, Winthrop rehabbed the massive Brayton estate, and the word *revitalization* was now everywhere. It was why the death of two middle-aged people had become national news. Poor folk were killed unremarkably all the time, but when rich people die, the world takes notice.

Tessa gazed at the stodgy structure more befitting a museum than a family. She scanned the windows, searching for a sign of *something*. Life. Warmth. Evidence. Then a shadow shifted. It was on the second floor. The shape was human, thin and distinct, with a swish of long hair that fell in a very familiar manner.

It was Mariella. Tessa knew it.

She's still living here. Tessa's eyes narrowed.

Mariella's parents had been hacked to death—let's just say by *someone*—on that very floor, and Mariella was still inside, roaming around like it was home sweet home. There were hotels. The Morses had money. Mariella could easily run from that crime scene. She could hop in a limo and go all the way to Boston if she wanted, escape the cameras and slip into big city crowds until the attention died down. She could deal with her trauma alone, in peace.

If in those early days of Tessa's grief, after her father's funeral, she'd spied a single camera, let alone dozens, trying to capture her pain, she would have crushed the lenses and danced on the shards. Even without the intrusiveness, Tessa had still fled the memories, dashing all the way to Massachusetts to hide. But no, Mariella Morse was sleeping within steps of her parents' spilled blood, knowing that exploitative cameras collected outside wanting to expose her every teardrop.

Tessa's eyes lasered in on the slender shadow, all her brain waves willing the girl inside to peel back the curtain—it was a focused gaze anyone would feel on the back of their head. *Look at me,* Tessa thought. *Come on, Mariella, you know I'm here. Look at me.*

Then the curtain shifted. A fluffy white cat tail sauntered by, swishing the fabric. A hand appeared, human and pale. It clasped the edge of the drapes and bared the slightest sliver of a high cheek and a single blue iris. It was Mariella. Her eyeball darted, erratic—at the cameras, at the reporters, at the cops handling crowd control, and then at its target. She found Tessa, of course she did. Even though Tessa was disguised in an unfamiliar car, wearing someone else's sunglasses and hat, Mariella knew who was puttering at her curb. She felt her.

The azure eye jerked so wildly, goose bumps pricked Tessa's flesh. Because Mariella didn't merely look grief-stricken or overwhelmed, she looked . . . wrong. With all the money and choices available at a flick of a touch screen, Mariella Morse had chosen to seal herself inside the tomb where her parents had died and watch the world through her closed double-paned windows.

Vik Gomez is a murderer. That was the last thing Mariella had said, at least publicly.

Tessa tugged her phone from the car's console and shot a text to the boy who knew Mariella best: *I'm down the street. Be there in two seconds.*

Phil immediately texted back: *Great. Coast is clear.*

CHAPTER EIGHT

TESSA

Lizzie Borden's house was situated in what Tessa would describe as an industrial part of town. It stood unremarkably across from a Catholic church, a brick apartment complex, and a boxy cinder-block courthouse. Graffiti of unreadable bubble letters marred the mailbox on the corner, and broken glass littered the gutter.

The home was green. Not an Irish kelly green; more like a forest green with evergreen shutters. It was simple, a residence that could exist in any time, in any state, and never be noticed by a single car churning by. It was a rectangular box with two neat rows of flat windows and a pitched roof.

Yet its utterly mundane exterior seemed only to add to the extraordinary legend.

Maybe in another hundred years, the Morse mansion would become a true-crime mecca, version 2.0, only with more glitz and glamour. Her brother's portrait might hang on the wall while people toured the preserved estate, snapping photos of where the bodies had been found.

No. Tessa gritted her teeth. She would not let that happen.

She parallel parked the SUV in the dead-end street directly behind the Lizzie B&B. It was one-way, hard to get to, and out of view of the news vans shooting B-roll. Tessa slid her hoodie over her cap, not a tendril of hair loose, sunglasses hiding her eyes on a cloudy day with mist in the air. Then she slunk alongside a chain-link fence, toward a large home divided into apartments, with multiple fire escapes extending from the windows and white siding. Phil had convinced the owners to let her cut through.

Tessa crept toward the front entry, then stopped short. Wedged between the storm glass door and the heavier wood door behind it was a gray, leathery-faced mannequin of a six-foot ghoul straight out of a Halloween horror display. It wore a Santa hat with reindeer antlers, a floral Hawaiian lei, and a pink tropical shirt that contrasted with deadly obsidian eyes and a gaping mouth that drooled blood. Above it, three skeletons clawed the building's exterior, two posed entering apartment windows and one dangling from a fire escape. The whole display could be chalked up to Halloween decor, 'tis the season, but something told Tessa these attractions were up all year, basking in the spooky proximity to the Borden massacre.

A shudder slunk down her back as Tessa snuck up the driveway, alongside the porch, toward a gap in the rear white fence. She emerged in a petite parking lot behind the Lizzie residence, next to a two-story evergreen replica of the Borden house that contained the gift shop and Phil's family. The Barkers lived in the second-floor apartment. This meant that not only did the Morses pay the Barkers' salaries, but the Barkers paid the Morses rent. Their families couldn't possibly be more entwined.

Tessa clung to the structure's shadows, ignoring the flock of pigeons loudly cooing and flapping under one of the Bordens' few remaining pear trees—Lizzie's juicy alibi for the time of her parents' murders. *No, I didn't hear my parents being hacked to death. I was too busy eating pears.* Tessa had learned that tidbit on the news this week. It was as though Victor Gomez and Lizzie Borden were now irrevocably bound together.

She stretched her legs, dipped her head down, and moved swiftly toward a metal basement door connected to the Borden house. It swung open as soon as she approached.

"Ya made it." Phil looked like he wanted to hug her, but he stopped himself when a pigeon dive-bombed the entrance. Tessa yelped, and Phil yanked the door shut with a thud. "Don't mind them. I think the birds are still pissed Lizzie's dad chopped up their ancestors."

Tessa's brow furrowed.

"It's one of the legends." Phil shrugged. "Lizzie had pigeons. I think they ate 'em."

A wet chill shivered through her as Tessa clomped down the four weathered concrete steps to the sublevel space. She shoved her sunglasses into her sweatshirt pocket and pulled off her baseball cap, smoothing her wavy hair as she scanned her surroundings.

The basement was musty, dark, and typical. Modern front-load washers and dryers sat in a corner, all rumbling; red gasoline jugs lined the walls; cleaning products filled the metal shelves;

and paint cans were stacked beside piles of crumpled rags. Electrical wires tangled against the cinder-block walls, and exposed pipes wove across the raw wood beams on the ceiling. There were folding chairs, brooms, shovels, and buckets. The space looked like any in America, except for two huge differences: one, the only lights illuminating the windowless cavern were eerie, glowing crimson bulbs, like in the photo darkrooms depicted in old movies; and two, there was a bedroom. In the middle of the concrete slab, behind an unfinished wood door begging for you to drag your hand and collect the splinters, was a queen-sized bed with a clean, modern gray tufted comforter.

"Guests sleep here?" Tessa choked, her open mouth inhaling the bitter mildew.

"Sometimes, but only when it's warmah. There's no heat down heah," Phil said, his accent twisting the words *warmer* and *here* in that familiar Massachusetts way that nixed the *r* sounds.

Who the heck sleeps in a basement? Tessa had spent her entire childhood afraid of the one in her abuela's house. The boiler was always banging, rattling the darkest parts of her imagination. Only here, that darkness had a history.

"People are weird," she muttered.

"Ya got that right."

They trudged up the curved concrete steps lined with caution tape that glowed in the ruby light. Then she whipped out her phone.

Tessa: I'm here. No issues.

Oscar texted right back. *Good. Let me know when you leave.*

She gave him a thumbs-up emoji, then followed Phil into a Victorian-style kitchen with lacy white curtains, rich oak trim, and an antique black iron stove with multiple small oven doors.

She slid her phone into her pocket, Phil's eyes on her. "My family's worried about me leaving the house," Tessa explained, gesturing in the direction of where she thought the front door might be, knowing there were camera crews clogging the sidewalk to catch B-roll for the evening news. *"Will the latest axe murders bring another Trial of the Century? News at six."*

"Your ma should be worried. *I'm* worried." Phil's gaze showed concern. "You are seriously brave."

Tessa scoffed at the suggestion. Brave? Tessa was so petrified her brother could be locked away for the rest of his life that her hands couldn't stop shaking. She'd hardly eaten. She'd spent half the night pacing, too afraid to check on her mom sobbing in the next room, because Tessa knew she'd just break down right alongside her.

"I am *not* brave."

Phil grabbed her hand. "There must be reporters staking out your place?" He said it like a question, so Tessa nodded. "Ya snuck past them to come here. Not to mention, ya visited your brother, walked through that mob of microphones, and past those picketers. Seeing him could *not* have been easy."

Tessa swallowed a hardened lump of bad memories, not wanting to remember the way Vik looked in that jumpsuit, the way his shackles clattered, or the way he smelled.

"You are the strongest person I know." Phil squeezed her hand tighter. "You kick ass."

Tessa blinked, because Phil's hazel eyes looked sincere. To Phil, this was who Tessa was. He didn't know what had happened back in Philly, other than her father dying. Phil didn't know her dad's last words to her or how she'd failed him. Phil only knew the girl who liked to study and stay home on Friday nights. Because that was who she'd become in Fall River. Phil liked Tessa for who she was *right now*, and there was something incredibly freeing in that.

"I don't know what to say." Her words sounded small.

"You don't need to say anything, you don't need to do anything. That's why I wanted ya to come here. So I can help *you*." Phil tugged her hand.

He led her toward the front of the ornate home, original wood floors creaking.

"I guess I'm finally in the Lizzie Borden House." She took in the interior, all decorated like it was 1892.

The textured floral carpet matched the endless floral wallpaper in a dizzying array of pastel patterns, trimmed by thick molding. A fireplace anchored every room. Lace swung by the windows, old books lined wooden shelves, and brass candlesticks sat on end tables next to ancient lamps with dusty glass domes. Black-and-white crime scene photos hung above velvet sofas alongside portraits of Borden family members. And just like in the basement—in true Disney World Haunted Mansion fashion—all rooms were illuminated with either eerie crimson or sickly green lightbulbs. The effect was disorienting, which Tessa assumed was exactly the point.

"Is it what you expected?" Phil asked.

"I'm not sure what I expected." Tessa's eyes fought for a place to settle. You know how sometimes a grieving family member might seal a bedroom after a loved one dies, morphing it into a shrine? (Her mom hadn't done that, but Tessa could understand the impulse.) Picture that scenario, only in an entire house, for over one hundred years, with spooky lighting. "At least I don't see any ghosts."

"Ah, wait till later. You already met the demon down cellar." But Phil said it like *cellah,* his accent making her smile.

"There aren't demons here," Tessa jeered.

"Ya sure about that?" Phil's smirk was teasing, and for a moment, Tessa almost laughed. Wow, she didn't know her body could still do that.

She scanned the formal dining room where they stood, taking in the mahogany table with a lace-doily tablecloth and untouched place settings. "Are there any guests staying here now?"

"They don't check in until evenin'. We usually give tours during the day, but because of all the reporters, we had to put everything on hold. We'll probably start back up again tomorrow."

"I can't imagine wanting to sleep in a murder house." And before Tessa could finish saying it, she pictured Mariella's silhouette standing in the window of what was now a murder home.

"You can take it a step furthah," Phil said, pointing toward the front staircase. "You can sleep in a lovely four-poster bed right next to where her stepmother's body bled through the floorboards. I can show ya if you want."

"No, thank you." Her response was quick, and she pulled out a dining chair, lowering herself, but Phil shot out a hand in warning.

"I should probably tell ya that this is where they performed the autopsies."

Tessa hovered mid-squat, the chair skidding on the flowery carpet as she caught herself before her bottom hit the upholstered seat. "What?" She stood back up.

"Not on this exact table. The autopsies were performed on that." His index finger extended toward a wooden slab with a cane woven center that leaned against the wall, nestled beside a china cabinet that held cracked replica human skulls, or at least she hoped they were replicas. "Her stepmom was cut open here. Her dad was over there." Phil pointed to an adjacent sitting room, sounding like the tour guide he was, giving a speech he probably spewed multiple times a week. "They didn't chop off their heads until the bodies got to the morgue downtown. But they took their stomachs out here. Is this too much information?"

"Yes." Tessa nodded.

"Sorry, it's hard to turn off. My dad gives the house tours, and I do the ghost hunts at night. I spit this info on autopilot." He crinkled his nose in apology.

"It's fine." Tessa's eyes skimmed the ten place settings of

delicate china, linen napkins, and polished silverware. "People really eat here?"

"Yeah, my mom cooks and serves breakfast here every mornin'. You know, we have some Portuguese chouriço left over if you're hungry. Ya don't look like you've eaten."

"I haven't." Her stomach rolled. "But there's no way I could eat sausage."

"Toast? English muffin?" He was genuinely trying to be a good host, and an even better friend, but she was incapable of small talk at the moment.

"That's not why I came."

"You're right. I'm sorry. Let's start over." Phil stepped closer, awkwardly raking his fingers through his styled blond hair. "How are ya? You okay?"

"No." Her answer was blunt. She realized she had asked Vik the very same question when she saw him, so she knew why Phil had started there, but she now had a fuller understanding of how ridiculous the concept of *okay* felt. "Everything's horrible. I don't know what happened that night, but I know my brother is incapable of *this*." She flicked her hands around the murder house.

"I'm so sorry." His face softened. "I haven't stopped thinkin' about ya."

He was worried about her the way she was worried about Vik, and it was sweet, but she didn't come here for sympathy.

"Phil, you're the only person I know who may have spoken to Mariella. Has she said *anything*?"

Phil sighed, glancing away with discomfort. "I mean, I haven't exactly asked for details. She just lost both her parents."

"I know, but"—Tessa's shoulders sagged with desperation—"she has to know something."

"She's talkin' to the police. As far as I know, she's told 'em everything. Maybe you should let the cops handle it?"

"How? The entire world's calling my brother an axe murderer!" she snapped.

Phil flinched. Then he paused before his next words. "Tessa, I'm not sure ya realize this, but Mariella has *no* family. Her grandparents are dead. Her dad's only brother is dead. If her mom had siblings, I've never heard 'em mentioned. Mariella is all alone now."

Phil was on Mariella's side. (Not that there were sides, but let's face it, there were.) Mariella was his best friend, and he was staying loyal to *her*.

A pang pierced Tessa's gut—a reaction she wasn't expecting, a feeling she didn't realize she had. For him. She felt strangely rejected.

"I lost my dad not that long ago. You know that." Her voice filled with the pain of never wanting to talk about this. "It's why we moved here. So I know how ugly grief is. I wouldn't put that on anyone. But Phil, blaming Vik isn't going to help. He *didn't* do it. Someone else did, and that person is still out there, getting away with it."

"Maybe. And for you, your family, I really hope you're right, but . . ." Phil folded his arms across his chest. "You saw the video of your brothah. You heard Mariella's statement. The cops found him holding the murdah weapon."

"The weapon was at his feet," Tessa corrected. Vik told her himself. Every detail mattered.

"I'm worried about *you*." He stretched for her hand. "Are ya talking to somebody?"

He thought she needed a therapist. He thought she was in denial. Maybe that was true, but there was no time to worry about herself. She tugged her hand away. "Forget *me*. Vik has no memories! Of holding an axe or even going into that house. Explain *that*."

"Maybe he blocked it out?"

"Or he wasn't in his right mind." Tessa shot him a look.

Phil's brows squished together. "Like, what? Drugs?"

Tessa shrugged. A week ago, she would have been insulted if someone suggested Vik did drugs, but right now, it might be the best-case scenario. Because she knew Vik wouldn't take drugs willingly. "We're still waiting on the toxicology report. But I know Vik didn't *do* drugs. You saw the reports about his biological father. Vik is terrified of addiction. He's never even had a beer. But do I think someone could have *drugged him*?" She let the words dangle in the air.

Phil stepped back. "Are you asking me if I think Mariella Morse drugged your brothah?" His accent was growing more pronounced as tensions rose.

Still, Tessa didn't take it back, because, yes, that was exactly what she was asking.

"Shit." Phil sounded surprised, then marched to the living room, or maybe in a house like this it was called a parlor. Tessa followed his steps, floorboards whining. "Ya know, Mariella and I learned to walk right there." Phil pointed in front of the charcoal-velvet, curved-backed sofa—the one where Lizzie Borden's father was slaughtered. Tessa knew this because the crime scene photo was blown up to poster size and displayed in a gold frame above the couch. What was left of the man's face was pulpy and unrecognizable. But Phil had toddled here as a baby. "Our parents have known each other forevah. We work for them. They haven't even been buried yet."

"I'm not asking you to betray her." Though maybe she was. "I just want your honest opinion. You're the one person who *really* knows her."

Phil assessed Tessa, then he let out a loud exhale. "I've never seen Mariella do drugs in my life." His tone was matter-of-fact. "Does that help you? Because I feel like I'm hurting you."

Tessa hung her head, and Phil stepped forward, wrapping her in a hug. She let him. "I wish there was something I could do to make this better for ya."

"So do I." Tears welled in Tessa's eyes, and she sniffed them back, her head on Phil's shoulder.

"If you ever wanna get away, not be *in it* for a while." His chin rested on her head. "Let me be here for ya."

Tessa nodded against his chest.

"I mean it, what you're doing for your brothah . . ." He spoke into her hair. "Vik is so lucky to have you."

Lucky? Tessa would have laughed if she were capable. But before she could respond, voices gathered on the second floor, bellowing toward them. Tessa stepped back from Phil's embrace and wiped her eyes. Then she spied Phil's mom with her thick black Portuguese hair pulled high in a messy bun, curly flyaways fluttering around her face. She descended the carpeted steps with an overflowing pile of bed linen in a white plastic laundry basket. Phil's father was just behind, wearing a black denim jacket and a gray newsboy hat. He was clutching an iPad, wire-framed reading glasses halfway down his nose, as his stocky frame shook the old wooden staircase.

"I don't know what we're supposed to do. We only have eight rooms. We couldn't meet this demand if we were a Marriott," said Mr. Barker, his tattooed finger punching the screen.

"How far out are we booked?" asked Mrs. Barker, her voice muffled by a mountain of sheets.

"Six friggin' months. That's as far out as our system will go."

"I already put a call in to the web designer," Phil cut into his parents' conversation. "He's gonna work on the backend, see if we can extend the reservation system by a year. But if we go any farther than that, we could end up with a bunch of no-shows." Phil glanced at Tessa. "It seems the media circus has increased demand. All the sudden, everyone wants to be where the axe murdahs happen."

Tessa blinked, a dust mote floating in her line of vision. It paused midair, round and perfect, bobbing unnaturally in the eerie green light. *Where the axe murders happen . . .* Tessa followed the transparent orb, trying to erase those words from her mind. Vik's tragedy was good for business.

Phil caught her face. "I'm sorry. I didn't mean it the way it sounded. What you and your family's goin' through, it's awful—"

"What *Vik* is going through," Tessa corrected, as Phil's parents shuffled into the kitchen.

"Yes, your brothah." His eyes turned apologetic. "It's just we had a wicked big increase in reservations and then our website crashed. And with Mariella's parents, like, *not heah,* we're not sure who's in charge or even what's gonna happen to this place. At least, not until they read the will. I mean, I guess Mariella owns . . . everything?" His face crinkled with confusion, then he continued to ramble. "But she's not even eighteen. And my parents have worked here for decades. Only their employers aren't around to sign their paychecks, and Mariella's grievin' . . ."

Jobs. Phil was afraid of his family losing their jobs. Income. Bills. Heck, even their apartment was tied to the Morse family. And while none of this compared to what Vik was going through, Tessa could step back for a second and understand their concern. There were likely a lot of Morse employees on the edges of their checkbooks right now.

"I get it." Tessa nodded, sucking her lips between her teeth.

"The Morses were like family to us," Phil added. "But that doesn't change how I feel about *you.*"

"I know." She bit her lips harder.

And she did understand, logically, in her brain—Mariella had lost both her parents. She wasn't the enemy, but for some reason, Tessa couldn't stop feeling like she was. She ran her fingers through her hair, an ugly resentment bubbling up from her chest. She couldn't see straight. Tessa didn't know what she felt anymore. About anything.

She shouldn't have come here.

She reached into her back pocket and pulled out her phone.

Her mother was back at the apartment; so was her family, and so was Oscar. Tessa hadn't even mentioned him to Phil, not that she owed Phil any explanation, but still it felt like a lie of omission. Her ex-boyfriend was in town, staying at her place. Tessa knew that would mean something to Phil—she just didn't know what it meant to *her*.

"Tessa, look, I get off work in a couple hours." Phil tilted his head with concern. "We could get suppah. You can unload everything."

But Tessa was done talking.

She stepped away. "I'm so messed up right now, you don't wanna be near me."

"I do. Believe me." Phil moved in. "Let me."

"So you can do *what*? Can you help me make sense of this?" Tessa swept her hair into a ponytail at the nape of her neck and squeezed, elbows pressed against her temples. "Somehow, my brother went from hooking up with his girlfriend in the woods to standing in her parents' bedroom, covered in blood, over their dead bodies. And he remembers *nothing*!"

"Wait, they were hookin' up in the woods?" Phil asked, as if that were the most interesting part of what she'd said.

"Yeah, why?" Tessa's eyes narrowed.

"Like, the Freetown woods?" He stared curiously at her.

"Why are you saying it like it's strange?" Tessa dropped her arms, suddenly feeling more alert. She hadn't dated in Fall River, so she'd just assumed the woods were a typical spot for teens here, the way she and Oscar used to park near the river in Philly.

"Because it is strange. The woods are mad haunted. I mean, *I* like them, because I work *heah*." Phil gestured to the living room crime scene. "But most locals stay out of 'em. It's called the Cursed Forest."

"Seriously?" Tessa's eyes bugged. "Maybe Mariella didn't know?"

"She definitely knew. She and I used to hike them all the time. *During the day.* But this was before she got with Vik. It used to be our thing."

"Mariella Morse hikes? In high heels?" Tessa shifted her weight to one hip.

"More like designer boots." Phil gave a knowing look. "Her family . . . wasn't perfect. It's not my place to say, but sometimes she needed to get away. I just can't believe she would go there after dark."

"Maybe she didn't believe in spooky stuff?"

"It's the Bridgewater Triangle." Phil held the tone of someone stating pure facts. "I know you didn't grow up heah, but the stories are real. Dark shit has gone down in that forest. There were wars between the colonists and Native Americans, satanic cults, Bigfoot sightings, a creepy rock with petroglyphs, a Lady in White, pukwudgies—"

"What the hell is a pukwudgie?" Tessa asked.

"Not important. You tellin' me Vik and Mariella went there on a Friday *night?*" Phil's voice was full of disbelief.

"Yeah. I mean, I'll check with Frankie, but I'm pretty sure that's where they went."

"That is weird."

Phil Barker, the guy who led ghost hunts in a house known for axe murder, thought her brother hooking up in the woods was *weird.*

Tessa yanked out her phone and pounded a text to Frankie: *Were Vik and Mariella in the Freetown woods that night?*

Three little dots appeared, and then Vik's lawyer quickly replied. *Yes. But can't talk right now.*

Tessa's brain scrambled with question marks—the woods, Mariella hiking, burial grounds, pukwudgies.

She remembered Detective Ertz's question, *Did Vik want to be a ghost-hunting YouTube star?*

A trained detective, with a badge and a gun, who grew up in Fall River, questioned whether Vik believed in ghosts or the supernatural. She knew the stories.

"Phil, I think you just helped a lot," Tessa said.

Phil smiled like it was all he ever wanted to do.

There had to be a reason Mariella Morse chose *that* location to take her brother that night and a reason he conveniently lost his memory.

Tessa's finger moved to her photo albums, and she scanned the images until she found a picture of a Post-it note.

Then she sent Detective Ertz a text: *I want to talk about the Freetown woods.*

CHAPTER NINE

The night of the murders . . .

MARIELLA

Mariella gazed at the blazing sunset above the Freetown–Fall River State Forest, and all she saw were putrid streaks of seeded mustard mixed with a sickly orange glow.

She slumped beside Vik, her jeans dusty from the colorful spray-painted surface of the Ledge, his arm slung heavy on her shoulders. A headache brewed, rising from the sun's offensively bright colors.

"It never gets old, does it?" Vik leaned in, his eyes shaded by the Oakleys she'd bought him for Christmas last year.

"Not with you," Mariella replied, her voice sweet, her words perfect, but her body feeling threatened. Something was watching.

In a forest where nothing lived and no animals scurried, Mariella felt eyes. Tons of them.

"You know the first time you made me hike here, I thought I was gonna collapse," Vik joked.

"That's 'cause we forgot water." Mariella nodded to the backpack. "I always remember it now."

"I know." He grinned, dimples flashing. His black hair dripped in a way actors probably had to practice in a mirror—his head cocked with a sexy soap-opera squint and a heavy brow. Vik exuded a natural spark. His dark eyes gleamed.

For her.

He pecked her lips. "It was more a city thing," Vik went on. "Back home, our woods have a highway cutting behind them. You're never really alone. But silence like this . . ." He nodded to the endless nature.

"Aw, you scared of the Big Bad Woods?" Mariella teased, her tone in no way conveying that he had every right to be.

There was a disquiet growing amid the trees, tonight more than ever, like even the shadows were alive.

Kiss him, the whispers ordered with a perverted tinge.

"Will you protect me?" Vik winked.

As directed, Mariella slid her fingers down Vik's cheek. She liked touching him and kissing him. She didn't need the whispers to tell her. She pressed her lips to his, and Vik knotted his fingers in her hair. A surge raced through her, and she shifted on top of him. Vik wouldn't let things go too far. Not here. He said it was because the spot was too open and too public. But Mariella wondered if he sensed something else, something closer to the truth.

The murky green water filling the rock quarry below was full of the dead.

It was why the Ledge was chosen. There was an energy that emanated from the very stones they sat on. It drew Mariella, reeling her closer. *Come here, little girl, come here . . .*

Vik sucked on her bottom lip, then trailed a line of kisses down her jaw so gently, her goose bumps felt permanent.

"You know that drives me crazy," she breathed, and for a moment, just a second, she felt clearheaded.

She inhaled Vik's scent, sweaty and citrusy in a way that made her muscles clench.

She enjoyed his fingers on her skin.

She felt alive and present.

"Wanna go to my car?" he whispered against her throat.

"Or we could stay here . . ." Her tone was playful and seductive. She wanted to cling to this sensation and to hold on to it longer, so much longer. She wanted to be this person, right here, right now.

"I'm not big on audiences." Vik flicked her ear with his tongue, and honestly, she could have exploded. Or melted. Or both.

Her hands slipped under his sweatshirt, under his T-shirt, her nails dragging lightly down the bare skin of his back.

He pulled away. "That's not playing fair."

"Never said I would." She didn't want to stop, because then she'd have to move on to what came next. And she wasn't ready.

Could she really do this?

"Later." Vik pulled back farther.

But later would be something else entirely, something darker.

Her hands fell into her lap, her bruises long forgotten.

"Next time, maybe we just skip the hike and go straight to my car." Vik nudged her shoulder.

"Sure, next time." Mariella smiled, her mouth filling with slush as she hoped that next time, they wouldn't be here. Because next time, they could be in her house, the one she'd share with her mother. Free from *him*.

Mariella took a deep breath, a light-headed buzz fluttering behind her eyes. All those hikes, and she'd never noticed how different the air was up here. It was so obvious now. The tea—it showed her the truth, the power this place held. And now Vik would see it too.

Her eyes shifted to the backpack.

You're ready, the whispers hissed. *Just a few hours. It'll all be over.*

Hours. The rest of her father's life was down to hours.

"You know, I'm starting to like this whole Bridgewater Triangle place." Vik gestured to the view full of shriveling leaves. It was funny how New England was famous for the season where everything died.

"You should be, because you're dating a potential New England witch." Mariella put one hand on her heart, and held the other to God, or whatever force was up there. Out there. "I'm serious. Lizzie Borden's biological mother, and uncle, both supposedly dabbled in black magic. I'm a descendant."

"You're not gonna hex me, are you?" Vik's tone was mocking.

But Mariella blinked. Once. Twice. She was unsure how to answer.

Much of the world was well versed in the notorious Borden

family, at least in how the parents died. But people tended to be less familiar with the Morses. When Mariella was old enough to Google, she'd fallen deep down a Morse family ancestral rabbit hole. She even visited the Oak Grove Cemetery, more than once, to lay eyes on the family plot. Each grave was marked with a simple ground-level, rectangular stone. Lizzie was buried beneath a horizontal slab that simply read, "Lizbeth." She was interred next to her sister Emma, and right behind the parents she was accused of killing. The mother who gave birth to her, Sarah Anthony [Morse] Borden, lay beside them.

Mariella had attempted to commune with Sarah's spirit a couple of times back in middle school. Sarah had died when Lizzie was two, so it stood to reason she might have a lot to say about the circumstances that befell her daughter. She might even know if Mariella's bloodline was cursed, or if the whole town was cursed for that matter. So Mariella sat cross-legged on the grave, marked only with Sarah's initials: S.A.B. There was a Ouija board, candles, and questions asked into the ether. But the planchette never moved. The wind hardly blew.

Maybe Sarah didn't want to talk. At least, not there.

The sky in front of Vik and Mariella now shifted to a tacky pink, the kind you'd see on a dress rack and immediately think, *Nope*. A breeze hit the nearby branches, lifting the hairs on Mariella's arms. Those eyes again. They were making themselves known, worming inside Mariella's subconscious.

"Think about it," Mariella said, feeling the whispers scraping her skull. "If places are haunted by a single deadly event, then what happens when tons of awful stuff goes down? Over and over. For hundreds of years?"

"What do you mean?" Vik's brow rumpled at the sudden shift in conversation.

"Lizzie Borden's aunt, Eliza, murdered two of her children, then slit her own throat with a straight-edge razor, in the house right next door to the B&B my family owns." Mariella's words were matter-of-fact.

"What?" Vik choked out, eyes alarmed.

He wanted her to smile and peck his lips, to tell him she was kidding, but the buzzing in her brain was overpowering. Her blood was steaming. "It's true. And this was decades *before* the axe murders. Don't you think it's weird that so much death happened right there. In one spot?"

"I mean, yeah, it's creepy." His face crinkled.

"Even these woods." Mariella gestured around them. "People were slaughtered here, again and again, going all the way back to the Pilgrims and the Native Americans. Probably before then too."

"Seriously?" Vik tried to keep his voice light, but his shiver betrayed him. He could sense the change in her now. Finally.

You see me.

"Yup." Mariella pulled her legs to her chest, wrapping her arms tightly around them, hugging herself. She couldn't put it off much longer. The whispers, the eyes, they were needy. Hungry. "The Bridgewater Triangle's not just ghost stories. The history's real. It's like a dark energy hovers over this place. This town."

"You don't have to live here." Vik looked at her. "You can leave. *We* can leave, after graduation."

Could they?

The whispers thrashed inside her skull, fighting her hesitation. But Mariella shoved back, pushing the intrusive thoughts, the wicked ones, the ones she knew weren't her own. She tried to find her true self. *My name is Mariella Morse. I'm seventeen years old. I have blond hair and blue eyes, and I hate my father.*

She did, didn't she?

Doubt crept in. What if her thoughts, all of them since the day she was born in Fall River, had *never* been her own? Maybe Lizzie Borden and her aunt Eliza, and the satanic cult rituals of the 1980s, and the Native American slaughterings of the 1600s, maybe it all happened *because they lived here*. It was possible that these atrocities didn't curse the land, but instead, the cursed land *caused* these horrible events.

"You okay? Are you cold?" Vik unzipped his hoodie, angling to wrap her up, to make sure she was comfortable. He cared so much.

The sky morphed to a dirty lavender fit for the bedroom of a kid with unicorn posters. The backpack's zipper caught the light, and a swarm of bees raced down her eardrums, stinging all the way. She squinted, fists clenched, her body rebelling against the disorienting sensations. The buzzing. The eyes. Where were those eyes?

My name is Mariella Morse. I'm seventeen years old. I have blond hair . . .

There had to be another way. Was this even *her* way? Her idea?

Do it. Now! The whispers burst through with a wave of vengeance. *It must be tonight! Now! Get! Up!* Each word was a foghorn that swallowed her thoughts and sense of self.

Her spine shook straighter, and her mind grew suddenly still. Without thinking, without wanting, her hand shot out; it pressed into the sooty painted bluff and pushed her to her feet.

Why was she moving?

Her body steadied, legs quaking like a newborn giraffe.

Then her eyes flung to the leather backpack.

"What's up?" Vik held out his sweatshirt, wanting to warm her and bathe her in his scent. But she stomped toward the bag.

"Thirsty," she replied. This was true.

Good girl, yes, the whispers hissed.

Mariella hauled the backpack onto her shoulder.

"I'm gonna use the bathroom." She pointed to a bush a few yards away. Her lips pushed into the shape of a smile. "No peeking."

Vik nodded. If he sensed anything was off, he didn't show it. Nearly two months of mental anguish, creepy nightmarish shadows, and vile muck on her tongue, and he never sensed a thing. Had he ever known her at all? Maybe he wasn't a good guy. Maybe it was okay to make him do this.

Exactly, the whispers agreed. *Keep going.*

Mariella marched across the spray-painted rocks, eyeing her favorite chunk of graffiti—a trippy *Alice in Wonderland* mushroom with Tang-colored polka dots. She'd always wanted to spray her own picture up here. Maybe she would, someday. She moved to a crop of trees festering with white-green lichen, the splotches of fungus bleeding onto the boulders that cowered in the shadows. The rocks, the sticks, the logs, everything was stained with mold.

She crunched to her usual spot, kicking a collection of crumpled beer cans. Since the first time she and Vik had made the hike, Mariella had been pretending to relieve herself at this location (as if she'd ever do that in the woods).

Her boots trampled a mess of twigs and shriveled leaves that ground to dust. She dropped her backpack, and it sloshed as it landed on a rock, clinking.

Mariella squatted, then unzipped the seam. She dug inside the bag, lifted a metal thermos, and unscrewed the lid. Then she swept the repugnant leaves from underfoot and revealed the treasure below—the etchings in stone.

A shadow crept overhead, chilling the air. Her icy fingers tingled as they skimmed the flat rock. The stone was small, about the size of a manhole cover, only heftier. A blistering rash of chartreuse lichen spread on its surface, covering the crudely drawn petroglyphs that had withstood the test of time.

The rock wasn't a secret. Mariella had been shown its existence the first time she'd come to the Ledge. People flocked from all over the country to see and experience it. It's said to have an otherworldly force flowing from the Earth's core directly to its granite top. If you spend a few moments touching it, opening yourself to its powers, an energy flows through you—a spiritual pulse that thrums in your bones and tickles your ears.

It was a good energy, right? That was what she had been told.

No one knew how old the carvings were. She'd done some research. The rock was standing, incised and waiting, when the first colonists arrived in the 1600s. Then blood was spilled all around it; towns popped up; legends grew, and the rock remained—drawing spirits, entities, eyes, and the supernatural.

A sizzle moved from its surface, against her boots, and into her belly, a tickling hum.

Mariella never heard the whispers here. It was as if they weren't allowed to speak. Or they weren't powerful enough to burst through. This spot, this point of light and life, was the heartbeat of the Bridgewater Triangle. It could be the heartbeat of the universe. She could sit here forever in its vibrating stillness.

Mariella dug her pointer finger into a fungi-infected, rudimentary carving of a human, a stick figure really. Her chipped nail burrowed in, grinding granite in a way that made her teeth clench. Rancid saliva filled her cheeks, matching the stench of ancient dirt beneath her fingers. She swallowed every drop of spit.

The whispers were right. She could feel it now, the stone's solitude was giving her clarity. *It was time.*

She pulled her finger away coated in lemon-lime fuzz. Her head grew dizzy, her eyes swimming as she brushed every speck into the sloshing thermos. Her thumb scraped under her nails, dragging out bits of dirt that had seen centuries, millennia, maybe even dinosaurs. She sprinkled it all into the tawny liquid.

The tea. She finally had enough.

The plants and herbs were collected from these woods—wild

roses, leeks, strawberries, vines, invasives, and lichen. Whatever forces her ancestors had trapped in this place were gulped into Mariella's body. The power was real—the whispers, her ancestors, emerged the day after she'd first drunk the tea. And they offered solutions. *This* solution.

Mariella clawed more blotches of rot from the rock's haunting etchings, her fingers grimy as a woman mauling her way from a grave. More. She needed more. She had to make sure. She had only one chance.

She slid a switchblade from the front pocket of her backpack and flicked it open in a swift gesture. The last remnants of weak sunlight glinted on the curved edge. The sky was fading to gray.

She didn't hesitate. Something was watching. Waiting. *I feel you,* she thought, and the hum from the rock intensified, slinking up her spine.

The metallic tooth—military grade, with a jagged lip—pressed into the flesh of her palm and she dug, a straight slice down her lifeline. She didn't even wince.

Her pulse throbbed down her arm and into her hand as she squeezed, forcing hot drips into the metal thermos. She didn't need much. Just a few globs. The whispers had prepared her.

A wet coppery stench rose up, adding to the death floating in the wind that lifted her hair. She capped the container with her non-bloody hand. Then she pulled out a baby wipe and cleaned her wound. It was shallow, nothing to cause alarm. She doubted Vik would ask any questions. He wouldn't have time.

One sip.

That was what made the plan so brilliant. It held no rational sense.

If for some reason, after all her careful planning, the events of tonight were not deemed an accident, then how would Vik, or anyone, ever prove *this* in court? *Your Honor, I was possessed by magical forces after drinking an herbal tea mixed with ancient dirt and my girlfriend's blood.*

Human minds weren't meant to accept concepts this far beyond logic.

Unless you were so desperate and terrified you believed only an act of black magic would end the torment that was your life.

Mariella shook the metal container, mixing the tincture—the plants, dirt, mold, and blood—melding together whatever forces came with it. Death, death, and death. She envisioned her father's face, his eyes gaping and lifeless. Gone from this world and from her life.

"Hey, you okay? You're taking a while," Vik called.

Mariella smiled, for real this time, because she was finally content. She'd gotten to the point she'd envisioned for weeks.

She rose from the ground, returned the thermos to the backpack, and marched across the spray-painted rocks, back to her boyfriend.

"We should drink something before we head back down." Mariella casually unzipped the bag and pulled out the thermos.

Vik glanced up, his tan face smooth as silk in the pale dusk of a crescent moon.

"I brought an energy drink." Her eyes sparkled as she held it out.

Victor Gomez took the thermos, his gaze trusting, and Mariella watched, silent, as this boy who'd kissed her cheek and held her hand took his first sip. Rusty liquid dribbled down his chin, and then his head snapped back.

CHAPTER TEN

TESSA

The crack of the gavel shook Tessa's rib cage as it echoed through the courtroom.

Bang.

Life over.

Bang.

Murderer.

Bang.

No bail.

It didn't seem real. Tessa, her mother, and her entire Puerto Rican family had gathered in that freezing government building, naively assuming Vik would be released. Bail would be high. It might even be astronomical, but he would get it, and they would find a way to pay it—mortgage homes, sell cars, set up a Go-FundMe, seek donations from the church, max out credit cards. They would find a way.

It had been two days since the police had handcuffed her

135

gore-soaked brother; they'd spent forty-eight hours "making their case." Now, they had not only Mariella's testimony but a statement from a pack of random dirt bikers dominating the news by claiming Vik had "assaulted" them earlier that night. Meanwhile, Vik had gone to a Philadelphia public school for the majority of his life and had never once gotten into a fistfight. But of course, the media didn't broadcast that. No, let's give airtime to the fame-seeking biker gang.

But that wasn't the worst of it. Chunks of the police report had been leaked to the press, and the details were vivid. Hearing them pulled tears even from Tessa's eyes. Winthrop and Catherine Morse had been mutilated. Mariella was found hysterical, covered in her parents' blood, begging the paramedics to save them. They had to pry her from her mother's nearly severed corpse. And the entire time, Vik stood, drenched in blood, completely stoic—no words, no reaction, no remorse shown to anyone at the scene.

The news portrayed Vik in the image of Frankenstein's monster—an unstoppable killer whose own father didn't want him. Vik's bio dad was serving time for manslaughter, after all. What do they say about nature versus nurture?

Looking back to that first meeting at the police station, Tessa realized Frankie had known bail was never going to be granted. She'd made that face, just once, when she'd mentioned the double homicide. She knew courts didn't let suspected murderers walk free in the community. But she'd tried her best. She argued that it was Vik's first offense. He didn't have so much as a traffic ticket. He was a stellar student with a steady job. He had friends and family who would support him and ensure he made all of his court appearances. He was a goddamn former altar boy. He deserved bail.

But the district attorney's response was powerfully succinct, "Your Honor, this is an open-and-shut case."

The gavel came down. "Remanded without bail."

Tessa's whole family inhaled one collective gasp. Mutters of "Huh?" and "What just happened?" were mixed with super-speed Spanish. Then Vik was yanked from the courtroom. Their final vision was of him in shackles as he tripped in the guard's burly arms, begging, "Ma! Ma, I'm so sorry!"

Their mother fainted. Paramedics rushed in.

"This can't be happening. This can't be real." Tessa's hands quivered as she sat in the SUV beside Oscar, leaving the court-house, heart thundering in her ears.

Autumn wind blasted her face from the car window, which she kept rolled down because she couldn't stop sweating, blood boiling beneath her skin.

"I'm so sorry," Oscar repeated. It was all anyone could say.

Including Frankie. She didn't give a statement to the press. She just grabbed Tía Dolores and Tessa, and muttered strategies. The evidence was mounting. And according to her, Vik's state of mind was worsening. Frankie said Vik was "seeing Mariella's face" and he heard her voice in his head. Best-case scenario—these were snippets of memories, which could be good. If Mariella had been at the scene *during* the murders, if Vik remembered seeing her in any way that countered Mariella's depiction of events, it could cast doubt on her credibility and hurt her entire eyewitness testimony. She could be charged as an accessory or a perpetrator. But the worst-case scenario was much more terrifying—Vik was having a mental breakdown, in a jail cell.

Tessa barely had a moment to absorb this information before she and her family were whisked down the courthouse steps and swarmed by reporters.

"Tessa, do you think your brother did it?"

"Did Vik abuse his girlfriend?"

"Mrs. Gomez, do you feel responsible for raising a murderer?"

"Why does your family attract death?"

They were told not to respond. No tears. No answers. No defense. The headlines would be written in bold ink, regardless of what they said, and her family would have to live with the Google repercussions forever.

Vik was staying in jail until his probable cause hearing, more than a month away. He could be staying in jail until his trial, whenever that was.

They had failed to stop this. They had failed him.

"We have to get him out," Tessa announced, her brother's helpless face lodged in her brain with the repetitive sound of the pounding gavel. "Us. *We.*" She gestured between herself and Oscar. She knew despite everything said in that courtroom, every vile detail splattered online, Oscar believed unconditionally that Vik was innocent. "*We* have to get him out of there."

"Like a prison break?" Oscar took his eyes from the road, and his gaze didn't say no.

"Not that. I mean, I would . . ." If Tessa thought she could, she'd show up tomorrow in a Wile E. Coyote T-shirt with a stick of dynamite. "But we have to find out what happened. Don't you think it's weird Mariella didn't show up today?"

"Well, it was a bail arraignment, not a trial." Oscar shrugged. "She didn't have to be there."

This was true, but still. "Her parents were murdered. And she says Vik did it." Tessa glared at Oscar's profile. "If she believes that, *really* believes that, wouldn't she want to face him? Wouldn't she want to see him put behind bars for what he did?"

"I have no idea. I've never met the girl."

Mariella's grief, and her feelings, did not matter to Oscar, at all. It was incredibly freeing—Tessa could say whatever she wanted, unfiltered, and he would believe her, even if her theories bordered on the bizarre.

Tessa told him about her phone call with Detective Ertz. Of course the cops had searched the Freetown woods. Apparently, Vik and Mariella both told the police that they were at "the Ledge," which didn't mean anything to Tessa but did to Detective Ertz. When Tessa asked if it was odd that two teens would be hooking up in that location, at night, the cop replied, "Abso-freakin'-lutely." Ertz knew all the same legends as Phil, and while she didn't say she believed any of them, she thought it was very possible that the two teens who often went there did.

Maybe it *was* an influencer thing? Maybe Mariella wanted to go viral? But Tessa had checked the girl's social media, and it was boring—selfies, mirror shots of outfits, latte foam, and cat pictures. Vik only posted images of cars.

There was not a single shot of the two of them in the woods, yet it was "their regular spot," according to Vik. Despite it being cursed, or haunted, or both.

It was also where Vik had lost his memory.

"We have to go to the Ledge." Tessa slapped her hands on her thighs.

Oscar slowed at the red light.

"Do you think you can find the place?" he asked, already agreeing to go.

"I don't know." Tessa chewed her lip. But she knew someone who could, someone who insisted he really wanted to help.

It took a surprising amount of convincing. Phil kept reminding Tessa how "cursed" the forest was, while also pointing out his actions might be seen as a betrayal to Mariella. "She hasn't left the house . . ."

In a different reality, one that didn't involve her brother facing life without parole, Tessa would respect Phil's loyalty to a girl he'd known much longer than her. She'd respect his concern at entering a supposedly haunted, supernatural forest. But in *this* reality, Tessa was not going to let him keep texting *I can't stop thinking about you* and *You're more than a friend,* then accept his refusal to *do* anything. So she laid out the truth—with or without his help, Tessa was going into those woods, and if the place really was as dangerous as he thought, was he okay with her going without him?

Yup, it was a guilt trip. And she was fine with that.

Phil said yes.

This was partly because she omitted certain details about the "family friend" who would be joining them. Oscar knew that Phil wanted more than friendship from Tessa, but Phil didn't even know that Oscar existed. Tessa couldn't risk Vik suffering the consequences if Phil stayed away, for any reason.

Oscar parked his SUV along a country road bordering the Freetown–Fall River State Forest. There was no sign, just a wide gravel hiking path and rusted metal guardrail with chipped yellow stripes, preventing a car from driving farther. Tessa stepped out, slamming the car door as Oscar hit the lock button on his keychain. Phil was already parked, and he emerged as soon as he saw them, his eyes scanning Oscar.

"Phil, this is Oscar." Tessa pointed innocuously between them. *We're all friends here.* "Oscar, this is Phil."

She thought of all the times she'd watched Vik and Zane try to dagger each other with looks over lunch. Tessa had always blamed Mariella for batting those doe-like eyelashes and raising the tensions, which she had, but now Tessa was doing the exact same thing. Only she was convincing herself it was for a far less selfish reason.

"Ya mentioned a *family friend.*" Phil ran his hand through his blond hair, which looked like he'd put pomade in it. "But I thought it would be an uncle or somethin'."

"Does it matter?" Oscar puffed his chest.

Tessa narrowed her eyes. During the car ride over, Tessa had begged Oscar to ignore any vibe Phil might throw her way. Phil was the only friend she had left in Fall River, and he also had incredibly useful outdoorsy information. These woods had twenty-five miles of hiking trails, and there was no way two city kids better skilled at navigating subway maps were ever going to locate a random "ledge" without his help. Phil had shown up for *her*.

"Yeah, Oscar and I went to school together back in Philly. He came up yesterday with his mom." Tessa chose her response carefully, leaving out the word *ex-boyfriend*.

Oscar shot her a look, unhappy at the omission, then assessed Phil, from his overly styled hair to his double-knotted hiking boots.

Silence hovered in the crisp air, then Oscar smiled wide, dimples flashing. "It's really cool of you to help Tessa."

Thank you. Tessa exhaled with relief. She knew it was the last thing Oscar wanted to say, but he did it.

"Anythin' for Tessa." Phil stepped toward her. "She knows that." He lingered a bit too close to be friendly, his gaze intense.

She'd cried on Phil's shoulder yesterday. She'd begged him for help. She needed him.

"You okay?" Phil asked, not breaking eye contact, and Tessa swallowed a gulp—from tension, from emotions, honestly, she didn't know.

"Can't get any worse," she replied. "Seriously, thanks." She rested a hand on the sleeve of Phil's maroon hooded sweatshirt.

Phil glanced at her fingers, then back into her eyes. "I told you. I'm always here." Then his gaze flicked toward Oscar. "Don't worry. I won't let ya get lost."

A golden sheen slipped through tangled branches that drizzled sienna-, crimson-, and lemon-colored leaves onto their path. Trails forked and turned over thick tree roots and makeshift wooden bridges that crossed above trickling streams. That was the only sound—water, bubbling and churning. The woods were so much quieter than Tessa expected.

Every hundred yards or so, a divide appeared; they could turn left or right along paths barely defined by footfalls. Though the one they were currently trekking was beginning to deepen, softly curving below their feet like it had been dug by hands. It was a trench, holding inches of rusty pine needles mixed with rich black soil, softening the ground so much they could barely hear their own steps.

"I can't thank you enough for coming with us." Tessa glanced at her phone. It wavered between one bar and no bars. GPS was useless.

"I'm sorry I made ya talk me into it. I had been textin' with Mariella right before you called, and . . . she's a mess." Phil took a swill from his metal water bottle. He'd brought a backpack full of provisions, because he'd assumed Tessa and Oscar wouldn't come prepared. He was right.

"Did she say anything?" Tessa asked, trying hard to sound casual.

Phil gave her a sidelong glance. "Not about that."

Tessa nodded, her sneaker slipping on a splotch of mud. They'd been hiking for barely fifteen minutes, and already her shoes were splattered with grit.

"I hope you know I would never have let ya come here alone." Phil reached for her arm, steadying her balance.

"She's not alone," Oscar said pointedly, hands shoved into the pockets of his Sixers hoodie.

Phil nodded. "You're right. Tessa's surrounded by people who care about her." Then he looked at her. "Fall River wouldn't be the same if you hadn't left Philly behind."

Oscar's lips pursed tight, awkwardness mounting. But before she could intervene, a pigeon flapped ahead. It landed in the trench, its iridescent green neck bobbing toward the earth, a coo breaking the silence.

The bird looked so out of place. Tessa was used to concrete city parks full of flapping gray wings that blended with traffic. But she'd never seen a pigeon in the woods before, not that she'd spent much time in the great outdoors.

The bird's beady crimson eyes shifted, catching the fiery sunlight; then its head grew motionless. Its gaze locked on Tessa. It didn't twitch, peck, or flap. Were pigeons' beaks always so sharp? Tessa's knuckles flexed. She was overcome with the urge to reach out, stroke its head, and slide her fingers down its neck; she lifted her arm, but the bird abruptly bolted from the path, whizzing so closely overheard that Tessa stumbled, her foot sinking into a puddle.

"Damn it." She grimaced. Her sneakers were far from waterproof. Same with Oscar, who was sporting an extremely pricey pair of high-top Jordans that were now smudged with so much muck they'd never be white again. Meanwhile, Phil's hiking boots had deep rubber treads, ankle support, and looked like they could withstand a snowstorm.

"Let me help ya." Phil held Tessa's hand as she unstuck her foot. A light breeze swept through, sending a colorful autumn shower cascading into Tessa's hair. Phil plucked a dried golden leaf loose, his fingers lingering in her strands in a way that felt intimate. Tessa didn't pull away.

"I heard about bail." Phil was inches from her face, and the air crackled between them. "You okay?" Phil pressed.

Tessa gazed, saying nothing, until Oscar coughed. Loudly.

Tessa pulled back, shifting toward the trees and smoothing her shirt.

Her eyes flicked between Oscar and Phil, the tension thicker than mud.

"You mean *lack* of bail," Tessa replied before clearing her throat and continuing to hike.

Phil followed behind. "I'm sure Vik'll be fine."

"Seriously? Vik is in jail." Oscar's tone was grave. "He's *not* fine."

"I just meant, I'm sure he won't be harmed."

"And you know this how?" Oscar stopped walking. "You know a lot of guys locked up?"

"No." Phil stopped, pumping his shoulders. "Do you?"

Oscar grunted, eyes blinking with offense. "Why, 'cause I'm Black?" The familiar edge in Oscar's voice meant: *I-swear-say-one-more-word-I-dare-you.* Tessa leapt between them.

"Hey, let's just take a second." Tessa held out her arms in a T.

"I didn't mean it like that," Phil insisted. "He asked me, so I asked him back."

"Oh, I know what you meant." Oscar's words were clipped.

"Let's just keep walking." Tessa's head swiveled between the two of them. "Okay? We don't need this right now." She dropped her arms, her body tired.

"Sorry," Oscar grumbled, eyes on the dirt.

"Me too." Phil said.

Well, at least they agreed on something.

The trio marched forward, and Phil took a swig from his thermos. "Want some?" he asked, holding it Tessa's way, his breath traveling on a breeze. It didn't smell like water. Was it alcohol? She squinted, trying to place it.

"It's a recovery drink, with electrolytes," Phil explained, noticing her reaction. "It's good for hikes."

Tessa shook her head. "I'm good."

"You sure? I brought more." He pulled on his backpack and looked at Oscar. "You?"

"Nah, but thanks," Oscar said.

That exchange was almost civil.

They plodded along a trench that only seemed to deepen the farther they went. The shadows were growing, and the walls (Were they dug by machinery?) crept increasingly higher. Tessa realized that if they had to, if they absolutely needed to scramble their way out, they would have to boost each other up. They'd need to claw and climb. Tessa wrapped her arms around her chest. It was impossibly quiet. She swore she could hear grass sprouting and pine needles plinking. There were no animals. Had she seen even a squirrel?

"Wait till ya see this," Phil said, his words booming in the stillness.

He pointed, and Tessa followed, slogging uphill, her thighs straining. The walls began to recede, and soon the air got fuller. The branches above them parted and daylight burst into a brightly lit glen.

Her chest relaxed as Tessa took in the green sea before them. Skinny trunks with branches too fragile to climb were enveloped with lush emerald vines. Or maybe ferns? Tessa wasn't good with plants. Limey lichen climbed everything from bark to rocks, while wispy white dandelions flirted with the breeze, sprinkling seeds in the air.

"It's like a fairy garden," Tessa said in awe.

"Believe it or not, it's mostly weeds," Phil explained. "They're called invasives. One day, someone dropped a seed, then, poof! They're all over. The park hates 'em." Only he said it like *pahk,* which she liked.

"What's wrong with them?" Tessa asked. The pretty jade backdrop was very much welcome after the reddish-brown trench they'd been stuck in. But then she noticed how dense the vegetation was, full of knotted vines and sticker bushes. They wouldn't be able to walk more than a few feet in any direction without being trapped and tangled.

The trench was the only way forward.

"The weeds choke the native species. People don't like it

when ya come in and try to take over. Neither do plants," Phil explained. "They start killing everythin', and the animals get confused."

"Where *are* all the animals?" Oscar asked, voicing the thought Tessa had already had.

Aside from the single pigeon, they hadn't seen or heard another bird. Not a tweet. There were no squirrels scampering up branches. No hawks threatening from the tops of trees. No rabbits or chipmunks scurrying in the undergrowth. No sticks breaking under the foot of a deer. There was absolutely nothing.

"There's more wildlife on our street back in Philly." Tessa's eyes scanned the forest. There had to be a squirrel somewhere. There had to be.

"They say animals can sense things people can't." Phil's tone held dark meaning.

So the woods were quiet because nothing wanted to live here? Or nothing survived here?

No. Tessa shook her head. Nature wasn't this desolate. Acres upon acres of empty forest?

"You had to have seen birds here." She searched in disbelief. "You've hiked here a lot."

"I have. But they don't call it the Cursed Forest for nothin'."

"Great." Oscar scoffed, wiping soil from his pricey Jordans, which were definitely permanently ruined, though he hadn't even complained. "How much longer we gonna be here?"

When you grow up surrounded by recycling trucks rattling over concrete, quiet like this makes you uneasy. The trees, the vines, the trench, it all pressed on Tessa's chest and prickled her skin. She knew Oscar felt the same way, and so would Vik—so why would he come here? Repeatedly?

"We're gettin' close, but we should keep going." Phil moved ahead. "Ya know, Mariella and I were out this way once. She thought she had an uncle who lived near here."

"What?" Tessa asked, brows crinkled in surprise.

"Not, like, a recent uncle," Phil clarified. They descended downhill, the trench's sides inching higher once more, creeping up to their shoulders, blocking the light. Tessa was growing to hate these dirt walls. "Mariella's great-great-somethin' uncle, John Morse, supposedly had a cabin out here. He was Lizzie Borden's biological mother's brother." He tugged on his fingers, relaying the lineage.

"Lizzie killed her mother, right?" Oscar asked, not having had the benefit of the murder home tour earlier.

"Not exactly." Phil flicked his blond hair. "Lizzie was *accused* of killin' her father and *step*mother. Her biological mother died when Lizzie was a baby. And John Morse was *that* mother's brother. It's one of the theories—people think John was trying to get himself named in the will. Or maybe he and Lizzie planned it together."

Tessa had honestly had no clue Lizzie Borden existed before she moved to Fall River. She came from a part of Philly where people were more concerned about the murders that happened last night than ones from a hundred years ago. And she could sense Oscar was thinking the same thing.

"Don't forget, Lizbeth was acquitted," Phil continued. "Some even think that Uncle John dabbled in the black arts. Bunch of story tellahs, if you ask me. But Mariella and I thought we could find his place."

"Did you?" A wind kicked up and lifted Tessa's hair off her neck. She rubbed her biceps, the air chilling.

"Pretty sure we found the right spot. I studied the maps. But"—Phil shrugged—"cabin wasn't there."

"It probably collapsed a hundred years ago," said Tessa.

"True. But we found these cool roses, strawberries, and leeks all over. Like the cabin sunk and a garden popped up." Phil zipped his sweatshirt. Yes, it was definitely getting colder. "We even had a picnic."

"You and Mariella Morse. Here?" Tessa raked her fingers through her hair, growing knotty from the mounting wind. "I cannot picture this girl you're describing." She shivered, staring at her now-constant goose bumps. She chose her next words carefully. "Can I ask you something? Yesterday, when we were at the house, you said that Mariella's family wasn't perfect. What did you mean by that?"

Phil's head wobbled, as though he was debating how to respond. "I guess, I mean, her parents are gone now, so I can probably say it, but her dad was . . . like, abusive. Verbally . . . physically."

"Shit." Tessa's gaze flung toward him.

"He hit her muthah." His accent was heavy on the final word, his emotions squeaking through.

"And Mariella?" Tessa asked, feeling suddenly nauseated.

"I don't think he hit her . . . or anything else. She talked to me a lot, and I saw how bad it could get with her ma." Phil twisted his hands as they walked, looking uncomfortable. "That's why Mariella liked it out heah. I think she felt free from all that."

"Do you think Vik found out? Tried to stop it?" Oscar gave Tessa a look that confirmed exactly what she was thinking.

If Mariella's father hit her, and Vik knew, he definitely would have intervened. But he also would have said something to Tessa. He would have asked for advice. He probably would have talked to their mom, and Frankie. Vik wasn't one to keep something this big to himself.

And he hadn't done any of those things.

Still, it made a lot more sense than any of Detective Ertz's ghost-hunting theories.

"Did you tell the cops?" Tessa asked. "Because that's a *real* motive. It could be a motive for a lot of people."

Phil's teeth set on edge. "I don't know if it's my place to say. They were Mariella's parents, and they're dead. I've been tryin' to get *her* to tell the police."

"Yeah, well, it's been days, and she's said nothing. Phil, my brother's being accused of *murder*! We have to do something." Tessa's tone was harsh.

Phil stopped short. "That's why I'm heah. Doing somethin'. I'm trying to help." His gaze was sharp. "You of all people should understand why I'm not draggin' my family into this. My mom cooks breakfast at a B&B the Morses *own*." He sounded annoyed, not at his social standing but that he even had to explain this. "Poor kids have a habit of bein' blamed for stuff when it involves rich people. Or hasn't that sunk in yet?"

"I get that, but—"

"But nothin'. I'm doin' what I can." He flung his hands around at the woods he hadn't wanted to enter. "Or do you really not see that?"

"You're right. I'm sorry," Tessa said.

Phil held her gaze for a couple of beats, and when he marched forward, she followed.

He was out here because she'd begged him, and if he didn't want to get more involved with the cops, she wouldn't force him. Tessa could tell Detective Ertz herself. If Mariella's dad was violent within their home, he might have been violent with other people. He might have had enemies. It was something. It was a start, a new direction.

The rumble of a motor rose up, and Tessa paused, twisting her head as the engine revved, bouncing toward them.

"What is that?" she asked.

"Dirt bikers," Phil answered.

Bikers.

Like the ones who claimed Vik had assaulted them that night.

For the first time, Tessa truly examined the curved earthen sides of the trench they were tromping through. The ground was soft and low, because it hadn't been dug out by hands, but by tires, heavy rubber tires, over decades.

This trench was for motocross.

"This a bike path?"

"It's a shortcut," Phil called.

"So the bikers on the news . . ." Tessa didn't finish the sentence.

"I wasn't sure if I should tell ya." Phil eyed her with sympathy.

Because he knew bikers hung out in these woods; he probably believed Vik had attacked those guys.

Did Phil think Vik murdered people too?

"This doesn't feel like a shortcut," Oscar cut in.

And Tessa agreed. The fact that Oscar—a guy who ran wind sprints for football nearly every day—was tired made her feel less embarrassed by the soreness in her legs and the huff in her voice. They were city kids. So was Vik. Her brother didn't play an organized sport or own any hiking equipment. Yet this was his "spot" with Mariella.

Phil twisted their way. "There's a wider trail we could've used, but it would've taken longah."

The stench of exhaust pushed toward them. The bikes were getting closer, and Tessa coughed. This wasn't the evidence she was hoping to find—confirmation that Vik *had* encountered bikers that night.

"We should keep goin'." Phil plodded ahead. "We wanna get there before dark."

CHAPTER ELEVEN

The night of the murders . . .

MARIELLA

The tea didn't hit Mariella like this, not when she drank it. She'd expected Vik to grimace; the foul taste had been lingering on Mariella's tongue for nearly two months. She had excuses prepared. "It's super healthy! I made it myself! It has electrolytes! Think of kombucha with a kick!"

Only she didn't need them.

One swallow and Vik's head wrenched back. His long lashes fluttered, the whites of his eyes exposed, as a foaming amber liquid drooled from the corner of his mouth. He didn't wipe it. She wasn't sure he felt it.

It.

Mariella stood with the stillness of the dead, gaping as Vik held the thermos to his mouth, his elbow locked. He gulped and gulped and gulped, his Adam's apple bobbing up and down. Chug after chug. He finished within seconds. Not even a burp.

His arm lowered mechanically, then released the thermos. It bounced once on the painted rocks below, splashing its last umber remnants onto Mariella's boot. The stench of fermenting leeks wafted as she bent, muscles tense, and returned the container to her backpack like a hiker cleaning up litter.

What was happening? When she'd first sipped the tea weeks ago, all she'd suffered was a buzzing in her ears, an annoying bout of tinnitus she initially blamed on allergies. By her calculation, it had taken hours for the whispers to hiss their first orders. Mariella had expected the same for Vik. The whispers had *told her* she'd have to wait.

But Vik was already feeling the effects—and very differently.

Her gaze skittered about the barren ledge. The sun had swiftly slipped, casting their surroundings in a dull midnight blue. They were miles from where they'd parked. She had arranged no special procedure to trek back to the Jeep. Mariella had expected Vik to walk, like she had done herself that first day. Sure, he'd be a bit groggy, maybe he'd complain of a headache, *Hey, do you hear that humming sound?* type of thing. But that would merely slow their pace.

Only Vik was currently standing stoic, seemingly unaware of her presence. Could he even see her?

"Vik, you okay?" Mariella cautiously approached.

No response.

"You feel all right?" She touched his arm, and his head whipped toward her at inhuman speed.

His eyes were swollen to a stormy gray. There was no hot-chocolate brown. No reflection of light. The whites and their thready red veins were now overtaken by a thick cloud covering. Something was wrong.

"We need to get back to the Jeep," she said, desperate to move him. "Can you walk?"

Vik's lips didn't part. No motion. Not even a twitch of a nostril.

What had she done?

The answer was simple: she had no idea.

Mariella had drunk that crap, and it had corroded her insides. Her reasoning had become so corrupted that she shared the liquid with Vik, all because some whispers told her to. She acted like those voices were friends, her mystical relatives, crossing cosmic lines to solve her problems. Well, if so, where were they now?

Mariella felt a sudden crush of abandonment—utter silence—in a dark, creepy forest, with a 180-pound boy who wouldn't budge.

A dirt bike, the whispers erupted, finally hearing her plea.

Mariella exhaled.

Not far down the trail. You heard the bikes, smelled the exhaust. Find help. The bikes will get you out of here, the whispers instructed with military authority.

Mariella nodded, dredging up a vague memory of a moto-cross track she'd spied weeks ago. The hike was off the wide main path, through muddy trenches with high, confining sides. It was a miserable trek, but dragging Vik there seemed a lot more do-able than dragging him out of the woods entirely. Mariella would simply tell the bikers that Vik had hit his head and that he had a possible concussion. Of course they'd offer rides.

She turned, ready to push, shove, and tug Vik from this graffitied ledge, but before she could speak, his entire body jerked, reacting to something that wasn't her. He spun with abnormal velocity, then he abruptly stomped back toward the trail. No words were spoken.

"Vik!" she called, clambering after him.

This was good, right? At least he was moving. But he looked so solid, so heavy. His back muscles rippled, biceps bulging above the heavy tread of his footsteps.

"Vik! Can you hear me?"

Vik started running. His arms pumped as he took off, suddenly diverting from the main path. He hurtled over logs and barely visible tree roots until he veered into a deep dusty trench, the curved walls rose to their shoulders in a way that blotted nearly all the moonlight.

It was the path to the motocross track.

Vik was headed in the right direction. The whispers?

Wait. Vik was moving, sprinting, without assistance. They didn't need help. Or bikes. And they shouldn't involve anyone else in what was going to happen next.

"Vik, stop! Let's just go to your car!" Mariella's squeaky voice held the panic of a person who knew they'd lost all control of a situation.

Vik darted farther down the trench. A breeze swept toward them, reeking so thickly of decomposing leaves, Mariella gagged. Then Vik cranked his head, his reflexes responding to a signal she couldn't hear. The whispers were talking to *him*. Not her. But they were *her* ancestors.

Vik accelerated his pace.

She sprinted—and she meant *sprinted;* she was moving at the full capacity her body permitted through inches of sodden earth. Her throat was already raw, stripped from ineffectively screaming in her nightmare, but now it flamed from the gulps of rotten air pumping into her lungs. She hadn't brought any water, only the tea for Vik, which was clearly a mistake. Maybe it all was a mistake.

Vik widened the gap between them, charging over branches and vines with the skill of a marine who did this every morning before six a.m. Was his body always this big? Her vision grew staticky, her eyes struggling to see through the blackness of night that drained the Freetown forest of color; all greens turned to gray and all puddles became ink. And the shadows were moving.

Mariella tripped, toe catching on *something* prickly and solid. Then her sole stomped on her shoelace, which swiftly untied and flopped as she ran. She couldn't pause, she couldn't fix it, or Vik might veer into a void and leave her cold and alone in a trench.

She yanked her phone from her back pocket and illuminated the path. A fork loomed ahead, and Vik hooked a sharp left, a hidden GPS burrowed deep into his brain, guiding his movements.

"Slow down! Where are we going? Are you looking for bikers?" Mariella shouted.

No sound responded other than the blood thundering in her ears. Icy thorns scratched her ankle and she ignored the sting, frantic to keep pace.

Then she smelled it. Exhaust. It was pungent and fresh.

An engine puttered, then revved.

The bikers. A sick feeling sank into the already growing pit in her gut.

"Vik, stop!" She doubted he could hear her—he was too far ahead—but she tried regardless.

When you see an impending car crash, you can swerve, you can slam on the brakes, or you can barrel straight into it. But you can't stop the other drivers. The wreck is out of your control.

Just like Vik was right now.

He kicked into a gear she couldn't compete with and Mariella stumbled, foot catching on another tangle of roots. She dropped her phone, then fell to her knees, scrambling on pine needles to retrieve her only lifeline.

An engine echoed louder, tires crunching.

"Oh, God, Vik, no! Stop!" She gripped her phone, scrambling to her feet.

Then the sputtering engines and snapping twigs abruptly halted. The air grew disturbingly silent, a gulp of gasoline-fuel smog pulsing in Mariella's throat.

Commotion erupted.

Screams tore through the trench as a yellow headlight appeared. The glow, the shouts, traveled closer, faster. She spied Vik's shadow heading straight toward the bike. He was going to get hit. In the woods. By a vehicle. Mariella took off, her shoelace whipping her calf.

"Get out of the way!" she hollered.

She heard four people (maybe five?) shouting from the top of the trench, nearly invisible in the shadows of the pines. Cries of "Stop!" echoed around her, but Vik kept moving, marching menacingly ahead. One rider was in the path, on a motionless bike pointed straight at Vik. A beer can—heavy and full—flung at Vik's head, and he dodged it with such skill, it seemed he knew it was coming. Then Vik extended his hand and snatched a branch poking vertically from the ground, the chunk of wood patiently waiting. *Here I am. Grab me!*

Mariella halted. She couldn't breathe as Vik held the branch like a bat. The rider's right hand flexed; then he sped forward. Boy vs. bike. What were they doing?

The headlight blazed, illuminating Vik as he swung for the fences, hitting the rider square in the chest with a crack of the branch. The driver flew, his thin body leaving the vehicle and soaring backward, airborne—one second, two seconds—then his helmet hit the ground with a scary thud.

The riderless bike careened toward the side of the trench, and the boy's friends clambered down the embankment, sliding and kicking, racing toward the injured body. A groan echoed, and the kid rolled, thankfully, his hand grazing the helmet that had likely saved his life.

Mariella exhaled. He was as okay, or as okay as you could be after getting hit and tossed from a motorized vehicle.

A deafening rev pulled her attention. She flung her eyes to see

Vik's legs straddling the leather seat. He was preparing to leave. If she didn't throw herself on the back of that bike *fast,* he was going to speed down the trench and leave her in a dark forest with a bunch of strangers who he'd just assaulted.

"Vik!" Her scream pounded in her throat. She raced toward him, panic fueling her movements.

The bike was built for two—even Mariella could see that from the long length of the seat—but she didn't have a helmet, and she wondered if Vik knew how to ride it. Then he confidently revved the engine, causing the owner's friends to charge with cell phones blazing and sticks in hands.

Ignoring all thoughts of *Is this safe?,* Mariella dove onto the back of the two-wheeled death machine and wrapped her arms around the boy who had held her almost every day for the past year. Gone was the scent of the citrusy shampoo snagged from his mother's salon. Gone were the hints of cotton-fresh dryer sheets clinging to his clothes. No, as Mariella squeezed against Vik's solid frame, all she could smell was the rank odor that had filled her mouth every moment since *that* day. It was wickedly familiar.

And very unexpected. For nearly two months, Vik hadn't been able to smell *her.* She had anticipated the same in return. But something was dangerously different.

"Hey!"

"Hey you!"

"Asshole! Stop!"

The mob was gaining, cell phone lights blazing, and Mariella stiffened her grip. They might not have needed the bikes before—when Vik regained mobility—but they did now.

"We have to go," she whispered.

For the first time, Vik's head shifted her way, much to Mariella's relief. He heard her. He sensed her.

"Now." Mariella's lips were at his ear. "We need to kill my father."

CHAPTER TWELVE

TESSA

The hike was taking much longer than Tessa had expected. During the time it had taken to convince Phil to join them earlier, he'd never once mentioned the setting sun. Yet it had been nearly an hour and they still hadn't reached the Ledge. Yesterday, Phil had been adamant no one should *ever* venture into the forest at night—too many potential creatures, from a Lady in White to a pukwudgie. (Tessa still didn't know what that was.)

Tessa checked her phone: no bars. It was five o'clock. The sun would set in an hour. Even if they turned around right now, they still might not make it to their cars before dark.

Even worse, Tessa was thirsty, and not for electrolytes or recovery drinks. She wanted water—plain, flat, non-protein, non-vitamin-enriched, water. It probably should have occurred to her to bring some.

"Okay, am I hallucinating or does that log say 'Help'?" Oscar pointed to a cluster of charred pines alongside the trench. Burned black soot stretched high up the towering tree trunks. It looked as though the flames had been recent; ashy soil covered the earth. There was no grass. One tree had fallen, and its scorched bark would have been hard to decipher against the unnerving shadows if it hadn't been spray-painted with four cherry-red block letters: HELP.

"What happened here?" Tessa asked, her voice a bit too high.

It could have been a bonfire gone wrong. Or lightning. Yes, it was probably lightning. That made sense. Her brain hung up the rationale like a sign: NOTHING TO SEE HERE.

"Probably just a bunch of kids with a wicked sense of humor," Phil said. Then he nudged Tessa's shoulder. "Or maybe it was a cult." His eyes were mocking.

A gust of wind pushed down the path, shoving her closer to Phil. The air was getting frostier. The farther they walked, the lower the sun hung, and the more Tessa felt a chill. Then warm breath tickled the back of her neck. A heavy pant. Her eyes whipped around. No one. But she felt a presence, somewhere. Her head shifted, scanning the shadows. Nothing.

It was the wind. It had to be. Yet her skin prickled.

"Hey, you okay?" Phil sounded concerned. "Ya know, I'm only kidding about the cult. That was, like, decades ago." He grabbed her wrist. "Come on, take a deep breath."

Phil pulled an audible inhale, stretching tall and filling his belly until it puffed full. Tessa did the same, closing her eyes and drawing in the scent of fall leaves. Her chest rose, then she exhaled through her mouth. Her gut unclenched, and all her muscles unwound at once.

Wow.

"Again," Phil insisted.

Eyes still closed, Tessa sucked in, slowing her exhale. In and out. The wind brushed her face. In and out. Was the breeze flowing with her? In and out. Her lungs kept pace with the trees, the rustle of leaves. In and out. She felt herself grow lighter, her body drifting. She peeled open her eyes, and the branches above them danced and rippled. The forest was swaying.

"Shit." She stumbled, and Phil gripped her tighter, helping her balance. "I think I'm light-headed."

"When's the last time you took a deep breath?" he asked.

"Sixteen months ago." Her answer was immediate, and her eyes shot toward Oscar, who was watching them silently, his look suggesting he didn't like what he saw. Then Oscar nodded, considering her words. He knew what she meant.

June 8th, that was the day before her dad died. And it was the last time Tessa had been truly happy, the last time she could really breathe.

Oscar's gaze fell to Phil's hand, still clutching Tessa's forearm. She pulled away.

"Well, then I'm glad we came out here," Phil said, eyes flicking between her and Oscar. "The woods can be really cleansing."

"Considering Vik lost his memory after coming here, I'm not sure he'd say the same," Oscar countered.

"I said the woods were cleansing, I didn't say they haven't seen their fair share of shit." Phil's boots crunched dry leaves as they hiked. "Did ya know one of the bloodiest wars in American history, King Philip's War, happened right here?" Phil gestured at the trees. "No one talks about it, but the local Native Americans were nearly wiped out by the invading colonists. King Philip, though that wasn't his real name"—he gave Tessa a look—"got his tribe to fight back, and more people died here, per capita, than in any wah in US history. Even the Civil Wah."

He said *war* without the "r" sound.

"How do you know this?" Tessa asked. She could barely remember which war the Battle of Saratoga was from—she was 90 percent sure it was the Revolutionary War, but she wouldn't bet her life on it.

"I work at a hundred-year-old tourist attraction. We do a lot of tie-ins with the historical society." Phil pulled a bag of trail mix from his pocket and held it out to her; she shook her head no. So did Oscar. Phil tossed some nuts in his mouth. "All of those bodies, all of 'em"—he munched—"they're still here. Somewhere. There's a swamp that way"—Phil pointed toward the makings of a trail in the distance—"called Hockomock Swamp. Literally means 'where spirits dwell.' FYI—do *not* go near that swamp. Like evah. Not even in daylight. It's haunted as hell."

"Awesome." Oscar glared at Tessa. "Tell me again why we're out here?"

"For Vik."

"Right, right. Vik's my boy." Oscar nodded, his cobalt hoodie covering his head. It had to have dropped ten degrees since they'd left the cars. "At least *he* kept in touch."

Tessa winced, turning away. "You know things have been hard."

"I do. And I get you not wanting to talk about it." She could feel Oscar's eyes on her. She always could. "But *I* think about it all the time. If we had turned on your phone, if we had gotten those cupcakes, then your dad . . ." his voice trailed off.

"Don't you think that's what's in my head every second of every day?" Her voice croaked with a toxic amount of regret.

"I'm not trying to upset you," Oscar said softly. "That's not why I brought it up. I guess I just want to make sure you know how sorry I am, about how things went down, back then."

"I know." Tessa nodded, sucking in her bottom lip to hold back the tears that accompanied these memories. "Really. I do."

That was true. But Oscar was so twisted up in what she thought of as the darkest time of her life. She had been touching him, kissing him, instead of doing the *one thing* her father had asked her to do. The last thing. The bakery was on her way home from school. She'd walked right by it. And she forgot. Tessa simply forgot. She didn't blame Oscar for that. She forgave him instantly, because there was nothing to forgive. But herself . . . no matter how many days passed with her dad's name etched on that tombstone, she'd never be able to forgive herself.

"Sounds like you guys have a lot of history," Phil awkwardly interjected.

Oscar cleared his throat. "Um, yeah."

"We left a lot behind," said Tessa.

"Looks like a lot followed you here too." Phil gave Oscar a look.

It was a dig, and Tessa didn't like it. When it came to this conversation, to her dad, to what happened—it had nothing to do with Phil Barker.

The two boys locked eyes, and the cool air around them crackled with the energy of a high school cafeteria right before someone yells, "Fight!" Tessa opened her mouth, prepared to interrupt the tension, but Phil unexpectedly pointed to their left.

The trench had suddenly grown shallower. The dirt walls were now lower. The crop of trees had thinned.

Phil smiled. "We're here."

For a forest so disturbingly silent, when the three of them stepped onto the wide, flat, rocky ledge, the first thing Tessa noticed was the sound. Water. It gushed, cascading from somewhere unseen and far below the steep drop-off. The Ledge was much higher than Tessa expected—maybe a hundred feet up from a pond surface as flat as glass. Across the way, fiery leaves rocked in a breeze that was wet, the sun slumping behind the autumn trees with a view that screamed *New England.*

"This is it," Phil said, gesturing like a tour guide.

Tessa tucked her hair behind her ears. Then she rubbed her arms, the friction adding some much-needed warmth. If it was ten degrees cooler in the shade of the trench than it had been by the cars, it was another five degrees colder in the open breeze of the Ledge. Forget a coat; Tessa needed gloves and a hat. These woods were far too cold.

Someone giggled. Maybe below them. Or behind them? The voice floated, young and light. *Oh, stop!* someone said.

They weren't alone.

"It's graffitied." Oscar stated the obvious, pointing at the colorful spray paint beneath their now-very-muddy sneakers.

The rainbow display of haphazard artwork reminded Tessa of a city sidewalk on a summer day—bright, childish, chalky, and while not supposed to be here, it still made people smile.

Tessa stepped onto a creepy, misshapen drawing of Pikachu, its yellow body oddly angular and its eyes large and strung out; the painting's massive scope could have held all three of them sitting at once. Nearby was a trippy *Alice in Wonderland* sketch of a cherry-red mushroom with tangerine spots. There was a Batman symbol and the comedy/tragedy masks. Black bubble letters with neon-pink trim were scribbled illegibly, along with words like *Acid* and *Coven,* and names like *Kaylyn* and *I Love Jayson.* There was an inspirational quote, *Your Rad Future Begins Right Now,* that contrasted with an ominous dare—the word *JUMP* was sprayed in cobalt all-caps letters with a massive arrow pointing to the perilous edge.

"Do people ever dive into the water?" Oscar asked, peering down what had to be at least nine or ten stories. They were so dangerously high, the water looked almost black. And still, impossibly still.

"Sure, to kill themselves," said Phil.

"What?" Tessa and Oscar asked in unison.

"It's a granite quarry." Phil waved at the sharp snags in the cliff. "The surface might look peaceful, but it's all rock down there. It's a popular place to un-alive yourself. I thought ya knew."

"You thought I knew Vik was making out where people jump to their deaths?" Tessa gave him an odd look. "No, Phil, you left that part out."

"I didn't leave it out." Phil shrugged, unaffected by the history. "People jump off bridges all the time, but that doesn't stop other people from kissin' on 'em. Look at the Golden Gate Bridge."

"Still . . ." Tessa turned to Oscar. "Does this seem like Vik?"

"Nope," Oscar replied simply. "I mean, it's pretty, but . . ."

"Mad haunted." Phil stepped toward the drop. "People have jumped off this cliff for hundreds of years. I told you about the Lady in White." He glanced at Tessa. "People have seen her divin' again and again, for decades. And they say if ya sit here long enough, ya might get the urge to do it yourself."

"Awesome." Oscar nodded. "So glad we came."

Tessa took in the sprawling, spray-painted granite perch. It was clear this was a place people wanted to be. You could plop down and watch a sunset on a checkered blanket, then make sure you got the right angle up on social media (which neither Vik nor Mariella ever did). But her brother didn't believe in the supernatural, and he didn't make light of the dead. He had been a pallbearer at their father's funeral. Tessa could see him following Mariella up here once—*It's an adventure! Let's hike the woods!*— but trekking to a suicide cliff, repeatedly, did not feel like her brother.

There was no way he knew the history.

Tessa skirted around an oily puddle, inching toward the woods behind them, looking for something, anything. Boulders popped up between the slender tree trunks, the rocks and bark slathered in greenish lichen. Weathered beer cans were strewn about—Busch, Bud, and Natural Light. She knew those weren't Vik's, but there had to be some clue as to why *this* was Vik's last memory, and not the bloodbath that came next.

"Look at this place," Oscar blurted, so loud his voice ricocheted off the bluff. Tessa twisted and spied him standing uncomfortably close to the edge, spinning in a careful circle, his arms spread wide to take it all in.

"What?" she asked.

"You could play a pick-up game of basketball on this ledge." He waved his hands around. "It's huge and wide-open. Vik told you this was 'their spot'?"

Tessa nodded.

"That makes no sense. Listen." Giggles rose up. Motorbike engines revved. She heard the faint and very welcome blare of a police siren. "This is the most noise we've heard since we stepped into these freaky woods. And it's the most exposed we've been. I'm sorry, but *your* girl, Mariella"—he pointed at Phil—"picked this spot for a reason, and it wasn't to hook up."

Oscar was right. Tessa moved toward the edge. "Detective Ertz knew all the same stories as you." She glanced at Phil. "She said all the locals do. So why would Mariella bring my brother *here*?"

Tessa inched forward, eying the dark water; it was so far below. The trees looked like bushes. She didn't see any people hiking. Where had those giggles come from? They were girls, right? A hollow woof rose in the breeze. Was that a dog? Her toes scraped the granite and she leaned, peering, straining to hear more, to see something shift between the shadows of tree trunks. She had to find someone. There were voices in the wind.

"Hello!" Tessa called, bending farther, her chest heavy, droopy.

Someone was near. She could feel it—their eyes. "Is someone there?" Her voice echoed. Down, down, down. Where were those eyes? Could they feel *her*?

She reached out her arm, leaning, bending.

"Whoa, there." Phil snatched her elbow and tugged her back a few steps.

Tessa blinked through a fog of confusion. How close to the drop had she just gotten? She'd thought she was a few feet away. She shook her head, cheeks flushed. Her toes had touched the precipice.

She was so dizzy.

"You okay?" Oscar asked, looking concerned.

"I . . . I thought I heard something." The stutter in her voice—she'd never admit it to them, but for a second, a distinct moment, she felt . . . out of herself.

"Why don't we hang out back here?" Phil tugged, liquid splashing from the thermos he was clutching. The droplets hit the granite and looked almost brown.

Tessa deepened her breath to clear her thinking. You know that feeling when something is itching at your brain, right there, scritch scratch, but you can't quite find the spot? *Almost there! Keep scratching!* That was how she felt. Tessa had come here, to this ledge, in these oddly silent woods, searching for something, only now she sensed she was *missing* something.

"Ya all right? Ya looked disappointed." Phil was still holding her arm.

She tugged her limb free.

"Maybe give her some space," Oscar snipped.

"I wasn't asking you."

"Well, she wasn't asking for *you.*"

"Actually, she begged *me* to come here today," Phil said. "Did she ask *you* to come up from Philly?"

Seriously, again? Tessa groaned, rolling her eyes. But before she could intercede, a wind pushed through the trees with a roar. Her shoulders shuddered. A gale snapped close behind, its bite much sharper. Icy needles flew across the water, the sudden breeze whipping Tessa's jeans against her thighs. It felt like a storm was coming. Only the sky was clear.

Tears pricked, and her nostrils filled with the stench of mulch. No, it was something worse, something familiar. She tossed up her elbow, blocking her eyes from the onslaught of grit in the air. A rip blasted from behind, old roots pulling from the earth. Instinctively, she turned toward the sound, and her balance was knocked off-kilter, the dizziness from earlier returning. It was more than a head rush. Red spots pulsed in her vision, and she tripped back a few steps, something slimy, maybe leaves, giving way underfoot. She fought to stand still, and Phil hollered, his voice struggling to soar above the gales. She couldn't make out his words. Then Oscar moved into Tessa's line of vision, and he reached protectively to help her.

Then Oscar slipped.

His wet, mud-slicked high-tops, with their smooth red bottoms, slid in an awkward jerk. Yes, the rock was flat, but it wasn't that flat. There were curves and ridges, angles and creases, puddles and muck, that were hard to make out in the hectic graffiti, especially with your eyes squinted and the wind pushing.

Tessa's mind snapped to attention, the scene shifting to slow motion. She reached for Oscar, peeking through her lashes, her hand outstretched to grab him. Then one—just one—fire-engine red sole kicked up, and Oscar crashed down solidly on his other knee.

There was a crack.

"Oscar!" Tessa shouted.

He screeched in pain.

CHAPTER THIRTEEN

The night of the murders . . .

MARIELLA

Vik maneuvered them out of the forest. He swerved the motor-bike down the soft trench, navigating around dropped branches with only his headlight and the moon to guide them. Mariella's arms locked around his torso, her heart drumming against his spine. Everything felt . . . wrong.

Vik still hadn't spoken. And his body simmered with hostility, a granite statue with a burning violent core.

They reached the Jeep, and she slid the keys out of the front pocket of his baggy jeans. Vik didn't fight her. There was no way Mariella could have wrangled for control in whatever super-soldier state he was in, but she also couldn't veer through town with a dangerous robot behind the wheel. Did he even know what a stop sign was right now?

So instead, Mariella slipped into the driver's seat and took control. It was the first time she'd ever driven without an adult. Mom had taught her when Dad wasn't around, *just in case.* Because her mother knew. In her soul, she knew a day would come when her daughter would have to run, or drive. Mom just thought it would be *away* from him, not toward him.

Mariella stared at the double yellow lines stretching ahead. For the first time, ever, she could go anywhere. She could steer her life someplace new. She could leave this town.

But not without her mother.

Mariella slowed at a traffic light, and the Jeep rumbled. There was no radio playing, the dense silence filled only by Vik's heavy breath. For weeks, Mariella had envisioned giving Vik that thermos; she'd pictured him drinking and the surge of victory when he joined in her plans. She'd imagined her father's lifeless body, stiff and sprawled in his bed. Mariella could see so clearly the beginning and the end, but she never pictured the middle.

Cowardice caused her mental block.

Yes, Mariella wanted her father dead (*let me count the ways*), but she feared that when it came to the fatal moments, she'd stop herself from doing it. Lizzie Borden was a badass (if you assume her guilt). Mariella had no problem, morally, with murdering the man who'd been terrorizing her household. He deserved to be gone, and her mom deserved to be safe. But Mariella didn't want to get caught. So she'd come up with a painless and plausible way to get the job done, yet still she feared the cops might decipher that Winthrop Morse's death wasn't an accident.

And that fear—of jail, of a cage worse than the one she currently lived in—was enough for Mariella to involve the sweetest boy she'd ever met.

Guilt flooded her body, sending waves of acid breaking in her stomach. She peered at Vik, his fists pounding unnaturally on his thick thighs, his clenched knuckles now a dingy yellowish white. His one knee jittered, bouncing anxiously and shaking the Jeep.

She could still feel his kisses.

The light switched to green, and Mariella drove, below the speed limit, delaying their arrival. Her house loomed ahead, a monstrous beast, up-lit to ensure it was noticed. She could pull into the drive, or she could keep going; she could fly down a highway until they ran out of gas; she could start a new life with Vik, right now.

Then she pictured Mom's bruises and remembered her cries. She heard her dad's slaps and the echoes of his words. She envisioned Dad's smile as they strolled through Fall River. *Hey, bud, good to see you! We gotta get that beer sometime!*

Winthrop Morse was a man of the people, a normal Joe who never forgot his roots. What a job creator! His picture was a regular feature in the local paper. *Businessperson of the Year.*

Mariella didn't know that man, nor the one smiling in her parents' wedding albums.

She knew only her father, and the fear she felt in the core of her being every time she heard his keys jingle in the door.

Mariella slowed to a stop at her front curb. A year of dating, and Vik had never been inside her home. Not until now.

And hopefully, he wouldn't remember even crossing the threshold. The whispers had promised that Vik would forget his actions. He'd think their date ended on the Ledge with kisses and an autumn sunset. He'd go to sleep in his bed, when this was all over—soon, very, very soon—and he'd awake to Mariella's tragic text. *My father died in his sleep.* He'd console her and hold her hand at the funeral. She'd cry on his shoulder.

Then they'd be together. For real.

The leather wheel felt slick beneath her clammy palms. Her lungs drew air polluted with the filthy sweat emanating from Vik's pores. He now secreted the same corroded, muddy stench as her mouth, his essence matching her own. Was that why she could smell it? They were as one now?

The Jeep idled, and Mariella glared at the driveway's cobblestone entrance. The next touch of the gas pedal brimmed with meaning. Last chance. Her heart rumbled, quaking in her rib cage, quivering her bones.

She pressed down. The Jeep rolled forward, turning onto the circular drive and igniting the sensors. White lights blasted. She touched Vik's forearm, out of habit and out of affection. His thin white T-shirt exposed flesh boiling with fever. For the first time since they'd gotten behind the wheel, Vik shifted toward her. His eyes simmered with smoke, but they weren't deadened. He was alive, somewhere in there. Vik was aware of her. She could see that now.

"Vik." Her voice was tissue-paper thin as she pressed the brake. "Before you get out . . ." She lifted her palm from his arm and stretched for the backpack resting on the rear seats. She unzipped the main compartment and dug her hand inside until she clutched the cool, smooth object she needed.

It was her weapon of choice.

"I just . . . I know what you're about to do. And I want to say *thank you.* For helping me. And my mom. You may not remember this tomorrow. Hopefully. But I need you to know . . . I'm . . . so sorry, for putting you in this position." Tears crashed into her words, clogging her throat. "I wish you didn't have to do this. I wish I were stronger"—she slid out the object—"but I'm afraid I won't go through with it. This should be quick. Painless. And no one will know. You'll be *fine.*"

The exterior lights of her property glinted against the metal tip of the syringe in her hand. She plucked off the clear plastic cap and held the plunger toward Vik. The barrel was full. He didn't move. So, she reached for one of his fists, and he let her pry open his fingers. He stared curiously as she placed the long medical-grade needle in his sweaty palm, closing his fingers around the object before it could fall.

"It's penicillin," she explained. "My dad's allergic."

Reflexively, Mariella's eyes shot toward the house of her neighbor, Mrs. Churchill. The raspberry-red Victorian home was lit almost as elaborately as her own. Its windows were dark, the old woman likely asleep, with her shih tzu curled at the foot of her mattress.

Her neighbor had suffered a serious bacterial infection recently, during which Mariella had cared for Rocky every day.

When Mrs. Churchill returned from her hospital stay, alone, she hired a nurse to aid her recovery. It was a young woman in scrubs, fresh out of UMass, who administered liquid penicillin until the old woman's health improved. The extra vials were stored in the kitchen refrigerator, right next to Rocky's wet food.

If anyone had noticed when Mariella snagged a needle, no one said a word. At least not to her. It wasn't like she'd pocketed oxy or fentanyl. Antibiotics didn't release a psychedelic high, and they weren't lethal to ninety-nine percent of Americans.

This made it the one time in her father's life it sucked to be part of the one percent.

"Inject him anywhere," Mariella explained, and Vik's charcoal eyes remained smoldering and unresponsive. She hoped he could hear her. "Push the liquid in." She made a bending gesture with her thumb. "And that's it. He'll die quickly, without ever waking up. The cops will think it was an accident. My dad's been part of an experimental therapy, and they'll blame it on that."

This was a kinder death than her father deserved, but it was one Mariella could live with. Winthrop Morse had an allergy so lethal, he had to wear a medical bracelet, which he hated for vanity reasons. And when you've got all the money a person could want, you can buy solutions. Her dad was currently paying out of pocket to participate in a penicillin desensitivity therapy trial. For weeks, he'd been going to the hospital and having bits of penicillin administered under a doctor's supervision, the dose slowly increasing. The hope was that over time, he would learn to tolerate the medication.

The potential dangers were obvious. Dad could go into

anaphylactic shock within minutes, hours, or even days after receiving the treatment. He had to be checked out by a nurse daily, he had to sign tons of paperwork, and her mother had to closely monitor him.

Mariella paid attention.

That was why it had to be tonight. Dad had completed his first round of treatment, and he'd just received his highest dose.

The whispers' plan was perfect. Or was it *Mariella's* plan? She hadn't heard a voice, hiss, or buzz since they'd left the woods. Part of her felt grateful—she desperately wanted her mind back, calm and quiet. But another part felt abandoned. Mariella was alone, handing a deadly syringe to a weapon shaped like the boy she loved. Were the whispers inside *his* head now? She didn't know how this worked.

But she knew what came next.

Mariella turned off the Jeep. The headlights powered down, and the black curtain of night fell around them, stars twinkling through the windshield. Mariella had never learned the constellations, but there was something romantic about looking into that never-ending chasm and seeing myths and zodiacs. It was legends that had brought Mariella this far, those of her ancestors. She hoped they were with her now.

She placed her hand on the door and turned back toward Vik. He hadn't twitched, and briefly, Mariella wondered if he couldn't follow through on the plan either. It was possible the part of Vik's brain that was still him was fighting back. Vik was likely stronger than Mariella, both physically and mentally. This plan could fail, and all this could be for nothing.

"Vik," she whispered, "if you're in there . . . *it's time.*"

They were the two magical words the whispers had promised would morph Vik into an obedient killer. *It's time,* two words that would ignite the final phase.

An invisible noose tugged on Vik's neck. He flung open his door and charged out. He said nothing, agreed to nothing, but there was also no hesitation. His footsteps were heavy on the gravel—a monster invading a village, only there were no torches or pitchforks. No one stood in his way.

Mariella exited the car and hid behind a hood that puffed heat from the engine. She watched as Vik thundered up the marble front steps. The porch was covered, useful when finding your keys in the rain, though the door was rarely bolted. You'd be surprised how many rich people's doors were unlocked. They relied mostly on intimidation, as well as fences, cameras, motion sensors, and alarms. But Mariella had already switched off the security system using her phone, and the camera footage would only show Vik Gomez storming inside, which she intended to delete. Not that the cops would ask for it.

Hell, if Mariella and her mom really wanted to, they might be able to sue the hospital, the doctors, and the drug manufacturers. *That therapy was irresponsible and not administered under the right supervision. Winthrop Morse should have been held overnight for observation. They never should have let him leave with such a high dose of a lethal allergen in his system.*

But Mariella wouldn't let her mom do that. They would both be too glad it was over.

Vik stood on the porch, his chest heaving, until his head abruptly jerked to the right. It was a movement too quick to be human, a rabbit's ear flicking at the crack of a stick. Only nothing was there. Dad insisted that front patio furniture was tacky, so the massive space stood barren, except for a stacked pile of wood regularly replenished from October through March. Mariella squinted, trying to discern the source of Vik's interest, watching as he pounded toward the sliced hunks of dead trees. Then her vision—her mind?—registered something that flooded her gut with dread. The scene shifted into slow motion.

The shadowy, hulking figure of the guy who tickled her lips moved his muscular arm toward the logs, and something dropped. There was a high-pitched plink, then a bounce as the plastic syringe hit the marble slab. Vik didn't bend to retrieve it; instead his hand clawed for an object obscured in a dank corner, far from view.

When his elbow pulled back, Mariella's mouth unhinged toward her boots.

Victor Gomez held an axe. An honest-to-goodness lumberjack axe, with a tan wooden handle and a dark steel blade that splayed from its base.

Mariella had never seen the weapon before, but it must have always been there. Why would she notice? What would it matter?

Only now, as Vik hoisted the hatchet to rest on his shoulder, his biceps powerfully flexed, the gravity of every decision Mariella had ever made pulled hard on her breath. Words collected, then piled, then fought in the back of her mouth, but no sound seeped out.

An ugly silence gripped her darkened soul as Victor Gomez marched into the Morse home, with an axe heavy in his hands.

CHAPTER FOURTEEN

TESSA

"Okay, try to stand." Tessa wrapped her arm under Oscar's armpits like she actually thought she could support his two hundred pounds.

Oscar balanced on one leg Karate Kid–style, puffing a few get-ready breaths, then he gingerly shifted his weight onto the ball of his left toe. His left knee flexed, and instantly, his jaw clenched in pain. A yelp escaped his lips and his leg popped back up.

Shit. Tessa was far from an orthopedist, but something was seriously wrong with that knee. "Okay, sit down. We'll figure this out." She held on to Oscar's torso as he lowered himself to the spray-painted rock.

They were miles from their cars.

The sun was setting.

The temperature was dropping. Phil should have told her to bring a jacket.

No, you should have figured that out for yourself.

Phil grunted behind her, in what sounded like pain. Tessa spun toward him. "Are you okay?"

She'd been so focused on Oscar, she hadn't even considered that Phil might be hurt.

Then she saw the blood.

She rushed toward him, his palm dripping, not a river, but a decent crimson trickle that splashed onto the granite below, creating splatters that accented the graffiti.

The wind kicked up once more, thrusting against her back, and Tessa immediately sank to a squat, arms wrapped over her head. Only the gust passed quickly. Almost embarrassingly so. Tessa rose, a blush warming her cheeks at her overreaction. She casually smoothed her sweatshirt.

"What happened to your hand?" Tessa asked, reaching for Phil's palm.

"I lost my balance." He pointed to a rocky point, now covered in splotches of burgundy. "Granite's sharpah than it looks."

"You're lucky that wasn't your head." Tessa shifted Phil's hand this way and that with delicate care. The cut looked shallow—at least, she thought so. She wasn't a doctor.

"I got bandages." Phil tugged at the zipper of his backpack, then yanked out a ziplock bag containing a fully stocked first aid kit, not just Band-Aids and bug spray. He had gauze, pills, and tubes of cream, like a mom on a playground armed for the apocalypse.

"How can I help?"

"Can you take off the cap?" He handed her antibacterial ointment.

"Of course." She unscrewed the lid, then cleaned the gash,

helping place a massive square Band-Aid on his palm that any kid who's fallen off a bike could tell you would never hold; Band-Aids don't stick to sweat. But it was better than nothing.

"Thanks." Phil packed up the supplies.

"What are we gonna do?" Tessa nodded to Oscar, who was seated on the ground, painfully trying to bend and straighten his left knee without groaning too loudly.

They had hiked for over an hour to get to this spot, through a mushy, root-filled trench, on fresh legs and with warmer air. Now they had to make it out in the icy dark with only their cell phone lights to illuminate the obstacles underfoot. And Oscar couldn't stand.

Phil reached into his bag. "I got ibuprofen and a bandage." He handed them to Tessa. "We don't got reception but"—Phil checked his phone again, knowing the bars were nonexistent— "I think I know where those dirt bikers were. That trench leads to a motocross track. Remember we could smell it?"

Tessa nodded.

"I'll see if I can get them up here to help, ride *him* out . . ." He pointed to Oscar.

Tessa could not picture Philadelphia-born-and-raised Oscar on the back of a dirt bike, in these bizarre woods, with his arms wrapped around a complete stranger. A biker. Like the ones who had been circulating on the news lately, claiming Vik had attacked them. Maybe it wasn't too late to get some of the answers she needed.

"You think you can find them?" Tessa asked.

"Positive." Phil slung his backpack on his shoulder. His

take-charge, I-got-this persona was incredibly comforting given the circumstances.

"So we should just wait here?" Tessa asked.

Orange streaks were already smearing ominously across the autumn tree line. There might be a half hour of sun left, max. If Phil didn't come back with a bike, they'd all be spending the night in a haunted forest. There was no way Oscar could maneuver that trench on one leg, in pitch darkness.

"I can hike a lot fastah than the pace we took up here," Phil said, his accent showing his nerves. "I'll be back in forty minutes. Fastah if I find the dirt bikers where I think they are." He pulled the two metal thermoses from his bag, one smudged with a bloody print from his cut. "Drink these. You're probably dehydrated. And he's gonna need all the strength he can get."

"I don't know what we'd do without you."

"Hey, I wouldn't let you come alone. I told ya that." Phil gazed at her intently. "Now, don't go anywhere."

"Like we could." She touched his arm. "Seriously, Phil, thank you."

He paused, holding her eyes for an extra moment, twinkling as though he liked what he saw there—New Tessa. There was no history. No tragedy. No drama. With Phil, she could start over. It would be so easy.

Phil brushed her cheek, lips parting like he wanted to do more, but he stopped himself. "I'll be right back."

Tessa dropped onto the rocky bluff beside Oscar. His left leg was stretched before him, his hands squeezing and massaging his joint.

"I feel like an idiot," he grumbled.

She held out two Advil. "People trip all the time. That wind was crazy."

"It was like a two-second hurricane. What *was* that?" Embarrassment colored his cheeks, which was unwarranted. No one could prepare for a trick of weather that unusual.

She offered the thermos, and Oscar unscrewed the cap, gagging before it even hit his lips. "Ugh. What is this crap?"

"It's a 'recovery drink,'" Tessa said as Oscar popped the pills and swallowed them dry.

Seriously? That bad? She took the container and sniffed, causing an instant reaction from the back of her throat. Damn. She breathed to the side. It smelled like the wind, a dirty rank wetness, and whatever part of the human brain cataloged scents struggled to bring up a memory. Maybe that summer camp by the Schuylkill River? Or the bay down the Jersey Shore?

"Told you." Oscar snorted at her reaction. Then he gave her a look, suggesting she might not like what he said next. "Hey, I know Phil's your friend and all, but don't you think he's a little weird?"

"I dunno." Tessa shrugged. Though she had a feeling it wasn't "weirdness" that bothered Oscar. Phil didn't work hard to hide his feelings, and if his intentions were clear to Tessa, she was certain they were clear to Oscar.

"It's the know-it-all crap. 'Did ya know that Lizzie Borden's real name was Lizbeth?'" Oscar mimicked, his mouth turned down in an exaggerated Phil impression. "'She had ten fingahs and ten toes. And she killed two white people a hundred years ago.'"

"'Allegedly.'" Tessa held up a finger, impulsively joining in. "'She was acquitted, but her house is wicked haunted.'"

Oscar snickered, fist to his mouth, and instantly, guilt rippled through Tessa's body. She had begged Phil for help, and despite his reluctance, he'd shown up for her. Tessa was sitting in the last spot Vik remembered, and if Phil didn't come back, she and Oscar might have to build a duplex on this ledge.

Besides, up until a few days ago, she and Phil were . . . what? Maybe, possibly, becoming more than friends?

But now Oscar was here.

"Stop," Tessa said. "Phil's really nice."

"I'll take your word for it." Oscar rolled his eyes.

A rustle shifted behind them, a branch cracking under the weight of a footstep. A human footstep. Tessa swung, heart swelling with hope, expecting to see Phil, or even a hiker—maybe one with a satellite phone and a helicopter on standby. A light breeze flowed, spitting bits of crumbled leaves, and Tessa squinted, hand held like a visor.

Only she saw nothing.

She heard nothing.

Her eyes focused where she'd heard the crunch, and for a moment, maybe a blink, she thought she spied a shift of a shadow. It slipped low and stealthy. Then the darkness sank, crouching in a movement that looked human.

"Anyone there?" she called, trying to sound hopeful, but there was unease in her voice.

If someone was coming, someone bad, there was no possible escape, nowhere but down. Very far down. They were backed against the cliff's edge.

A frozen finger scraped down Tessa's spine, and she remembered that feeling from earlier, the one that nudged her toward the precipice, that had her leaning a bit too far. "H-hello?" her voice was even weaker.

Oscar gripped her hand. "What is it?" he whispered.

"Nothing. I just . . . feel something."

They sat in silence for a space of time, the air growing colder. Thicker. But there were no more cracks. No snaps. No footsteps. Not even a draft.

"I'm losing my mind." She shook off the bad feeling, blowing out a stale puff from her lungs. "And you should probably drink something." She nodded to the metal container. "Crap or not. You need your strength."

"Strength is not my issue." Oscar cocked his brow, the one with the scar cutting through. In ninth grade, some drunk threw a beer bottle, not directly at him and his friends, but close enough that the glass caught Oscar anyway. He'd needed stitches, and he loved every ounce of character it gave him. "I'm more worried about Coach."

"Coach is the reason your knee popped." Tessa shot him a look.

Oscar was a running back who had started every football game he'd played in since the second grade. *Walk it off! Walk it off!* might as well have been painted in white chalk in the end zones.

Tessa handed him the roll of bandage. There were two metal clips in the box to fasten it. Very old-school. Oscar tugged up the wide leg of his jeans, and Tessa could see fluid already puffing below his dark skin. The joint was beyond grapefruit sized.

With the efficiency of someone who'd done this before, Oscar wrapped his knee and secured the clips.

"I wonder if Vik saw the sunset that night?" Tessa pointed to the lemon-orange threads tangled on the horizon, highlighting the fall leaves of a collegiate brochure.

"Probably," Oscar said. "Did it help? Coming out here?"

"Not really." The restless feeling of missing something hadn't left her.

Tessa didn't know what she'd hoped to find—maybe a poorly discarded note with the header, "How to get away with a double murder in three easy steps," or a pill bottle with Mariella Morse's name on it, or an abandoned cell phone with a video of the entire night's events. Tessa wanted a clue. If this were a movie, she'd be able to come here and find the exact hidden item the police had overlooked that would prove her brother's innocence.

But there was nothing.

Vik was in jail. Tessa was failing. Just like she'd failed her father. Just like she'd failed her mother by making them move to this cursed zip code.

Tessa hung her head, wavy hair concealing her face. "I have completely screwed up my family."

"What?" Oscar's face whirled toward her. "How can you say that?"

"I keep messing up. I'm trying to be *responsible*"—she remembered her father's final words—"to make up for what happened. But I never should have made them move here. If we'd just stayed in Philly—what the hell was I thinking?"

Oscar pulled her close, her vision blurring with the regretful tears that were always bubbling.

"Look, I'm not gonna argue with you about leaving Philly." Oscar's breath was hot against her cheek. "I want you home, like, tomorrow. But you can't keep spending your life thinking you're to blame for everything. Your dad's death was an accident. *You* weren't the one texting and driving."

"I know." She swallowed the apple-sized lump in her throat.

"Do you?" Oscar pulled back, forcing her to meet his stare. "Not many people are gonna say this to you, but I'm gonna. Vik's not a child. And he's not an idiot. There's a reason they're charging him as an adult."

Tessa jolted, shoving a hand at Oscar's chest.

But he continued, not holding back. "I'm not sayin' Vik did anything wrong. I'm just sayin', he made his own choices. He picked his own girlfriend. He came to this spot. He knew the hike. He knew it was getting dark. Whatever happened that night, it wasn't their first time here. Vik said so himself."

Tessa tugged at the strings of her hoodie, head drooping toward her lap, crisscross-applesauce. She'd already considered every point Oscar was saying, but none changed how she felt.

She tucked her hands in her sleeves. The sun had almost completely slipped away, and the temperature was probably down to the forties. She'd never considered they would be out this late. They weren't supposed to be in the woods after dark.

"Something shady went down here that night. We know that," Oscar went on. "But it had nothing to do with *you*."

"But Vik wouldn't even be in Massachusetts if I hadn't—"

"Girl, you were sixteen years old when you moved!" Oscar cut her off. "How much power do you think you have? You think your mama would just leave her job and her family, because *you* said so?"

"No, well, I mean, I don't know. It was *my* idea." Tessa was getting confused.

"No, it was your Tía Dolores's idea. Your mom's *sister*," Oscar corrected. "You think you're the only one who talked to your mom?"

"So, it's my aunt's fault?" Tessa yelped.

"It's nobody's fault!" Oscar insisted. "That's what I'm trying to tell you. You forgot to get cupcakes—well, you know what? You could have gotten them the next day. There was plenty of time. Your dad *chose* to do it that night. Your mom *chose* to move in with her sister. Vik *chose* to come here with that chick. You've gotta stop putting everyone else's choices on *you*."

That wasn't what she was doing.

Was it?

Tessa blinked at the sky shifting to a pretty purply twilight.

She hadn't skipped the bakery on purpose. She'd simply forgotten—an accident, just as Oscar had said. But Vik,

Fall River—Tessa had been so full of grief when the decisions went down regarding the move that the memories of who talked to who, and when, were fuzzy around the edges, blurred and smudged.

Shit.

Was it her mom's idea? Did it even matter?

Oscar inched closer and put both palms on her cheeks. "Am I finally gettin' through to you?"

He held her face until she looked at him, really looked at him, and the box she'd tucked all her feelings away in instantly ripped open.

God, she had missed him. Her forehead fell against his. "If I didn't say this before, I'm so glad you came."

"So am I."

Tessa hovered in the moment, their breath mingling. It was so familiar. Enticing. Oscar didn't move an inch, nor did he push. This was her choice, and they both knew it. The entire hike up, all the tension between Phil and Oscar—it was because Tessa didn't know what she wanted, or even *who* she wanted. She'd tried so hard to put everything that happened in Philly in the past; she'd tried to forget. She wanted to be the responsible girl her father had needed that night, but her dad wouldn't want her constantly trying to be someone she wasn't. He wouldn't want her to live as half a person. New Tessa wasn't real, because Old Tessa never went away.

Oscar knew that. He looked at her and didn't see just the person she'd become this past year; he saw all of her. The *real* her.

And she saw him. Every night, when she closed her eyes.

She'd wanted to call him, she'd wanted to visit, but she was so scared to open that box, so terrified of the pain that was packed deep inside, that she forced herself to forget all the love. That was what she saw in Oscar's eyes right now. That was what she felt. It was why she could never go out with Phil.

Because Tessa hadn't stopped being in love with the boy she'd left behind.

Tessa leaned forward, closing the space between them, and the air grew warmer. Her fingertips tingled. She shut her eyes and pressed her lips to his, just a flutter, soft and tickly. Oscar slid his hands into her hair, and goose bumps raced down her skin, her body reacting the way it always did. For him. His lips opened, teasing; he wanted her to like what he was doing. And it worked. Every. Single. Time.

Tessa wrapped her arms around him, and her fingers skimmed the fade on his neck. He held her tighter; his lips pressed firmer.

Then a sudden burst of wind shoved at their backs. Icy and rough. It was a stormy gust as strong as the first and way too cold for October. They both pulled back, squinting at the horizon as if expecting snow to blow their way.

Only that wasn't what they saw.

Through Tessa's fluttering lashes, she made out slivers of sky that looked *wrong*. Gone were the yellow sunset bursts and the calm lavender blues. There was no grayish cast, or navy blanket peppered with stars.

Instead, Tessa peered at lights, intensely bright, formed of aqua, sapphire, and celery. They were beams, ribbons, as distinct in the atmosphere as the strobes of a Hollywood premiere. And the colors weren't coming from the sun or even the direction where the sun had dropped. They weren't coming from the sky at all.

Tessa had never seen the aurora borealis, and she was guessing most people hadn't, but she'd seen pictures. And that was what she was looking at now—a nuclear, swirling neon cloud hovering above the trees. Its odd light beams reflected on the pond below—or did they come from there? Tessa peered down, down, down. An hour ago, the water lacked a single ripple, now frothy white foam waved across its surface.

And the strobe lights were growing. Rising. Building.

Then the voices started.

CHAPTER FIFTEEN

The night of the murders . . .

MARIELLA

Mariella stood motionless in her driveway.

It's said that when human beings are faced with potentially deadly situations, they react in one of three ways—fight, flight, or freeze. It's an automatic reaction, a survival instinct. And you don't get to choose.

Mariella stiffened as she watched Vik stomp into her home with an axe (or was it a hatchet?) hanging heavy in his hands, the steel blade scratching along the tumbled marble tiles of her entryway. Her mind switched off. Shut down. It wasn't that she couldn't decide what to do, it was more that she couldn't remember why she needed to do anything. Should she walk? What was walking?

An ocher light glowed from the wide rectangular shape ahead. That was the front doors, wasn't it? They were open.

A creature shot out—small, fluffy, and white. Fancy. Her cat. She was loose; Fancy never left the house. Mariella should chase her, catch her, and make sure her cat was safe, but she couldn't make her legs move.

Why wouldn't they move?

A deep whirring filled the cavern of her skull, the cogs of her brain spinning so fast, steam gushed below the deepest layers of her skin. Sweat broke out under her arms and inside her bra. She glared at her hands, expecting blistering pustules to be sprouting from the blaze, but there were only freckles.

Then a scream cut through the air, high-pitched and terrified. Too big for this world.

Mariella's head swung toward it, a clump of blond hair sticking to her lips.

She knew that voice.

No, no, no, no, no . . .

Mariella's legs left the ground before she had made up her mind, speeding at a pace she didn't know she was capable of. Finally. She could move, sprint. Her heart accelerated, the rhythm of war drums.

What had she done?

Her foot stomped on her loose shoelace, and she tripped onto the front stoop, her sole skidding on the slick tiles. She caught her balance, then scrambled into her shiny foyer decorated with gold this and marble that. It was so obnoxious. Why did she live here?

A thud, gushy and wet, sounded from the second floor. Her

stomach flopped, bile bubbling. She thundered up the mahogany staircase, gripping the polished railing as her toes frantically slipped, step after step.

"Vik Vik Vik please stop oh my god Vik!" Mariella shouted, her throat painfully chafed as her lungs pushed beyond max capacity. "Stop you have to stop don't do this I take it all back I swear Vik stop please don't Vik no!" she yelled, blubbering, her bootlace flapping, its plastic end tink-tink-tinking against the varnished wood. God, why hadn't she tied her freakin' shoelace yet?

Then her hands clawed the stairs, her body half bear-crawling, half running until she reached the ornate Turkish carpet that sprawled down the hallway's center. She stood, eyeing her parents' bedroom at the far end of the haunting corridor, walls stretching and swelling in time with the sickening moans.

Who was moaning?

Mariella's stomach clenched, a foul liquid rising.

"Vik," she creaked, then swallowed, gagging on bile. Her legs moved of their own accord, because surely her brain wasn't telling her to go. She didn't want to enter that space. She didn't want to see what was inside. The threatening vomit that burned in her esophagus mixed with the mulchy saliva on her tongue, reminding her of what she'd done, and why they were here. This was *her* fault. "Vik, please please please stop. This is a mistake, not this, please God no please."

But God wasn't here. Not in a place like this, not at a time like this. No, the forces in this home, right now, were much more infernal, leaching from a forest—a triangle—that had seen so much death and destruction that supernatural powers were drawn to it. From it. Even animals stayed away.

An ugly amber light glowed from the bedroom. Dust floated in the beams, spinning and dancing with the unnatural shifts of ghost orbs. She'd learned once that these pretty spiraling specks were mostly human skin cells, bits of dead flesh. Seemed fitting.

Mariella shut her mouth and burst through. Vik, or the body that used to be Vik, towered at the foot of her parents' antique four-poster king bed, facing the sculpted wooden headboard, his strong legs spread in a wide V. The muscles on his back rippled beneath what had once been a white T-shirt, but now . . . now . . . that couldn't be blood? Veins and tendons bulged on his forearms. One fist anchored the base of the the wooden axe handle, while the other clutched high near a blade that dripped red. She couldn't see the mattress or what lay there. Who lay there. Vik's hulking frame blocked the scene. Had he grown?

Mariella watched stoically, head tilted, unsure what was unfolding. The axe sliced through the air with the whistle of a bomb, a high-pitched, draining squeal that cut off with a final thunk. Blood splashed, no spurted, no blasted, onto Vik, dousing his head, his shoulder, and his T-shirt. *God, had it* ever *been white?* His black hair oozed with slimy burgundy fluid. A chunk dripped off his chin. The floral beige-and-gold wallpaper, expertly hung to ensure every seam lined up perfectly (*Do not mess up the pattern!* her mother had warned the decorators, over and over), was splattered with drips of crimson and bits of— Flesh? Muscle? Brain?

Mariella could have stepped to the side; she could have shifted slightly, to see who was on the bed. But her legs stayed locked, her brain protecting what was left of her soul.

Vik yanked on the weapon, which had sunk into its target and was now lodged into something . . . human. He grunted, foot braced against the frame, thigh muscles squeezing as he worked to free the blade from whatever resistance kept it from him. Abruptly, the axe shot up with a slurping gulp, the momentum tossing the steel end against Vik's shoulder, his body twisting to the side.

Then Mariella saw it.

Saw her.

Her mother.

Mom was lying on her back, wearing what once was a silk-and-lace ivory nightgown with spaghetti straps, something far too revealing for Vik to see. Her mother always wore a robe, white silk to her ankles, belt tight. She'd hate being exposed like this, though it was more than just her skin showing. Apple-red blossoms bloomed on the fabric, spreading from a fresh chasm in her lower abdomen. A fountain gushed from her thigh. Both thighs? The mattress was a growing scarlet pool.

Mariella recoiled, choking, a metallic taste in her mouth. It was blood. Her mother's blood.

Where was her father?

Mariella's eyes darted about. The floor. The sheet. The plush white settee. No, it was Alabaster, not white. Her mother had agonized over the color choice—when was it? Two years ago?—when they renovated the room.

Mariella, do you prefer Eggshell? Alabaster? Or Winter White?

They all looked the same. But now that same sofa was riddled with droplets darker than any merlot. Because this wasn't a spill. It was a loss of life.

The wrong life.

"M-mom." Mariella sobbed, doubling over. Hot tracks burned her cheeks, dripping off the tip of her nose. Her stomach retched, but she hadn't eaten since lunch. There was no relief.

Vik jerked her way with an inhuman tic as his mind (what was left of it) finally registered her presence. He heard her. Yes, Mariella was here. She wished she weren't.

He raked his cloudy gray pupils down her body, this boy with the velvety lips and the seductive smile. He turned over the axe in his hands, crimson streams dribbling from the tip. He pointed the edge her way, and it was in that moment, that very instant, that Mariella first realized she was in danger. She swallowed her breath along with her screams, then assessed the blade.

Mariella had put a lethal plan in motion, and she'd just assumed she'd be unscathed. She thought she could wipe this boy's soul from his body, hand him a weapon (granted not *this* weapon, but *a* weapon), and trust that, of course, he wouldn't turn against her.

Vik lowered the axe, his right wrist swirling the blade near the ground in the circular pattern of a ballplayer toying with his bat. A spray of crimson released, bits of her mother sinking deep into the white carpet fibers.

Mariella didn't flinch. She didn't look for an escape.

No, she was ready. She was done.

Her lashes squinted shut, her arms falling limp at her sides, palms facing Vik. Mariella dropped her head back in surrender. *Do it. I deserve it.*

She welcomed the blow.

After everything Mariella had done, after what she'd let be done *to* her and to her mother, this plan was finally in motion, and the man she wanted dead, the one who truly deserved an axe to the chest, wasn't even in the room. He'd probably gone for drinks at the local speakeasy with a corporate crony. He was likely kicked back in a tufted leather wingback chair, listening to jazz, and smacking some waitress's ass—*I'm just kidding, sweetheart*—while his wife lay dead, and his daughter faced her final moments.

Her father was going to win. He would get the house and the money, and he'd score a do-over on life. He'd find a newer, younger model to marry. He'd terrorize a different unsuspecting woman. He'd make her bear his child then emotionally ravage the offspring from the moment it wailed its first cry. Poor baby, that wouldn't be its last.

Mariella waited. What was taking so long? Where was the blade? Her jaw tightened, longing for the whistle, the swing, and the last act of justice.

Then a gurgle rose up.

It wasn't from her.

Or Vik.

No, this was a slight did-you-hear-that? sputter from a woman Mariella had heard choke and sob so many times. Mariella's eyes sprang open and flicked toward the mattress. Blood popped from the gash in her mom's stomach, little burps made by air. Or breath.

Mom wasn't dead. Not yet.

An ambulance. Cops.

Mariella could fix this.

Only Vik's hand slid up the slimy handle, and his head twisted toward the only family that had ever meant anything to Mariella. He wrenched his shoulder back, arm swinging once more, and her mother rattled again, a spray of garnet gargling from her downturned lips.

Mariella dove. Her body leapt without giving her notice. Airborne, her thin frame collided with Vik's chest, her long arms latching onto his back and wrapping around his throat. Both her legs twined around his hips, forcing him to carry her weight, her movement so sudden he actually dropped the axe, the weapon falling with a thump onto the plush carpet. He crooked his arm and threw an elbow, slamming into Mariella's eye socket. Her face erupted in pain, a white haze blinding her vision. A ringing filled her ears. But she didn't let go.

Instead, she tightened her grip, her right forearm crushing his Adam's apple as her left fist struck the crown of his head. She locked her legs, teeth grinding, and his left arm shot up to backhand her face. He busted her lip, blood spurting, the coppery taste adding to the muck on her tongue. She welcomed the flavor, because *it was hers*. From her body. She didn't know what forces—what evils?—were in that tea, what darkness she'd ingested, but her blood, yes, *her* blood was her own. She was still human. She was alive. And if she could, if it was at all possible, Mariella was going to save her mother.

"Get off!" she screamed, slamming her fist again and again on

Vik's skull, bruising her knuckles and straining her already sore wrists. "Stop! Wake up! Stop! *It's time! It's time! It's time!*"

Mariella shouted the magic words, but Vik didn't listen. He didn't stop. He continued to buck, trying to toss her. She clung on tighter.

Then a thud rose up. Heavy treads. Footsteps. On the stairs. Down the hall.

It was her father.

It had to be. He was coming. At last. Vik would have a new target. A distraction.

Mariella let go, her body abruptly dropping from Vik's back and landing heavy on the carpet, her limbs slack and exhausted.

She turned toward the doorway, Vik's movement matching her own.

They waited together.

Mariella wouldn't interfere with whatever Vik wanted to do to that man. Her father would draw Vik's attention away, long enough for Mariella to apply pressure to her mom's wounds and call 911.

It would all be okay.

Vik squatted slowly, eyes on the doorway, and lifted the axe. He adjusted his grip. Mariella leaned toward her mother, stretching for the mattress and finding her foot. *I'm here,* she thought. *Just hang on, Mom. Help is coming.*

A figure emerged.

His clothes were clean and unwrinkled. His hair was slick and styled. He looked too put together for the carnage of this room.

Then he walked, confidently, into the bloody massacre and Mariella's muscles relaxed, her chest slumping.

"What the hell happened?" he asked.

"Phil?" Mariella said it like a question. "Thank God, you're here."

CHAPTER SIXTEEN

TESSA

"What the hell?" Oscar yelled, swatting at Tessa as his muddy Jordans kicked the granite, damaged knee be damned.

An iridescent blaze illuminated the night.

"What is that?" Tessa tried to point, but the screaming wind pinned down her arms.

Ultramarine, emerald, cobalt blue, and zinc yellow sullied the sky Van Gogh style, a *Starry Night* painting come horribly to life. It was overwhelming and pulsing. Swirling. Bringing with it an unnatural stench of iron and rot—the stink of it so overpowering that it rammed down Tessa's throat. No, it invaded her throat; it invaded *her*.

"Is it coming from the lake?" Tessa struggled to peel her lashes more than a crack.

She pulled onto her hands and knees, fighting the rank-scented gales. Then she crawled, inched, struggling to look into the cavernous depths, searching for the base of the lights. The pond's surface, once a lifeless black, now glimmered with the source of all color. It was an acid spill, only instead of flowing deeper into the liquid, the color rose up, clawing higher and higher. The strobes were reaching for something. Someone.

A heaviness tugged on Tessa's torso. Had she ever seen anything like this? The Manic Panic colors blended and whirled with a wickedly beautiful shine. She reached out a hand and was surprised that she could. Had the wind stilled? She wanted to touch it. Grab it. See what color felt like, let it brush against her skin.

The light—it could swallow her whole if she let it.

A crumb broke off the cliff, more like a chunk. It plunked into the cauldron below, into the rainbow, and rippled, gentle circles ringing outward.

Yes, that was what Tessa needed to do. She needed to dive. Jump. She could make it. That was where she needed to be. They didn't have to hike. She would instantly reach the bottom. It was so simple. Why hadn't she thought of this before? She'd be there in seconds; she just had to fall. Tessa leaned, her head, her eyes, her chin stretching toward the precipice, all the weight in her toes ready to push. *Just jump. JUMP!*

Someone grabbed her biceps, fingers digging hard. She was yanked back, until she rocked onto her side. She blinked. Dazed. The fog dissipated from her brain.

What had she almost done?

"We have to go!" Oscar yelled over a roar of wind louder than any clap of thunder.

The air smacked her. Gusts screeching, filling her ears like a swarm of bees, buzzing into her brain.

Go . . .

Leave . . .

Who said that?

Her head whipped toward Oscar, but he stared with his mouth closed. Sealed.

Now!

Run!

Oscar's lips didn't twitch. All the warmth in Tessa's body spun down a drain inside her and exited her pores. She pressed icy palms to the sides of her skull, kneading, rubbing. These weren't her thoughts. These weren't Oscar. Someone was speaking to her. Inside her.

"Tessa, what are you doing? Let's go!" Oscar bellowed over the chaos, over the voices. He grunted, putting all his weight on a quivering arm and shifting himself to a low squat. Then he balanced, teetering, until he stood on his unhurt leg.

HE is coming.

You must go!

Quickly!

The voices shrieked, scraping inside of Tessa's cranium, clawing their way down her eardrums. She needed to breathe. Tessa sucked in a gritty burst of wind and suddenly, her mind stilled. Total and complete calm overtook every cell in her body, washing out her panic with the invasive voices.

Tessa rose to her feet. Whether the shouts were friend or

foe or the source of all color personified, it didn't matter. The ledge wasn't safe. Granite was falling. Crumbling. A landslide was threatening.

And Oscar needed help.

"Can you walk?" She reached for him.

"I'm gonna freakin' try." Oscar placed a heavy palm on Tessa's shoulder, and for reasons she couldn't understand, his weight didn't register. She could have carried him through the forest like a newborn in a swaddle.

She boosted him, and they stumbled toward the path. No, toward *a* path. There were so many. Which way had they come? It had been a trench, but there was more than one. She dove into a trail, skidding over rocks and sinking into sandy earth.

They couldn't communicate. They couldn't hear each other's voices, or even screams. The noise was all-consuming, matching the train wreck footage that had dominated the news mere months ago. A cell phone camera caught twisted metal, jack-knifed dining cars, squealing wheels on melted tracks with hunks of sharpened debris raining hot from the sky. That disaster was quieter than what Tessa heard right now. The grating sound raked up her spine as they tripped and hobbled. Away, simply away. Behind them, fluorescent lights flared—not constantly, not even regularly—more like erratic camera flashes.

Stumble, trip, hobble.

"Phil!" Tessa hollered, knowing her friend wouldn't hear her even if he were standing right next to her. But she had to try. "Phil!"

God, the taste—what was in the air? She fought a gag, the rotten flavor on her tongue, then desperately scanned trees, which were morphing into blackened silhouettes.

"Phil! Where are you?" she shouted, holding up her hand to bat away branches.

"Phil!" Oscar joined in her cries.

She could hear Oscar! Thank God! They both screamed. There was no way she was leaving Phil, and Oscar knew that without even asking.

Together, they yelled his name again and again, until a boom rocked the air, shaking Tessa's chest.

Smoke exploded and debris flew. A whistle rose above the cacophony with an ever-growing *ssss*. She scanned the trees. Something was coming down, growing closer and closer. Louder and louder.

The wail was deafening. Then Oscar wrenched her arm nearly from its socket.

Stumble, trip, hobble.

Tessa crashed into him, and he crashed into the bark of a tree, their backs sliding down the lichen.

A massive branch fell, too dense to see light through to the other side. It crashed into the path where they had been faltering, its drop so great that the fractured limb shot back up. It actually bounced.

Tessa lengthened her arm toward the branch, fingers quivering and her heart somewhere near the back of her teeth. She plucked off a burnt-sienna leaf.

"That could have killed us." Her voice held wonder.

Run. A voice said—from inside her skull. This was no survival instinct. She was certain of it. This was a shout, a warning, coming from somewhere beyond herself.

Tessa laced her fingers with Oscar's, a grip so tight she could have crushed his bones, and tugged him back toward the path. They weren't on the right trail. There was no trench. No dirt walls edged toward their shoulders. This path was low and rocky, and it was meant for hiking, not dirt bikes. But they had hiked *up* to get to the Ledge, so now presumably, they needed to go *down*. And down they went.

A squawk rose. Oscar? Tessa's head whipped toward him. No. Phil? Her ear cocked.

The howl rang out once more. A call.

A battle cry.

The voice didn't sound human.

Stumble, trip, *sprint*.

With lungs gulping rancid air, they ran from an angry wind.

Minutes passed, maybe more, Tessa wasn't sure. She was fighting the vines and the trees. Fingers, long, thick, and very much alive, reached for her wobbling ankles and slithered against her skin. The touch was wet and far too cold. But she never stopped, not even when the unseen plants grew teeth and bit. Tessa's flesh was bleeding. Somewhere, below her jeans, above her soggy sneakers, crimson trickled into her socks. She continued sprinting, propping Oscar's weight, with their internal compasses pointed down.

The forest had to end. The chaos couldn't last forever.

"Phil!" she continued to holler desperately, her throat stripped and aching.

They had driven to this park on a road, so eventually, blissfully, they had to reach a potholed, double-lined paradise. Even if they emerged nowhere near their cars, they'd still be in civilization. This was Massachusetts. Home of the T and Fenway Park. The state had woods, not wilderness. These trees had to end.

Damn, why hadn't she stayed in the city?

A branch, or maybe a sapling, crashed behind her. Or was it beside her? Leaves flew at her face, tangling in her sweaty hair. Oscar twined his fingers tighter, running like someone in a full leg cast. Painfully. Awkwardly. But he was an elite athlete, and despite a busted knee, he was matching Tessa step for step. In fact, it could have been her slowing their pace. Her lungs were an inferno, her legs not used to bolting for anything other than a school bus.

And though it could be wishful thinking, she swore the switch on the monstrous northern lights above them had lowered to a flicker. The endless trees were now illuminated with a muted, unnatural aqua. The wind was lessening and visibility was increasing, which meant Tessa could finally see what was right in front of her.

And that only increased her fear.

There were plenty of people in this world who were petrified to stroll down a city street alone at night, their keys between their fingers—most identify as women, because being alone in an unknown place with a strange man was the most dangerous thing a woman could be. And sure, there were times in Tessa's life when she'd heard footfalls behind her on a Philly block, and she'd slid her phone from her pocket, her thumb unlocking the screen, ready to dial for help. But typically, the guy would turn a corner or hop into a cab. If he didn't, then she was still in a big city, never more than a wailing scream away from another person. A crowded restaurant. A car at a traffic light.

But now, in these woods, she was trapped in some *Blair Witch* shit. Tessa had been screaming since the source of all color exploded. How long ago was that? It felt like they'd been running forever, and no one had heard them. Not even Phil. Especially not Phil. Their cries were being gobbled by a wind that reeked of death.

Only she didn't feel alone.

Trees were being hurled their way—yes, hurled. Something was throwing them. Something was watching. It was following. It was brushing against Tessa's skin with clammy fingers and whispering in her ears, inside her skull. Inside her.

Her back pocket buzzed.

Vibrated.

Her phone! Cell reception. 911.

She slid out the slim electronic miracle device and sent up a prayer with every ounce of goodwill she'd earned from years of Sunday school.

God, please let my phone work. Please let my phone work. Please let my phone work . . .

She looked down.

One bar.

One freaking bar!!

Thank you, thank you, thank you.

She dialed 911, then clutched the phone to her ear.

"I have reception!" she yelled to Oscar, who hobble-sprinted beside her.

He immediately yanked his phone from his pocket.

Only 911 wasn't ringing. It wasn't connecting. There was only the sound of deadly quiet air failing to locate a network.

Don't panic. You can do this. Try a text.

But who? Her mom would completely lose it, her sanity stretched too thin. Tía Dolores would tell her mom. Then the entire family. They'd know she was in danger, but that wouldn't get her *out* of here. Frankie could tell the cops. Cops! They might not be able to stop a supernatural tornado, but Tessa knew at least one officer who would believe such a thing existed.

Detective Ertz.

Tessa scanned her text messages as a vine—a branch—closed around her foot, thorns scratching her ankle. Tessa kicked it off in the single fluid movement of a person who didn't have time for these games. Not now. Throw your trees later.

Her eyes stayed on the screen.

"I don't have a signal!" Oscar whined.

She heard him clearly. Yes, the wind was definitely dying down. And it was darker, no swirling lights. Her phone was the only glow in front of them.

Oscar steered her past a fallen log, guiding her, as she opened her chat with Detective Ertz. Her right thumb pounded while her left hand stayed locked in Oscar's, not releasing his grip.

Tessa hammered a message, autocorrect to her aid: *Help! In the Freetown Woods. Lost. Being chased.*

Send.

Three little dots appeared. Blink, blink, blink.

It went through. Oh sweet Jesus!

"I don't have any bars. Why is my phone not working?" Oscar groaned.

"Mine is. It went through! I texted the cop!"

Detective Ertz texted back: *Where are you? Who's chasing you?*

"Send a pin! Can you drop a pin?" Panic bled from Oscar's words.

Tessa opened her Map application, a tiny azure dot pulsing in a sage-green sea of nothing. Absolutely nothing. There were no white lines with streets, no beige squares of neighborhoods. Just an ugly, angry green, green, green. And a splotch of pale blue smaller than a pinkie nail.

Was that the pond? The one below the Ledge?

They should have gone farther than that. They had to be close to a road by now. They had to. If not, that meant they were running in the wrong direction in a five-thousand-acre haunted death trap.

Tessa held down the surging blue dot and hit send.

Three little dots appeared.

Dots!

It sent!

Detective Ertz had a pin of their location!

Then the dots disappeared.

Tessa's eyes flicked to the top of her phone.

No bars. *No! Nooo!*

"I don't know if it went through!" Her voice cracked, not from the fire iron scorching her throat, or from the hollering and panting, but from fear. Maybe that was what she was tasting in the wind, toxic fear grown over centuries in this cursed and wretched place.

"Hopefully she got it!" Oscar yelled, running without a grunt of pain.

"We're in the middle of nowhere." Tessa's voice was helpless. She coughed, a cramp in her side digging for her spleen. She was tired and painfully thirsty. The metal containers from Phil were still up on the Ledge. They had nothing. They were abandoned. "The map, there were no roads. Anywhere. We're going the wrong way!"

She stared at the map. No dot. No bars.

"What the hell is the *right* way?" Oscar shouted. "Back the way we came? Where the wind was chucking trees and the sky looked like a freakin' alien invasion?"

"I don't know! But this—"

A branch cracked. Like the sound they'd heard earlier, back on the Ledge. A footstep. It was right over Tessa's left shoulder. Then her skin pricked, triggered by the part of the human brain that sensed eyes.

They were being watched.

There were no animals in these woods. They'd been here for hours and not a single squirrel had scampered by. No, these weren't the yellow irises of woodland creatures. This was something else. Someone else. A bad feeling pulsed behind her breastbone.

Tessa skidded to a halt, her Nikes slipping on the slimy mess underfoot. She kicked at the wet blackness. Then she pointed her phone's flashlight down. She and Oscar were standing in an emerald sea of climbing plants—only this one lacked the feel of fairy wings fluttering from dandelion wisps. These invasives were wet. Tessa yanked her foot from the sopping ground, her other one sinking even deeper.

"Why did we stop?" Oscar tugged at her arm.

"Something's wrong." Crushed ice slid down her spine, matching her freezing, soaked toes.

"No shit! We're lost in a goddamn hellscape!"

"No, not that. Well, it *is* that, but . . ." Tessa's voice trailed off. Where were the eyes coming from? That feeling . . .

The orbs of light were now extinguished, returning the sky to a rich black with just the slightest eerie hint of an unusual green. The light was subtle, but enough to cast shadows, lots of them. Hair stuck to the back of her neck as her gaze flung around, a creepy sensation crawling beneath her skin.

"I feel someone," Tessa whispered. "Looking at us."

Oscar's body grew rigid, and his hand clamped even harder around her fingers, his head darting in all directions.

Another crack.

When had it gotten so quiet? Tessa suddenly realized the freight train that had been barreling toward them since they started sprinting was suddenly gone. Or maybe they'd successfully outrun it. The air was now stagnant. Musty.

And alive. Very alive.

She lifted her sneaker to the sound of a slurp.

A shadow shifted. It was a darkness slightly blacker than the star-speckled sky.

Tessa's eyes flicked in time with Oscar's. To their left, maybe six or seven trees away, a shadow was moving.

It lifted a limb, a human limb.

Then it coughed.

Tessa immediately recognized the sound. "Phil!"

CHAPTER SEVENTEEN

Nearly two months before the murders . . .

MARIELLA

It had started weeks ago. Well, actually, it'd started long before that, but in terms of Mariella's current circumstances, it all began during the last blasts of summer. They were in the Freetown–Fall River State Forest. Mariella and Phil had gone on a hike—it had become their thing.

They were searching for her great-uncle's cabin. Only instead of finding a rotted pile of logs once belonging to Lizzie Borden's uncle, John Morse (which would have been seriously cool), they found a field choked by vines and lichen. Wild white roses mixed with leeks that reeked of onion. Tiny low-lying strawberry clusters spread specks of vibrant color. She and Phil gathered specimens, a way to remember their journey, or so Mariella thought. Then two weeks later, they trekked to the Ledge for the very first time, right before the school year was about to begin.

Phil handed her a thermos. "Drink." He nodded with his chin. She sniffed, nose crinkling at the stench. "Ugh, what is it?"

"You're not gonna believe this, but"—Phil's eyes flashed with excitement—"all those plants we collected, it was 'cause I found this book at the historical society, with a recipe for some kinda special tea. The book had 'Morse' written on the inside cover."

"Like my family?" Mariella stared curiously at the metal container. "You made the tea?"

"Yeah, I'm tellin' ya. Your family had power. Remember those séances we had as kids? In the graveyard?" Phil asked. Mariella nodded. During their occult phase, Phil had accompanied Mariella to Sarah Morse's gravesite. They'd failed to communicate with the dead, several times, then eventually grew out of the hobby. Or, at least, Mariella had. "Well, I thought maybe those didn't work because the spirits weren't *at* their graves. If John Morse really was a witch, or a warlock, then it's possible his spirit remained where he *lived,* and the power he possessed may have seeped into the ground . . ."

"What exactly are you saying? You think if I drink this 'special tea,' I'll inherit powers?"

"I dunno." Phil shrugged. "That's what the book seemed to be sayin'. Worth a shot, ain't it? Some extra strength might come in handy with your father." He gave her a meaningful look.

Mariella lifted the thermos again. "What if it's poisonous?"

"I already tried some yesterday. It's fine."

"Do you feel magical?" She sounded dubious.

"No, but I'm not a direct descendant. You are." Phil pointed her way. "Maybe it'll only work for you."

They'd been pretending to be witches and wizards since they were little kids, making voodoo dolls and talking to Ouija boards. Still, Mariella hadn't realized how much of the supernatural Phil had continued to research. Though he did work in a haunted murder house, which gave him every reason to believe in the un-explainable.

The question was, did she?

It was seductive—the idea she could drink a magical potion, straight out of a fairy tale, and somehow summon ancestral pow-ers that would stop her father's destruction. Damn, what could be better than that? And if anyone could help her do it, she be-lieved Phil could. For her. What was the worst that could hap-pen? Mariella might throw up. She trusted Phil not to poison her. And she didn't see how drinking a tea could possibly make her circumstances worse. She was desperate enough to try any-thing. Including this.

Mariella held out the thermos for him. "You take a sip."

"No problem." Phil snatched it from her and sucked down a huge gulp. Then he lowered the container, wiped his mouth with the back of his left hand, and handed the thermos back. "See?"

Mariella wrapped her fingers around the cylinder, eyes search-ing his. He wasn't gagging or choking. Mariella had joked for years that she was a potential New England witch. Look at all the murder and violence in her family lineage—it was so unusual that she'd suspected her family was cursed. But maybe that was the wrong word. Maybe her family was *powerful,* and they'd simply forgotten along the way. Spells and secrets had gotten lost in the family tree, but not lost on the family land. It was possible. There could be ancestors up there in the heavens right now, just waiting to assist in her father's demise.

Mariella stared at the thermos, and before her brain could talk her out of it, she pressed the metal edge to her lip and swilled the earthy fluid.

Ugh, how did Phil not spit this out? It tasted like liquified soil. But she swallowed four times in quick succession, because when Mariella Morse decided to act, she went all the way.

She lowered the container, its stainless steel clinking on the cliff. The sound of running water trickled, cascading somewhere down the artfully spray-painted Ledge and into the green pool below. The sun hung high above the horizon, painting the summer trees with a goldenrod brush. And the air smelled fresh.

"How do you feel?" Phil asked, reaching for the thermos, and for the first time, Mariella noticed a Band-Aid stretching across his right palm. Had it been there all day?

"Fine," she answered honestly.

They sat together on the Ledge, sharing drippy pears that smelled of autumn—the last luscious food Mariella truly remembered tasting. An hour later, her saliva turned to mud and her legs buckled when she tried to stand.

"Whoa, ya okay?" Phil grabbed her elbow, steadying her.

"Head rush, I guess." A dizzy wave flushed her skin, her mouth bitter.

They hiked down the wide path, back toward Phil's car, and she stumbled, her body veering toward the woods, a force yanking her chest.

"Watch it." He grabbed her arm. "You don't wanna go that way. It leads to the swamp. Trust me, even I don't go there."

She let him hold her elbow as they trudged toward his car, a strange buzz building in her ears. Its pitch was high and not completely unfamiliar. Mariella assumed it was a reaction to pollen. They were in the woods, surrounded by plants. It was an allergy nightmare.

They kept plodding, but the buzzing grew louder. It got to the point that she struggled to hear the clomp of her own feet. Her head roared as a black-and-gray pigeon swooped above, flapping so close, she felt the wind of its wing before she heard the coo from its throat. Two more soared next, sharp beaks open wide, but their sounds were muffled. Or was it her ears?

"Pigeons? I thought they were city rats," Phil noted.

"I don't think I'm feeling so good." Mariella halted, swaying on wobbly legs. She placed the back of her hand to her forehead. She felt cool.

"Ya look pale. Ya all right?" Phil gazed with concern. "Is it your stomach? The tea? You hardly ate."

"No, it's my head." She could barely hear him, the internal rattle rising to the din of cicadas. She scratched her ears, fingers digging, searching for bugs squirming toward her brain.

"Let's get you home." Phil's hand was warm. "You'll be fine. I'm here."

And for a moment, just a second, she thought she heard his voice *inside* her skull.

～

The night of the murders . . .

"Wow, ya really screwed this up, didn't cha?" Phil strutted into the room, smoothing the hem of the black polo shirt he always wore to give ghost tours at the B&B.

Ghosts.

Mariella cringed, lifting a hand coated in warm, crimson life. *No.* She crammed down her fears and swung her wrist, signaling Phil to hurry.

"I heard her breathe! Not long ago, I swear. And she twitched. She's alive. Call 911!" Mariella's voice clawed from deep in her throat. She kept one hand pressed ineffectually to the gurgle in her mother's open abdomen, trying to do something. Anything.

Vik stood beside them, showing no reaction.

"Seriously, what the hell?" Phil glanced about the grisly room, once an ultramodern suite in hues of gold and white (no, alabaster) now showered with the sudden scarlet downpour that had come from her mother's chest.

Mom's eyes were open. Her emerald gaze stared vacantly at the crystal chandelier dangling from the coffered ceiling with the slow swing of a pendulum keeping time. *I will not put a ceiling fan in this house! They are tasteless!* Mom admonished the decorators. She'd sooner set the air-conditioning to sixty-five

226

degrees than deign to look at bulb lights attached to rotating blades.

Mariella's fingers spread impossibly wide, compressing the sickening wound. She'd tried to manually pull the gash in her mother's stomach back together, the way you'd force two ends of fabric before fastening a zipper. Only the gap wouldn't stay closed. Instead, Mariella's hands slipped inside, squishing against something hot and soft.

Mom's blood was no longer gushing.

No, no, no, no, nooooo . . .

"We have to help her. Phil, please. Call an ambulance!" Mariella whimpered, tears raging a river down her cheeks and into the open cavity. Why wasn't he helping?

You. Are. An. Idiot. The words hissed inside her skull.

The whispers. They were back.

Mariella's teeth snapped together, so aggressively she heard a crunch.

Maybe this was good. Mariella stilled, listening carefully for instructions and assistance. Then she realized that the words had echoed. Not inside her skull . . . but inside her ears. She'd *heard* them.

No, she was just in shock. Everything felt wrong right now.

Mariella lifted both hands, gummy red slime cascading from her pinkie fingers down to her elbows, a surgeon not about to give up. She reached for a nearby pillow, tugging off what used to be a high-thread-count-cotton case. Yes, the shade was definitely alabaster.

She balled the fabric—if she remembered correctly, the sheets were Kate Spade—and pressed the lump to her mother's gut. She needed to keep pressure on the wound, right? The blood would clot to the fabric. That was what happened in movies.

Where was her phone?

"This scene is a mess." Phil surveyed the slaughter.

"I don't care about the *scene!*" Mariella yelped between sobs.

This wasn't real. It was a nightmare. Another one. Like the shadow. Now she needed to wake up. She always woke up. "This isn't happening . . . My mom . . . her leg twitched . . ."

"Jesus Christ, Mari, snap out of it. She's gone. It's over." Phil's words were so cruel, they lanced her chest.

"No, she made a sound. I heard her . . ."

"Dying's a noisy business." Phil shoved a palm in her face. *Enough.*

Then Vik jerked her way. He took a menacing step, closing the space between them, the blood-streaked axe still clutched in his monstrous grip.

Don't make him use that on you, the whispers growled.

Only they weren't merely whispers in her heard. No, she definitely heard the words spoken this time, ricocheting audibly. In this room.

From him.

Mariella's gaze shot from Vik's blade to Phil's satisfied face. "What did you do?" Fire brimmed in her voice.

"Ah, ya finally catchin' on?" Phil cocked his head, a blond lock of hair falling loose from his gunked-on pomade.

"What? I mean, how?"

There was a ghost of a grin as he spun his hand in a circle like *Go ahead, think it through. I'll wait . . .*

"Did . . . did *you* do this?" Mariella sputtered, her words—her thoughts—tangled in knots. She turned to her mother's ashen (let's be honest, slightly blue) face. Mom hadn't blinked in a while. The pillowcase was no longer white. "No, you couldn't have. This plan, the penicillin, it . . . it came from the whispers, my ancestors."

"And who told ya that?" Phil cocked his head, wearing a twisted smile.

"No." Her head shook defiantly. "My mom, you wouldn't. Vik . . . he was supposed to kill my *dad*."

"It's not my fault he wasn't heah." Phil tsked, a don't-blame-me tone in his voice.

She didn't recognize him.

Mariella's eyes moved from her mother's still—far too still—frame to Vik, the lethal soldier wielding a hatchet and waiting for orders. From Phil? No. Mariella clenched her teeth. The whispers were powerful beings from the Morse bloodline and the Bridge-water Triangle; they were cosmic entities aligned with Mariella and her mother's need to survive.

So why was an axe pointed in her direction? "What is wrong with Vik?" Mariella asked.

She considered the weapon. They actually thought they could still hurt her, which was almost laughable. The worst had already happened. Her mother was dead. That was true, right? Mom wasn't breathing.

"There's nothing wrong with Vik." Phil's gaze glimmered too brightly, and she saw excitement there. He'd been waiting for this moment—the big reveal. Phil wanted her to know he was behind this. He wanted the credit. Hell, judging by the smile in his eyes, he looked like he wanted a thank-you.

Phil leaned toward Vik. "Drop the axe." His voice took on a commanding quality, a look-at-me-I'm-the-big-bad-boss bullshit bravado.

Vik released the weapon. The axe instantly fell to the carpeted floor, the blade missing his toes by less than a few inches. Vik didn't flinch.

"Clap your hands. Once," Phil instructed.

Vik clapped, one time, then held his hands in a clasp, awaiting further instructions.

"I can make him do the Hokey Pokey and turn himself around. Wanna see?" Phil wiggled his eyebrows, enjoying this.

"Omigod. Why? The woods . . . you said . . . I was descended from witches . . . You said, I was your *friend.*" Mariella tripped over the words, eyes casing Phil's and straining for a glimpse of the boy she'd known her entire life, a boy she'd trusted more than anyone. Mariella considered Phil her best friend. No, more than that—a brother.

"I am your friend, duh." Phil gestured at the room ravaged by a tidal wave of death. "That's why I came. To *this.*"

Somehow, he'd known to come. Mariella's quivering hands fell to her lap, the bitter metallic taste of her mom's blood mixing with the permanently rank flavor of the tea on Mariella's tongue.

After she'd drunk the concoction that *Phil had given her,* he had asked Mariella, only twice, if she felt different. The first time, she'd lied and said that she'd felt stronger. The second time, she'd admitted that she was hearing voices. Only she didn't get specific. She didn't tell Phil she planned to kill her father—how could she? Instead, she'd said that there were all these new thoughts in her brain, whispers of plans to fix her life, all coming from ancient ancestors. Phil's reply was so transparent in hindsight: "You should listen! That's why we drank the tea. Holy shit, it's working! Do what they say!"

Mariella should have wondered why he never asked again. Phil didn't follow up, and she had been grateful, because it meant Mariella didn't have to reveal her patricidal plans.

She'd never considered that Phil was behind them.

"What did you do?" Her words were daggers, and her eyes were stretched so wide she felt a blast of cold air on her pupils.

"Nothing you didn't want," Phil replied.

"You think I wanted my mother *dead*?" Mariella choked on the final word, pointing to her mother's . . . corpse. That was what she was now, a corpse. "You were supposed to kill my father!"

"No, *he* was supposed to kill your father." Phil pointed to the statue that was Vik.

Mariella flung her hand, sending a splash of blood against the wall. One more stain. "I wanted to *stop* my father. But *this,* every screwed up second of it, came from constant whispers in my head. It came from *you.*"

Phil's lips smushed into a hard line, saying nothing, disputing nothing.

Mariella rose from the bed, a sinister calm overtaking her being. She breathed slow. *In for four, out for four.* Her eyes locked on Phil, not a speck of blood on him.

She inched closer. The fire that had lapped beneath her skin oh-so-many times for nearly two months now drafted into an inferno. Flames licked up her throat and out from her ears.

"*You've* been in my head," she spat. "So did you tell *him* to do this too?" She gestured violently to Vik. Dear God, if you spilled a bucket of paint on him while finishing a barn in the country he'd be less covered in scarlet than he was right now.

Only this was blood—her *mother's* blood.

Bubbles burst in her stomach, and she swallowed back vomit.

"I never told Vik to pick up an axe." Phil chose his words carefully. "And it was *you* who wanted your father dead."

"With a syringe of penicillin!" Mariella shouted. "Not like this! And not *her*!"

The next three things happened so rapidly that they were almost indistinguishable to the human eye:

1. The door to the en suite bathroom slammed opened, crashing into the nearby drywall so hard, it left a hole in the gold-patterned wallpaper.
2. A figure charged out, a shadow backlit by the daylight bulbs that glowed from her mother's

vanity. A straight-edged razor glinted in a fist.

3. The antique silver blade swept toward Mariella, so close she could finally register the figure's face.

It was her father.

CHAPTER EIGHTEEN

TESSA

"Omigod, Phil!" Tessa rushed at him, squelching on tiptoe in whatever disgusting muck slopped beneath her sneakers. "I thought I'd never see you again." She flung her arms around his neck. "Are you okay? Did you find help?"

Phil's arms wrapped tight around her waist. "I'm fine, but I didn't make it to the bikers. How are ya?"

"Been better." She pulled back, gesturing wildly in the direction they'd escaped. "It was like a freakin' UFO landing—lights, wind, and I swear I heard voices . . ."

"Voices?" Phil and Oscar said in unison.

Tessa peered at Oscar first. "I didn't say anything because I thought you'd think I was losing it, and we were running for our lives. I don't know if it was the wind, or my panic, but I swear I heard something telling me to *go*."

"Yeah, your common sense," Oscar huffed.

Phil touched her forearm. "Ya must've been scared to death.

Maybe you're dehydrated? I finished my thermos. You have yours?" he asked, concern in his voice.

"No, we left them up on the Ledge." Tessa's tongue could have sanded the baseboards in her bedroom. "Seriously, I'm dying." She slumped over, her hands on her knees, the stitch in her side deepening to a battle wound.

"We've been out here all day! That's why I gave ya drinks," Phil snapped.

Tessa's brow wrinkled with a look of *Really, Mom, not now . . .*

Phil caught her expression. "Sorry, I've just been so worried about ya."

Oscar placed his hand on Tessa's lower back. Protective. Intimate. "How did you find us?"

Even without the orbs of fluorescent ghost lights, even with a half-moon casting the world into shades of midnight blue, Tessa caught Phil's eyes flick to Oscar's hand. She could have shrugged it off or she could have stepped away, but she didn't. Tessa had made her choice, and now she had to deal with it.

Phil cleared his throat, eyes on Tessa as he spoke. "I made it halfway to the motocross track when the wind kicked up. I doubled back to find ya, and I thought I heard screamin'. When the sky went crazy, I caught enough of your trail that I was able to track you here."

"You were able to track us in the dark?" Tessa was seriously impressed.

"Yeah. I'm not gonna letcha get hurt. I told ya that."

"Damn." Oscar didn't hide his regard.

"Do you know how to get out of here?" Tessa asked.

"I think so." Phil nodded. "We're not in an ideal location. But yeah." His eyes kept returning to Oscar's hand resting near Tessa's hip. Phil deserved an explanation, but she was exhausted, and this was a conversation best had when they weren't running for their lives.

"You lost your bandage." Tessa pointed her cell phone light at the garnet blood spewing from Phil's palm.

"Yeah, during whatevah the hell that was." Phil gestured in the direction they'd escaped. "I was grabbin' like mad at trees to not fall ovah." Thick drops plopped from his fist, and Tessa leaned toward him, wanting to check his cut. But her foot squished, sludge seeping between her frozen toes. That was when it hit her—with her lungs slowing and her panicked brain unfogging— she was standing in liquid way too deep to be a puddle and not enough to be a pond.

This was *muck*. Mire.

Swampland.

Tessa's spine sprang straighter. "You said we weren't in the ideal location." She pointed her cell phone down, illuminating the blackness. There were reflections—in water—of trees swaying and shadows shifting. "Where are we?"

"Don't wantcha to panic." Phil held up his palms, insisting everyone remain calm. "We're in a swamp."

"*A* swamp?" Splinters painfully pricked from her throat to her gut. "Or *the* swamp?"

"There's only one."

Tessa's flight instinct kicked in with the desire to go. Away. But in which direction? Her head whipped around. Phil said never to go into the swamp. Not even in daylight. Maybe that was why everything stopped—the orbs of light, the deranged winds, and the murmuring voices.

There was a sudden stillness around them that felt final.

"We have to get out of here." Tessa looked at Oscar, his eyes reflecting similar warnings.

"Absolutely." Oscar tugged her arm.

"Wait." Phil reached for her in the thick, wet air. "The swamp is huge. If we go the wrong way, we'll end up deeper in it."

"So what's the *right* way?" Oscar snipped.

Tessa cut him a look.

"Sorry. I just want to get the hell out of here."

"We all do."

"Not sayin' you gotta listen to me." Phil's voice was curt. "By all means, don't wanna give another wicked boring history lesson." Then he gave Tessa a pointed stare, and her stomach sunk to basement level.

Crap. The Ledge. He heard us . . .

They'd been mimicking—no, call it what it was—making fun of Phil's historical expertise and his interest in the local lore. He must have still been within earshot. Could he have been the eyes she felt watching them? No, he was long gone by then. Right?

"Phil, I want you to know how awesome you are." Tessa sloshed toward him, her toes likely a deep shade of indigo. "You've done so much for me. I am *so* grateful."

"Yup, good ol' Phil." He cocked his head, watching Oscar's grip entwine tighter around Tessa's fingers, not letting her go. "The loyal puppy."

"You are *not* a puppy." Each word was a guilty stab. "You're my friend."

"Friend." Phil said it like an insult.

Tessa did not want to have this conversation right now.

"Hey, if it weren't for the bandage and the meds"—Oscar spoke up, pointing to his knee—"I'd still be on that ledge. I should've said thank you right away. So, thanks."

"Glad I could help." Phil's smile in no way touched his eyes. "Seems you guys *made out* all right."

Yikes, what was she supposed to say to that?

"We need to get out of here," Tessa replied, choosing to ignore his innuendo. "It's not safe. If the same crazy stuff happened *that night* on the Ledge with Vik, it could explain his amnesia. And I don't want it to happen to us."

She glanced at her phone. If the sun had set at six o'clock, then that meant they'd started running over an hour ago. How long had it been since she'd texted Detective Ertz?

"Were you able to get reception?" Tessa asked.

"No." Phil shook his head.

Tessa's lips parted to tell him about her texts with Detective Ertz, but a sudden breeze stopped her. The cool air kissed her cheek and sent leaves pirouetting in spirals. White moonlight cut through the branches, shooting a beam of starlight directly into Phil's eyes.

Tessa blinked at the sight, startled.

Phil was blond with pale skin and memorable golden-green eyes that were arguably his most notable feature. And right now,

Tessa was staring into the pallid face of a man whose eyes were nearly black, a pewter inkblot unnaturally swelling.

Was he high?

Tessa's chest heaved, but words skidded to a halt in her throat. Every woman is born with an innate instinct that tells her when she isn't safe and it's time to disengage. *Get up and pretend to go to the bathroom. This man shouldn't get any closer—move away, far away.* And right now, Tessa's insides were screaming.

She stepped back.

"Wish I could've gotten ya a dirt bike." Phil gestured to Oscar's knee.

"I've been managing." Oscar shrugged.

Tessa inched to his side.

"Whatsa mattah? Ya feelin' okay?" Phil noticed the distance she was creating and splashed her way, hand extended, close enough that she could smell his sweat.

No, it wasn't sweat. Tessa could smell his breath.

Her eyes reduced to slits.

That drink. The woods. The smell of death. It *was* familiar.

What Tessa smelled was . . . Vik.

That first day, when they visited him in the police station, Tessa had thought Vik's smell was off. She had assumed it was from the prison soap or the filthy holding cell. But it wasn't that, or not just that. Vik smelled like *this* place. These woods. Phil's breath.

"Tessa, ya don't look good." Phil words were garbled inside her eardrums. "Take a deep breath."

And she did. When someone says, "Look up," you do. And as soon as the air sucked deep in her nostrils, her vision blurred. A blackness began to pulse—a steady blob—and the dizziness from earlier returned.

"Tess?" Oscar gripped her elbow. Her balance tossed off-kilter. She couldn't find her center, and Oscar winced when her weight slumped his way.

"Lemme help ya." Phil moved closer. *Squelch, squelch.*

Tessa tried to swing at him, but her arm was heavy. The air was gelatin. She shifted away. "What . . . is . . . happening . . ."

"It's the swamp." Phil sounded worried. "It's why I didn't want us anywhere near heah. I know you guys don't believe me, but this place . . . all the death . . . it builds up. It hovers, in the water, in the air. The more you're exposed . . ."

"You've gotta be kidding me." Oscar scoffed. "Tessa is light-headed because she's dehydrated and we ran full sprint over un-even ground for who knows how many miles while something was chasing us."

"No, it's not that . . . I mean, I just realized, it's the drink," Tessa murmured, anything louder seeming impossible.

Slowly, the black spots thinned. Tessa could make out the trees. Branches. Leaves. She tried to focus, her eyes squinting, but the trees kept moving. Stretching. Bending. Only she felt no rush of air, no wind pushing through.

The trees grew taller—no, the shadows were growing from them. Lots of shadows. Yet there was barely a moon sneaking through the canopy, and definitely not enough light to create these shadows, not this many and not so dense. They were solidifying.

"What?" Phil gripped her arm, his fingers digging far too tightly. This wasn't him supporting her balance. This was him grabbing Tessa.

"Get. Off." She yanked her arm free.

Instantly, Oscar wedged himself between them. "She said back off." His voice was deep and menacing, as though he'd been waiting to say that for a while.

"What is wrong with you guys?" Phil feigned confusion while his eyes swelled to bricks of smoky charcoal.

Tessa reached for Oscar, pressing her lips to his ear. "The drink . . . from the thermoses. I think it's how Vik lost his memory."

CHAPTER NINETEEN

The night of the murders . . .

MARIELLA

Mariella would've liked to say she had intrinsic super-reflexes with matching inhuman strength that allowed her to lift a car, or in this case repel her father and his straight-edged razor, with a flick of her arm, but that was not her body's natural response. Fight, flight, or freeze. Again, Mariella froze.

Vik—she didn't know if it was the part of him that was actually Vik or if it was the part of him controlled by Phil—rammed into Mariella's dad with abnormal force, striking her father in the throat with a fist, then elbowing his eye socket.

Dad went down. Hard.

"Shit, he was hiding in the bathroom this whole time?" Phil said, like he wanted to add the word *Respect*.

Her dad had almost gotten away with his life. If he had just stayed hidden.

Mariella stared at his fit middle-aged body, writhing on the ground in black silky pajamas with white piping along the collar and down the edge of the button-front seam. They were rich-guy pj's—a gift from her mother last Christmas? Or the Christmas before? Mariella wasn't sure.

Dad gripped his throat, hand clamped like a vise around his Adam's apple, coughing, back arched as he fell to his side. His salt-and-pepper hair was soaked with sweat, bangs matted to his fore-head (which was more Botoxed than her mom's). The weapon he had rummaged out of the medicine cabinet, a straight-edged razor that had been in the family for over a hundred years, now lay half-buried in the carpet fibers. It was out of his reach. Phil kicked it away.

"Well, at least this isn't a total loss." Phil looked at Mariella. "We can at least kill the right person, and everyone gets what they want."

"Gets . . . what they want?" Mariella repeated the words, try-ing to comprehend Phil's meaning as she peered at this stranger she had known since before she could walk. "What the hell hap-pened to you?"

"What's happened to *me*?" Phil snapped, flicking his blond bangs aside. "Well, thanks for finally noticing. Because, yeah, I've changed a bit."

"Are you hearing voices too?" She was confused.

"Oh, come on, Mari, think!" Phil smacked a backhand to his palm, glaring in exasperation. "We've been researching the super-natural since we were kids! Difference was, you were playing, and I wasn't. I've been harnessing this power for *years*."

"Power? You said the recipe came from *my* family?"

"It did." Phil shrugged. "So? You didn't know how to use it. Mari, ya added your blood to Vik's drink tonight. Did it evah occur to ya, that you drank mine?" Phil smiled with perverse pride. "The whispers, the buzzing, the nightmares . . ."

You really didn't recognize me? the whispers asked, the words echoing in her mind and in her ears. *You really didn't sense it was me, every night, in your dreams?*

All the blood surging through Mariella's head suddenly whirl-pooled down her body. She bent over, gasping, hands on her knees for support. Her *nightmares?* No, no, no . . . The shadow? Phil. No!

She dry heaved toward the blood-speckled carpet, her mind picturing the shadow crawling up her immobile body. Helpless. Exposed. She remembered the bruises on her legs and the licks to her neck. He'd touched her. He'd. Touched. Her.

Her stomach hacked but nothing spewed.

All those nights, no matter how hard she'd tried to scream or swat, the shadow's talons roamed her skin. She couldn't stop it. No, she couldn't stop *him*.

"You . . ." Mariella choked; a flash of those devilish crimson eyes had her heart beating somewhere outside of her chest. Maybe in her throat? How could that be Phil? "No, it's impossible . . ."

"Mari, we have been building to this our entire lives! I told you about your ancestors. I gave you your first Ouija board. I helped you make a voodoo doll. I got you into hiking. I brought you to the Ledge. I gave you the tea . . ."

He'd used their past against her. Their childhood. The betrayal.

Phil was the only person Mariella had ever trusted completely, so much so that she would drink a thermos full of *anything* he handed her, because she never thought he'd harm her.

Her stomach cramped, wrung dry, as she turned toward Vik. He had trusted *her* that much. He'd drunk what she'd given him. But she'd never meant for any of this to happen. It was supposed to be a simple needle stick—guiltless and painless. Vik wasn't supposed to be standing stone-faced with her mother's life dripping off of him. "Why is Vik like *this*? I never turned into a zombie."

"Are you kidding? You're a zombie every night I come into your dreams. You just lie there while I drip more tea—"

"No, those were nightmares! It wasn't you. I screamed and punched and cried. You wouldn't do that." Tears leaked, expelling the final remnants of who she was before tonight.

Because this was it. There was no going back. You can't go through annihilation like this and then putter off to college and study art history. Sometimes, there are events so tragic that they are simply life killers, whether the victims continue breathing or not.

"Ya know the truth, Mari. You were foolin' yourself."

"Stop calling me Mari!" she snapped. That was Vik's nickname for her. Not Phil's. Not anyone else's.

"I feel like I know ya just as well." Phil blew her a kiss.

"You're disgusting." She thought of all the times the whispers had emerged as Vik caressed her skin and touched her lips. The whispers felt perverted because they were—they weren't mystical spirits; they were the leering eyes of a teenage Peeping Tom. Her stomach rolled once more, trying to force something up—maybe her soul. "Were you ever my friend?"

"Yes." Goddamnit, Phil actually looked insulted. "Of course! I'm the *best* friend you've ever had. I came *here,* didn't I? I didn't do all this just for me. It's for *us.* For you. To free you from *him.*" Phil pointed at her father.

"Mariella." Dad coughed and stretched an arm toward her. He'd stayed silent this whole time, but he'd heard everything. He knew her guilt, her humiliation, her shame. "Mariella, stop this. Help me." His left eye was swollen shut and turning indigo, while one hand still massaged the base of his throat.

Vik had only landed two hits. How strong was he?

"Dad." Tears spilled harder. Mariella sniffled, wiping her nose with trembling fingers. "I'm so sorry."

And she was.

She hadn't meant for any of this to happen. Yes, maybe she'd put this in motion, but it was supposed to be different. It was supposed to be him and a needle in the comfort of his bed. He never should have woken up. He shouldn't have felt a thing. Not anything like the pain he'd caused her and her mother for years.

But Mariella never should have done it.

And would she have, if she hadn't drunk that tea? Was any of this really her choice?

"Oh, don't let yourself off that easily," Phil grumbled, hearing her thoughts. Because of course he did. He was in her mind. Hers and Vik's. That was why the whispers got quiet today, after

Vik drank the tea. Phil couldn't be two places at once. He had to pick one brain to infiltrate. So if he was in her mind right now, did that mean there was a chance that Vik's mind was free? Maybe Vik could wake up.

"Doesn't work that way." Phil eyeballed her, but his voice was wary. She could tell he didn't like the way she was drawing lines between the scattered dots. "Don't strain your pretty brain. Trust me, this is beyond your comprehension."

Mariella's teeth gnashed at the insinuation that she was some dancing marionette and Phil was the grand puppeteer. *Yeah, well, puppeteers are stupid. They're cowards; they're so scared of real humans that they have to hide behind giant curtains. Just like you,* she thought, eyes firing at Phil.

Then she spun toward Vik, his smoky pupils vacant and lifeless. "Can you hear me? Vik? Listen to me. Hear my voice."

She reached out her hand, but she didn't dare touch him.

If I can snap him out of this, then maybe—

"Maybe what?" Phil asked, irked by her plan. "What are ya really gonna do? If you were capable of murdah, Mari, you would have killed your fathah yourself. And trust me, that would've been a whole lot easier than all this." His hands twirled around the room, his thick accent showing his nerves.

"Stop calling me Mari," she spat through her teeth. She honestly didn't know what she was capable of right now, but it felt like the answer was *anything,* absolutely anything.

She glanced over her shoulder at her mother's body: her skin was drained of the color of life, and her elbow was bent with her hand almost touching her sallow perfect face. Her body was a chalk outline in the making on a California king mattress. Mom was the reason Mariella had done any of this, the reason Mariella was here in this world. If Phil had been controlling Vik when he swung that axe, then this was Phil's fault. All of it.

But why would Phil kill her mom? Mariella pulled her eyes from the mutilated body and turned to Vik, who was picking up the axe off the floor.

"Vik, can you hear me?" Mariella leaned cautiously. He stood ramrod straight and his taut fingers gripped the axe with its blade pointing perilously at her father. "Vik, wake up. Snap out of it. *It's time.*"

She repeated the words the whispers had given her, and this time, Vik's dark eyes twitched.

The hatchet moved.

She swore she saw it.

So did her father.

"Mariella, run!" Dad's voice was husky as he rolled over, grunting as he tried to stand. "Call the police!"

"If you call the police, you'll go to jail right along with him," Phil countered. "Look at you—you're covered in blood. Your DNA is all over the scene."

"Because I live here!"

"You'll look like an accomplice. Who has the most to gain? You. You inherit everything." Phil threatened her with every step; his eyes zeroed in with warning.

"Mariella, don't listen!" Dad rubbed his fingers to his swollen eye, which looked just like Mom's when he would hit her.

Dad swayed unsteadily, a dazed look suggesting a concussion. "I'll protect you."

"Like ya protected her mothah?" Phil threw him a look. "No one would be here right now if it weren't for you, Mr. Morse."

"You don't know what you're talking about," Dad rasped.

"Yes, he does." Mariella's voice cut through them without needing a blade. "You have terrorized Mom and me in this house for *so* long . . ."

"I've provided for you!"

"You beat her! Did you really think I couldn't hear you? She was covered in bruises." Mariella marched forward.

"Your mother was no saint." Dad shook his head of prematurely gray hair (*I think it makes me look distinguished, don't you?*), sending beads of panicked sweat dribbling down his forehead.

He was finally the injured party—his eye purple and egg-shaped, his legs teetering, and his voice pained. He looked weak, this man she'd been too afraid to confront her entire life. "My mother is the only thing that has kept me alive all these years. She's kept me safe from *you*."

"Yeah?" Dad snarled. "And you just killed her."

The words exploded in Mariella's heart like cluster bombs. The destruction was complete. And it was absolutely warranted, because it was true.

She'd. Killed. Her. Mother.

Do it, the whispers urged.

No. No! Mariella scrunched her eyes, forcing Phil's voice out of her head.

She couldn't pretend these were magical fairies anymore. This was Phil—a messed-up, lying, betraying, perverted psychopath with a narcissistic bent.

You know it has to happen, the voice hissed. *There's no other way for this to end.*

Mariella clawed at her ears. *Shut. Up!* The bugs, swarms of them, tiny and biting, itched under her skin. She grabbed two tufts of hair, pulling hard to force her mind to focus on the pain. Physical pain.

"Mariella, what's wrong? Are you okay?" Dad's words were garbled, glubbing under water. Drowning under a buzz that was mounting. Overwhelming.

This is why we're here. It'll all be okay once it's over. You know that. You do . . .

She couldn't. This wasn't who she was.

Her index fingers pressed into her ears. She had to find the bugs. She had to get them out. Her nails dug into her cartilage, a cold sweat sliding down her back.

It's what you want. He deserves it. Think of all the times he hit your mother.

Stop.

Think of the nights you heard her up late, sobbing.

Don't.

Think of her on the bathroom floor, curled in a ball, terrified of another blow.

I can't.

He took your money and locked it away. He won't let you drive or get a job. He isolates you. He hates your boyfriends and friends because he needs to control you . . .

"Mariella, listen to me." Her father's words tried to slam through her mental chaos. "Do something smart for once in your life."

Hear how he talks to you? Even now? It will never end. Your whole life, decade after decade. He'll be there. Crushing you. Berating you.

"God, you're as pathetic as your mother."

Mariella peeled open her eyes and caught her father reaching for the straight-edged razor in the carpet's plush fibers. He was going to attack. She wasn't sure which one of them he'd swing at first, but her dad had made the decision to fight. Had she?

You're ready, the whispers pressed.

Her hand jerked, the movement sudden. Then she stomped, three steps, toward Vik.

He didn't twitch as she approached; his haunted foggy eyes pointed straight ahead, void of all comprehension.

Now. Right now.

Her dad stood in a squat, clutching the silver antique blade in front of him. (Had it belonged to the Borden family? She thought maybe it had. Lizzie might have touched it. Or maybe Eliza used it when she cut her own throat.) His elbow was bent as he waved the edge wildly around him, securing a perimeter. His pupils shook.

Come on. Do it.

In one smooth motion, Mariella snatched the axe out of Vik's hands—he didn't resist. The weapon jerked free, her right shoulder swinging back. The momentum of solid steel stretched her arm long, too long, and her limb windmilled through the air.

Listen to it whistle! The edge—no longer dripping, instead sticky with burgundy splotches—swept in an upward arc until it found its mark. There he was!

The blade sliced, a deadly uppercut thunking into the underside of her father's jaw, then burying into his throat.

Dad's eyes widened with a look of *What just happened?* He dropped the razor, his body limp. And she realized it was just her hatchet holding him to his feet. She tugged the vicious tooth, yanking it from her father's flesh with a wet suck. A massive blood spray exploded with the force of a fountain. An artery severed. The carotid. Hadn't she learned that in anatomy?

He stumbled for a second, maybe longer, on his bare heels, then he collapsed face-first in his black silky pj's, a pool of crimson spreading through the thick alabaster carpet.

His limbs twitched, all at once, then his body stopped.

Motionless.

Winthrop Morse was dead.

And Mariella held the hatchet.

CHAPTER TWENTY

The night of the murders . . .

MARIELLA

"What did I do?" Mariella's joints were locked, and the axe was bolted to her hands, splashed with blood. *She* was splashed with blood.

Her father's lifeless body was facedown on the carpet, stretched alongside the bed, oozing a terrible red pool. "What . . . what happened?"

She hadn't swung the axe. No, she couldn't have done that. She wouldn't. She wouldn't even squish a spider. She'd trap it in a glass and slide it onto a sheet of paper before releasing the eight-legged nightmare outside. She. Could. Not. Kill. That was why she had involved Vik to begin with.

But Vik wasn't a murderer either.

And look what he'd done.

No, Mariella couldn't have swung that hatchet, not of her own free will.

"So you're gonna blame this all on me?" Phil asked, hearing her thoughts. "Because the way I see it, I'm the only one here who *hasn't* axed anyone to death."

"No, no, no, no, no . . ." Black spots swooped before her eyes, her head flushed with fever. The axe was still clutched in her quavering hands. It was heavy, so heavy. She forced her fingers to unclench, straighten, release the slimy wooden handle, the drop of weight so sudden, she reached for the wall to steady herself.

Phil snatched her arm in midair. "Let's not leave any more fingerprints, okay?"

His voice echoed inside her head. It whispered. She couldn't see him. She couldn't see anything. Just blood. Her pulse thudded in her ears, her throat, and her eyeballs. Sweat poured down her chest.

"I think you're going into shock." Phil's voice, or was it the whispers (did it matter?), sounded irritated. With her.

Mariella tried to respond. Her mouth opened, air glubbed in, but no words came out. She was thirsty, so thirsty. Her muddy saliva had dried to sand, her cheeks a crusty desert with her tongue desperately smacking the roof of her mouth.

"I'd tell ya to sit down, but the place is a little covered in blood." It sounded like Phil was making a joke.

Mariella had killed her parents.

She had swung an axe at her father's face. His face!

I'm going to jail. For the rest of my life. I'm going to jail. They're going to put me behind bars. They're going to torture me. I'm only seventeen. If I get life, that would mean sixty, seventy, eighty years in a metal cage. I'd be better off dead, wouldn't I? Yes, I would. I could just . . .

Her eyes caught on the straight-edged razor poking from the dense carpet, glinting in the recessed lights.

"Whoa, now." Phil plucked the blade from the ground, hearing her unspoken plans formulate. "None of that."

He marched into the bathroom. She heard water running from the spigot. She wasn't sure for how long, but it felt like a while, then she heard a metallic plink and the medicine cabinet closed.

She stared at her hands, palms up. Her skin was coated, the blood darker in the creases, that Rouge Noir color popular for painting toenails in the fall. But on the rest of her flesh, the streaks were a peppy cherry red, detailing every wrinkle, every pore. Would it ever wash off? No, of course not. She'd see this forever.

"Mariella, we're gonna have to get ya cleaned up." Phil slowly approached her, his brow low with a look of fear. He was scared—of her, like he wasn't sure what she might do. You know what? Neither was she. "I'm gonna need ya to shower. Scrub every speck of this off ya. Then we'll clean the bathroom. The drain. We'll dry your hair. We'll put ya in some pj's. And you'll call the cops and claim ya woke up and found your parents like this."

Her eyes shot toward Vik, a reflexive jerk. Poor Vik. Sweet Vik. He still hadn't moved. How long had he been standing like a granite statue of destruction? Was he even still in there?

"I will wake him up once you're ready," Phil said.

"Ready for what?" Her body jolted—she'd spoken, the words loud as rifle blasts through the room. She could speak—her voice painfully raw but still operable.

"Ready to handle what comes next. The police. The cover-up."

"We can't cover up *this*." Her eyes narrowed at the gruesome, blood-strewn havoc that had once been her home. What was it now?

A crime scene, the answer was clear.

"We can cover up your involvement. Look at him." Phil gestured to Vik. "He's drenched in blood. The axe has his prints."

"It has mine too."

"You'll tell them you picked it up, to get it away from him. You were afraid for your life."

No, no, no. Mariella shook her head, blond hair smacking her face, strands sticky with blood. Her father's blood. She couldn't do this. "Vik was supposed to walk free. Both of us were. With my *mom*." Mariella's voice cracked, her lower lip blubbering. "Oh God, Mom!"

"Stay focused, Mari," Phil snapped. "The syringe plan is dead. There's no walking free from this. Someone's gotta take the fall."

"But why did Vik pick up an axe?" She pointed accusatorily. "This is *your* fault! You told him to."

"I never said *that*." Phil raised his palms in innocence. "Your boy went a little rogue. Somethin's off with him. I can smell him, but I can't smell you. Anyway, it doesn't mattah. We can fix this. Vik's an out-of-townah, drippin' in blood, standing over an axe, with a fathah serving time for murdah. The cops won't look any furthah than him. Everyone suspects the boyfriend, especially when he's poor and his girlfriend's got money."

Phil tried to convey control, but his accent betrayed him. He was nervous.

"What if Vik tells them the truth? What if he remembers?" asked Mariella. She wasn't agreeing to this, was she? No, she couldn't.

"He won't remembah a thing," Phil insisted, placing a hand on her shoulder. And she let him. God help her, she let him. Someone had to hold her up.

"But I remember everything." Mariella wished she didn't. Maybe Phil could wipe her memory too, because she'd gladly accept the offer.

"It doesn't work like that." He winced in sympathy.

"You keep saying that, but how do you know?" She met his eyes (had they always looked this cruel?), and just that subtle shift of movement sucked all her energy. She was so tired. She wanted to sleep. For days. Forever.

"Seriously? You still don't get it?" Phil words should have been insulting, but her mind, her body, was too exhausted to care. She couldn't even tie her own shoe right now. Literally. The lace of her boot was still untied. Her eyes widened. That meant there were footprints, tread marks, everywhere.

"We'll take care of that," Phil said, giving her arm a patronizing squeeze. He was handling her.

"Was it all lies?"

"No." Phil shook his head with a genuine look of sympathy.

"Don't think like that. I wasn't lyin' about your ancestors. John Morse may have been a witch. Hell, Lizzie's bio mom may have been one too. I don't friggin' know. But his cabin was in those woods. We *did* find the spot. And the plants and lichen we collected that day, it was just *part* of the tea. But a lot of the rest of it . . . came from the swamp."

Mariella's mind clicked through memories. The path. *It leads to the swamp. Trust me, even I don't go there.*

"Ah, ya do remember!" Phil clapped once in appreciation. "So many people died there. The colonists put a Native American chief's head on a spike for two decades. You won't find that in your Massachusetts history lessons." He let out a dark chuckle. "Ghosts are all over the place. And not just from the wah. Animals were slaughtered. Human body parts were found. Satanic cults held rituals. I dunno if all that death caused the Bridgewater Triangle, or the supernatural shit brought all the death. But there's a wicked dark energy in those woods." Phil smacked his lips. "And we drank it."

"Drank what exactly?" She should have asked this sooner. Months sooner. How completely she had trusted him.

"All of it." Phil shrugged. "All of those invasives you saw twining and chokin' the trees—well, they're inside us now. So is the lichen, and the plants, and the swamp water. We ingested the Bridgewater Triangle."

"Then how come *you're* not possessed?"

"I am. That's where my power comes from," he explained like he wanted her to understand. "Mari, I wasn't born with money. I knew I'd need something else to get me out of this life."

"So you used me?"

"I helped you."

"But what about Vik?" Mariella had cut her own palm; Vik had drunk a tea with *Mariella's* blood, so shouldn't she have maintained control? She'd given him a syringe. "What went wrong?"

"I don't know about the axe." Phil sighed remorsefully. "But your blood was already infected *by me*. So I kept control, somewhat. Besides, I'm the one who gave ya the thermos."

Mariella blinked.

"I brought it, when I came to visit ya, in your dream." Phil read the questions in her mind. The shadow. That disgusting perverted shadow had delivered the thermos. Mariella had just added to it.

"This is all because I drank a sip of tea . . ." Her voice trailed off, her mind unable to comprehend the magnitude of the consequences.

"Well, not just a sip. I've been feeding you a little more when I see ya at night." Then the asshole winked, as though they shared an inside joke. "But even I'm a little surprised at how well it worked. I'd been slipping it to ya in bits over the past year, a drop or two in your Dunkin'. But nuttin'. Then one day, I felt a shift. I felt ya heard me. So I took ya out in the woods and gave ya a big chug. Next night, bam! I was in your dream." There was pride on his face. *Hey, Ma, look what I can do!*

"You sadistic son of a—"

"Easy now." Phil rolled his eyes. "To be fair, you were already infected. All of us are. Everyone living in this stinkin' triangle is. It's in the air you breathe heah. That's why you feel light-headed hikin' sometimes. The energy is purer in the woods. But regard-less, it's a part of Fall Rivah."

Mariella considered his words, her mind skipping through tragedy after tragedy, century after century, just in her own fam-ily. Sure, bad things happen everywhere, but hadn't she said that to Vik earlier? It seemed that horrible violence fed off this place.

"Bingo," Phil said, enjoying her thoughts. "Darkness . . . it clings to events and to locations."

"And *you* can control it?" She sounded dubious.

"I told ya. I've been working on this for years." Phil ran his hand through his hair, completely casual.

"But my parents . . ." Mariella squinted her eyes and tried to see him clearly. She tried to see anything clearly. "Why the hell did you go after my parents? And my *mom*? If you have all the power in the world, then why not—"

"Well, I wouldn't say that." Phil bobbled his head, pretending to be modest. "I started small, with your fathah, because I figured it was somethin' easy that would benefit both of us. I told you, I did this for you too."

Mariella waited, without a twitch, for him to continue, be-cause she had nothing to say. Winthrop Morse's death would af-fect a lot of people, her especially, but how would it *benefit* Phil? He could lose his job. So could his parents.

Holy shit, Mariella could fire them tomorrow! She could evict them from their apartment! A surge of excitement entered her blood, jolting her awake. She wasn't powerless, not with all that money. Screw Phil.

"Don't get ahead of yourself." Phil snorted a laugh at her threats. "Ya really should read the emails from the family lawyer. I did. When your pop redid his will, cuttin' you out 'til you're thirty, he added a bunch of new stipulations. If he died, everything he had went to your muthah. But if they *both* died, you got the house, his cash, and most of his businesses. But some of his assets he left to charities, his old university, and a few close friends and loyal employees." Phil held her eyes with dark intensity. "Do you see it now? If both your parents die, your fathah left the Lizzie Borden House, our apartment, and the entire business that goes along with it to my mom and pop."

Mariella's jaw fell, and she inhaled a gulp of coppery blood. Phil was right; she hadn't read the whole document. It was long and written in legalese. She'd focused on the one page relating to her and had shown it to Phil, to highlight the section about her trust. Phil must have read the entire thing. But for Mariella, it was illogical to consider stipulations in the event of both her parents' deaths—they were in their forties.

"Turns out years of washing dishes and changing bedsheets was finally gonna amount to somethin'." Phil's voice was matter-of-fact. "I guess I didn't wanna wait . . ."

"That's . . . why you did . . . all of this?" Mariella's words dripped with disbelief matching the blood in the room. "To me. To them. You killed my parents . . . for *money*?"

"No, *you* killed them," Phil corrected. "My family will just benefit from it. And why not? You're not the only one your fathah terrorized. The way he yelled at my mothah! Just today—he freaked out over burned toast! And that time when he refused to pay my pop, because he got bronchitis. Heaven forbid Winthrop Morse provide decent health insurance."

Oh. My. God. Phil was a disgruntled employee. All those years of company Christmas parties and Halloween spooktaculars—it was all bullshit. Her entire childhood.

"That's not true." Phil held up a hand, objecting. "I really *am* your friend. That's why I tried to keep your hands clean of this. The syringe was a good idea! I didn't expect Vik to go anothah way. I still gotta work on my control. There's a lot of power in those woods, and it's leakin' outta Vik. That's why we smell it." Phil sounded frustrated, like he was messing up an assignment. "Anyway, I knew your ma was gonna have to die. I thought maybe a little air bubble in the needle after your pop. It wouldn't hurt. And Vik's a great patsy. All the pieces were there. Look at the end result! The money is yours! Your fathah is gone. Ya can live your life. It's ovah."

Phil thought he'd done this for her. He thought this was friendship. Mariella could still feel her hands sinking into her mother's chest. There were bits of her parents in her mouth, in her ears, and under her nails.

"I'll clean ya up. I'll get this staged." Phil's voice was determined, and it once again rang inside her skull—it whispered. It buzzed. It ordered.

Mariella's eyes flicked to Vik, immobile and ready to do the Chicken Dance upon request. Had Mariella swung that axe because she'd been forced to or because she'd chosen to? Phil was worming through her mind, making her question her choices and actions. He was invading her very soul, and he would continue to do so forever.

"It won't be like that," Phil said, hearing her concern. "After we get past this, it'll be better. I promise. I just need ya to do what I say *right now,* and then you'll walk away clean. You'll inherit everything. Ya won't have to wait till you're thirty. Ya won't have to live in fear of your fathah. You'll be free."

With you in my head, she thought, looking directly into his eyes, making sure he heard her.

"With me at your side." Phil ran his hand down her bloody cheek, a gentle gesture that was probably meant to mimic Vik. But Phil was no Vik. "Now I need you to get in the shower, and don't miss a spot."

Mariella could have resisted. Or she could have at least tried. But she didn't.

Mariella did as she was told. She stepped barefooted in every tread mark left by her boots on the carpet, every sneaker print left by Phil. She squished and smeared the fibers with the soles of her feet, confusing the evidence. Then she cleaned herself up under scalding hot water with the movements of a body clicked to autopilot. Afterward, Phil washed the shower and cleaned out the drain. She dried her hair with hot tears streaking down the sides of her nose. She couldn't stop the constant drip from her eyes, and Phil said it would make her more believable. The grieving daughter.

But they were real tears, right? She thought they were.

She tugged on her dirty pajamas from the night before, so she'd look more rumpled, more convincing. Her prints, her DNA, her footmarks were everywhere. But this was her house. Her parents were dead. She was hysterical. She couldn't be held responsible for her actions, for ruining the scene.

And Phil was right about Vik. He was a head-to-toe waterfall of gore with a murder weapon lying at his feet. Besides, he wasn't even Vik anymore. He hadn't so much as scratched his nose in—how long had it been now?

The boy she loved was gone. Zombified. If Vik took the blame at this point, he might not even realize. The cops would strap his catatonic body to a prison hospital bed.

The damage was already done.

So Mariella applied her night cream and tied her hair in a messy topknot, making herself a vision of sleep. All the while, Phil watched, standing in the hallway, away from the scene, his shoes in his hand so as not to track any blood out of the room and corrupt the story he'd so carefully concocted.

Then he told her to call 911, "and make it good."

It wasn't hard to sound hysterical when telling the world your parents were slaughtered by an axe. She just had to leave out the part where she'd held it. At least, once. Her father's wounded face, his artery, his blood, she could still see it all. She would forever.

The operator told her to stay on the line, but Mariella hung up. She dropped onto the bed, lowering herself beside her mother, and she stroked her hair. Then she pulled up the sheet so Mom wouldn't be exposed to a bunch of police officers, who likely already knew her from fundraisers and town celebrations.

Phil left, abandoning Mariella to deal with all of this. Alone. Two dead bodies. A flood of gore. And a teenage killing robot who couldn't speak.

Then when she finally thought she could deal with her guilt and grief and shame, privately, in the dreadful silence, Phil's voice echoed up the steps, through the hall, into the bedroom, inside her ears, and down into her soul. It was a domineering tone, a whisper scarier than any shout. It was *the* whisper.

And the command held just seven simple words.

Vik, it's time to wake up now.

That was it.

Vik's lashes fluttered. His tongue licked his lips. He wiped his mouth and glanced about. He saw the blood. He checked himself for wounds, frantically patting his chest and head. He felt the stains, once dripping and now drying, on his skin. His shirt. His hair. His hands. Everywhere.

He saw the axe.

He twisted wildly, a ghost mask of fear and desperation on his face. His eyes had returned to brown but were unbearably confused. "Mari, what . . . what happened?"

Vik was back. The boy she loved was back. He was with her. Right now.

And the cops were on their way.

The sob that ripped from Mariella's chest could have split the world in two. *I'm so sorry. Vik, I'm so sorry.*

Mariella howled, collapsing onto her mother, releasing everything she'd held in, everything she'd done, everything Phil was probably keeping tied together with his presence. Phil was gone, and she could feel herself again—or what used to be herself—and her soul unraveled.

She'd done this. To her mother. To her father.

To Vik.

Mariella let it out, all the tears, the screams, and the nightmares.

She sunk into a swamp of grief on the mattress and hugged her mother.

Mariella wailed, until the police arrived.

CHAPTER TWENTY-ONE

TESSA

Tessa wasn't sure who lunged first. But as soon as she registered the familiarity of that decaying stench and connected the stink to her memory of Vik, fists and kicks started flying. Oscar was on top, gripping Phil in a headlock, utilizing every muscle from his endless football workouts. But his knee was wobbling, destroying his balance, and it gave Phil an easy target.

Phil no longer had to be stronger; he just had to be accurate. He squirmed within Oscar's grip, bent his leg, and donkey kicked Oscar's bad knee. *Sweep the leg!*

Oscar went down.

"What the hell are you doing?" Tessa yelped, reaching for Oscar.

"Defendin' myself!" Phil shouted. "He came at me!"

Oscar clutched his swollen joint, grimacing but still holding in his agony behind clenched teeth.

Phil wore a grin of superiority, though he wasn't tougher than Oscar. Or Tessa. He wasn't smarter than them either, though he probably liked to think he was. Tessa didn't know how, or why, Phil was involved in the Morse murders, but she knew Vik's scent was connected to this boy.

"Phil, what happened that night?"

"What makes ya think I know anything?" His voice was coy, playing dumb, while his eyes shifted to a milky gray.

Then he winked. And that one gesture sent the Rube Goldberg machine in Tessa's mind churning into action—a toy car hit a row of dominoes sending a cue ball down an incline that swings a golf club that fires a cannon that splatters some paint. Click, click, boom. Phil had taken Mariella hiking; he'd said so himself. His breath smelled rank like her brother's—from a drink he'd practically begged Tessa and Oscar to ingest. He knew the history of these woods, this town, and the Lizzie Borden House he worked in.

The house he worked in. The last marble fell into the slot that sparked her intuition.

"You said you were working the night of the murders."

"I was." There was a challenge in Phil's gaze. A confidence. He knew she was piecing it together, and he was enjoying it.

"That's not far from the Morse mansion. If you knew that Mariella's father was violent, and you saw ambulances racing to her house, wouldn't you have assumed, wouldn't you have been terrified, that *Mariella* was hurt?" She asked the question but didn't wait for an answer. "But you said you didn't go there that night. You didn't check on her."

"I told ya, poor kids get blamed for bad stuff. My ma told me not to go." He crept toward her with the menacing look of a guy who thought he was still in charge.

Only Tessa didn't move. Not for him. This was her brother's life she was fighting for, and she was not going to let Phil take it.

"But Mariella's your *best friend*. Wouldn't you have wanted to make sure she was okay?"

"I sent a text." He slurped forward.

Tessa stood her swamp ground.

"You texted a girl to ask if she was *murdered*? No." Tessa shook her head. "You weren't at the Lizzie Borden House, because you were *already there* that night, weren't you? At Mariella's house, when it happened?"

"Tess, back up," Oscar warned, then groaned excruciatingly as he tried—and failed—to put weight on his knee. He couldn't stand. Whatever fit of strength had allowed him to sprint through the woods was gone. His leg went from hurt to damaged. He dropped onto the mucky earth.

Phil's grin was nasty. "Gotta hand it to ya. At least you're smartah than your brothah. And Mariella." His accent spewed. "She didn't put it togethah 'til the first body hit the ground."

The admission glided along a tight rope from Phil's mouth to her ears, then inside her brain, where it teetered and crashed. Tessa blinked. It's not often a person suspects the worst in someone, then hears it confirmed from their own lips. How often do cops get a confession? Probably not as often as it looks in the movies. That was why no one believed Vik. Jails were full of people pleading not guilty, but someone *had* to do it.

"What . . . what happened? You framed Vik?" She eyed the stranger who stood in front of her smirking with cloudy eyes. This boy she'd almost dated.

Now Tessa wanted to reach out, grab his stupidly styled blond hair, and yank it all out. Only she'd never been in a fight before. She didn't even know how to make a proper fist. Were you supposed to tuck your thumb or not tuck your thumb?

Her hands balled at her sides, thumbs untucked. Phil didn't weigh an ounce more than she did, and Tessa wasn't injured. She might not possess any real athletic ability, but she'd also never sprinted for her life before, and she'd managed to pull that off. Besides, there was one thing going for Tessa that Phil couldn't counteract—rage, a live volcano simmered so intensely inside her chest, she was surprised that lava wasn't erupting from her pores.

"Was my brother even there that night?" Tessa bit out the words.

"Aw, Tess, hate to break it to ya"—Phil gave a fake pout—"but your brothah's a murdering psychopath."

Tessa flung her body. She didn't lunge. She didn't swing. She couldn't jump; her feet were too bogged down in the swamp. No, Tessa threw her entire weight at his torso and landed a direct hit. Maybe it was luck, or maybe it was the years she'd sat in the bleachers watching linebackers try to tackle Oscar. *Lead with your shoulder! Drop your weight!* But somehow Tessa propelled herself at Phil, slamming her shoulder into his thighs, with her arms wrapped tight around him, and Phil toppled.

He never saw her coming. Men often grossly underestimate

what women can do when pushed to their max. Phil went down. In the swamp. His head submerged in the two feet of gloomy muck, and Tessa sprang onto his back and rammed her knee into his spine. Phil wrenched in pain, gurgling black liquid, then pitifully tried to stand. He clawed at the mud for support, but her knee dug harder, power coursing through her.

She wasn't trying to drown him. And she wasn't irrational. Sure, her head was a little dizzy—maybe Phil was correct about the dehydration, or maybe the air really was thinner. What Tessa wanted was to scare the truth out of him. For Vik. Tessa gripped Phil's blond hair at the base of his skull, her fist in his baby-fine strands. She yanked him up for a breath, through lips that had almost kissed her, then she shoved him back down. Phil choked, water bubbling deep in his throat. In his lungs. A person might be surprised at the strength they can summon when the life of someone they love is threatened.

"What did you do to my brother?" Tessa shouted.

She ripped Phil's head up for another watery gasp. "It burns!" he gagged, spitting a thick glob of something. Mud? Leaves? "I can't . . . breathe. It . . . burns."

She thrust his head again, rubbing it in the mess of twigs and vines and thick, thick liquid. He thrashed back and forth, arms slapping desperately at the surface. "What? Did you do? To Vik?" Tessa yanked his head back up. "Tell me what happened!"

"I happened."

The words came from behind her.

Tessa stiffened, eyes blinking too fast.

She knew that voice. That *girl's* voice.

"We both happened," the voice repeated. "Me and Phil. It's our fault."

Tessa turned around and saw Mariella Morse.

She was holding a hatchet.

CHAPTER TWENTY-TWO

MARIELLA

When Mariella Morse spied Tessa Gomez idling in a car outside of her house yesterday, she knew it was over. Not that she thought Tessa had figured it out. What rational mind could fit together the warped, jagged puzzle pieces strewn about her parents' bloody bedroom that night?

No, Mariella simply knew the lies were too big.

She'd had enough.

Only she kept that thought to herself, locked in a trunk and tucked so far back in her mind, even she didn't dare hint at its existence. Mariella carried on.

She woke up this morning in the house where her parents had met their gory ends and made herself coffee. She didn't shower. Her face was greasy, and her teeth were fuzzy, but the home was clean.

After the police had inspected and searched every inch of her parents' bedroom, every drop of their blood analyzed and photographed, they declared the scene closed. Dead.

Her family's routine cleaning staff showed up at their regularly scheduled time and determined that the gruesome job was too overwhelming for their capabilities. They hired specialists. A team in lemon-yellow hazmat suits arrived, and Mariella transferred whatever funds were needed.

It was her money now. That was what the accountant said. And soon she'd be declared legally an adult, according to her lawyer. She had one now. Phil was right—it was the guy who'd sent the email about her trust. But that didn't matter anymore. Mariella now had more money than she could ever spend, and no family to share it with. Someone was trying to locate her mom's long-lost sister, but so far, no luck. She might be dead too.

Instead, Mariella received an influx of phone calls and visits from lawyers, estate planners, financial advisors, the new acting chairman of the board of her father's largest company, and her dad's college roommate—whose wife filled the freezer with lasagna and soup. There were text messages from the lady who did her mom's nails on Fridays, the guy who mowed their lawn, and everyone Mariella had ever gone to school with. The principal and all her teachers emailed, "Take as much time as you need." Old Mrs. Churchill from next door stopped by, and the mailman left a condolence card.

Flower arrangements piled on the front porch, alongside the ominous woodpile. God, had she even noticed the axe before? It was in an evidence locker somewhere downtown. Disturbingly, a new, much smaller, hatchet was put in its place, by the home's maintenance crew, in case Mariella ever wanted to light one of the home's original historic fireplaces. *Yeah, let's get cozy with a cup of cocoa.*

Mariella never answered the door; there were too many reporters and a few were clever enough to pose as pizza and floral delivery drivers. That was when someone hired security. It might have been the college roommate. Within twenty-four hours of the camera crews arriving, men were stationed on the front lawn to make sure no one stepped too far. Josephine, the member of the cleaning staff who had hired the hazmat team, hardly left. She busied herself doing Mariella's dishes and washing her clothes, but it seemed she was really there to keep an eye on her.

Everyone was worried Mariella might do something harmful. This wasn't conjecture. They said it to her face. Even the accountant. *Are you okay? Do you have anyone to talk to? I have a great therapist . . .*

Mariella assumed she didn't look well. But how was someone supposed to look in this situation? From their points of view, both her parents had been axed to death by her boyfriend. That alone was reason to be holed up behind locked doors with dark circles under her eyes and grease building in her hair.

But if they only knew the truth . . .

No, no, no. Like she said, Mariella kept those thoughts locked away.

She couldn't let *him* hear.

Phil wasn't whispering to her anymore. He'd tried that the first night, while the police were trampling about, bombarding her with questions. The whispers, or more specifically Phil, coached her on what to say, how to act, and when to cry. He stuck around in her mind the next day, trying to tell her it would all be okay. *There, there.* She'd make it out of this all right. She just needed to *trust* him.

His voice, his whispers, made her nauseated. Literally. She couldn't eat. Her hatred for the boy who had been raised alongside her blackened her insides and consumed the hateful abyss once held by her father.

Mariella wanted Phil gone.

So she clamped noise-cancelling headphones over her ears and blared a steady stream of death metal. Eventually, Phil slunk away, but she knew he was still there, burrowing through her brain matter and twining around her soul like—what did he call them?—invasives. His shadow likely still watched her sleep, but he no longer made himself known. He probably thought he was being magnanimous by giving her silence. But she knew he was lurking. He always would be. Forever.

His prisoner.

Mariella made no conscious plan. She couldn't. If she'd made a decision, if she put steps into motion, Phil would know. Instead, she waited. She figured the only thing on her side was spontaneity. Mariella couldn't think about doing anything. She just had to do it.

Then she felt him enter the Freetown State Forest. Mariella wasn't sure how. She guessed that since she was connected to him, and they were both connected to the woods, then when one of them got close to the source, the other one felt it. She really wasn't sure.

It was a new sensation, a little tingle walking on tippy toes down her spine, the kind that made you shiver, but a good shiver. The trees, the vines, the moldy fungus, the swamp—it all welcomed Phil back. With vengeance. And she was betting that he had no idea the cord that bound them together was tied on both ends; he didn't know she could feel his presence in those haunted woods. Because if he was in her mind when she grabbed the new hatchet off her porch, if he sensed her picking up the keys to her father's BMW and driving (without a license) toward the swamp, he didn't let out a whisper.

No, Phil was too busy. Distracted. He was with Tessa and whoever the boy was she'd brought with her for some reason. Mariella knew Phil didn't like him. She didn't need a creepy supernatural connection to feel that.

And they were easy to find. It was as though something, somewhere, wanted Mariella in this wretched place. A dark something. Mariella was drawn to the spot. The vines stretched to greet her as she slipped by, petting her skin and waving hello. *You're home, child. Come in. HE's waiting, and he's angry . . .*

The hatchet might have been smaller, but it felt like an old friend. Her muscles remembered that swing, and it was time for Phil's plan to swing right back on him.

Mariella's eyes adjusted to the dark, almost too easily, allowing her to spy skinny Tessa Gomez drowning Phil Barker in a few inches of cloudy water. Liquid gargled in his lungs and sputtered from his lips, and Mariella swore she could taste the earthy sediment on her own tongue. She could smell the fear in Phil's sweat. She could sense the rage in Tessa's heart.

Branches, plants, hell, even the moonlight, seemed to lean longingly toward Tessa, offering encouragement as she yanked Phil's face in and out of the blackened swamp. The forest had been used, just like Mariella. Just like Vik. And a ferocious reprisal was now mounting.

Flickering shadows leached, spiny fingers stretching and grabbing for pieces of . . . Phil.

Couldn't anyone else see it? A fantastical heavy presence was leaking around them, from not just one spirit or one ghost. Something big and beautiful was converging. Pulsing.

Mariella couldn't have looked away if she'd wanted to, and she didn't want to; this was the show she had come to see.

"Tell me what happened!" Tessa's yell ricocheted off the tree bark, her fist in Phil's hair. She was totally in control and winning this round.

Well done.

"I happened." Mariella stepped forward, and into the beam of a cell phone light being held by whoever that new boy was. Mariella dangled the hatchet, light glinting off its blade. She wanted Phil to see it and feel the magnitude of this final moment. "We both happened," she explained. "Me and Phil. It's our fault."

"Mariella?" Tessa gasped, with shocked innocence. She really didn't have a clue. "What are you doing here?"

"I'm here to see Phil, my best friend forever." Mariella smiled, then licked her lips in anticipation. "Surprised to find you guys, though. Phil, I thought you were afraid of the swamp?"

Mariella approached, hiking boots sinking into inches of pine needles upon sodden leaves upon mucky fluid. Thin trees with chipped white bark poked all around them in a vast dank wilderness, and the air reeked so richly of mold Mariella could scrape it off the inside of her cheeks.

"Don't . . . do anything stupid." Phil's rasp was wet as he coughed, then spat a wad of dark gunk.

"Stupid?" Mariella arched her brow, twirling the hatchet in the light of the half-moon. It wasn't the same weapon from that deadly night, but the petite new edge really gleamed. "Seems like you went from boiling a few leaves to drinking straight from the source. I mean, if anyone's stupid . . ."

"What are you talking about? Does this have something to do with that thermos?" Tessa's head bounced back and forth between Mariella and Phil.

"Oh, so you have figured some of it out. Good for you." Mariella meant it. "Phil is quite proud of his hard work."

She watched him stagger, a black frothy brew hacking through his pained lips from a neck so strained, she could strum his tendons. A burn blazed down her esophagus; it was coming from him. She was feeling his pain. Only to her, it was a welcome sensation. She wanted more. She wanted this fake friend, this false brother, gone from her mind and from this world.

"What's the matter, Phil? Need a drink?" Mariella inched closer, slopping into a mound of soggy leaves. She rocked the hatchet his way. "Should I get you some tea?" Her head swung toward Tessa, her long blond hair whipping over her shoulder. Funny, she wasn't even sweating. "You didn't drink it, did you?"

"No." Tessa shook her head.

Score one for the new girl.

"Stop," Phil ordered. A command. A whisper. Inside her skull.

Mariella felt it: the authority he held over her life, the choices he stole the night she swung that axe. Only it didn't stop her. Mariella kept moving, squelching in the sludge that froze her toes and stiffened her joints. Her movements remained her own, and her mind didn't even buzz.

"Huh." She grinned, looking Phil dead in his cloudy gray eyes. "Doesn't seem to be working anymore. Maybe it's all that swamp water you just gulped. You said so yourself, thousands of people died here. Now that darkness is inside you. Can you feel it? *'Cause they feel you . . .*" Her voice singsonged.

"Can someone tell us what the hell is going on?" asked the random guy.

Mariella's head shot toward him. His hand was intertwined with Tessa's. *Interesting.* Vik had said that his sister had a boy-friend back in Philly, and that was why she was stringing Phil along all those months.

I wonder . . .

"Are you the long-lost love?" Mariella gave him a side-long look.

"What?" The boy pursed his lips.

"This is Oscar. From back home," Tessa explained.

Mariella looked at Phil with a teasing expression. "That must've really ticked you off." She let out a chuckle. "Having a bad night, Phil? Trust me, I know how that feels. I watched my mom bleed out, remember?"

"Mariella." Tessa's voice was cautious. "You said *you* happened that night. You and Phil. What did you mean?"

"I meant—" Mariella sucked a breath between her teeth, inhaling the wicked bite in the air, until her brain filled with a nice buzz. Ah, that was better. She needed that feeling if she was going to continue. And what was a little more Bridgewater Triangle infection at this point? "Your brother shouldn't be the one in jail."

Tessa and her boy gasped in unison. *How cute.*

"What are you talking about? What do you know?" Tessa asked hopefully, sounding breathless.

Don't breathe in too hard, sweetie. It's these woods.

"Everything," said Mariella, catching a shadow prowling low to the earth. She squinted, straining in the blackness, tracking the agile form. There were so many silhouettes. Yes, something was waking up. The eyes—all those eyes—that had always stalked her, they were here. "I know it goes against my image, but my life was shit. My dad . . . let's just say he wasn't a good person. Your brother didn't know. But Phil did." She swiveled his way. Was it the light, or were Phil's eyes growing stormier? Yes, it was happening. To him. "Phil was there for all of it. He helped me through some of it. He was my chosen family and I trusted him, until he poisoned me, with tea. Somehow it let him control me—you sick, twisted, freak. Then I poisoned your brother."

"You *what?*" Tessa shouted, more of a yelp, and the boyfriend grabbed her arm, holding her back.

"Believe me, I'm not the one you should be pissed at." Mariella was here for only one person. Her foot slurped, then the twigs, leaves, maybe even the universe, parted to make room as she slogged closer to Phil.

Phil watched her approach, but didn't move. Maybe he couldn't. The shadows—honestly, did no one else see this?—were practically piling on top of Phil's head. They clung and mauled, distinct smudges lit by the pinholes of stars. Mariella lifted the hatchet, then placed the edge flat against Phil's smooth face. He didn't jerk away. And while it was hard to tell in the staticky gloom, she swore she saw the outline of a black claw gripping Phil's chin and holding him still. For her.

Mariella scraped the steely edge teasingly against his skin.

"Don't!" Tessa screamed. "I don't know what's going on with you, but you can't! You're the only one who knows the truth. Stop!"

Mariella halted the blade's motion against Phil's cheek, and their breathing synced. Their minds tangled. *Can you hear me, Phil? It's my turn to come for* you. His swollen gray pupils jittered with fear. Desperation.

Good.

"You're a gross, demented pervert. I can't believe I ever trusted you. I can't believe I ever thought you were my friend. All those years, and you betrayed me. You killed my mother. My *mother!*" She pressed on the shiny tooth—not too hard, just enough that he knew she could. Crimson trickled a tear track toward his chin. Fear raged in his eyes. Perfect. She wanted him to feel what she had every time that shadow came into her room and she couldn't move, she couldn't scream, and she couldn't stop it. She wanted him to sense the confusion she'd suffered when she'd swung that axe at her father. She wanted him to experience the agony that had demolished her while she watched her mother bleed.

And she wanted him to scream as she had when Vik awoke and saw what he had unwillingly done. "This is the end. You feel it, right?" Mariella slid the sharp tip down Phil's already-bleeding flesh, giving a nice slice. His breath hitched almost musically as the garnet stream flowed, off his jaw and into the ancient water below. Phil's life would soon be yet another spirit dwelling here.

"You will never control me again." Mariella spoke with her lips only inches from his face, her blue eyes locked on his panicked gray gaze. "No man will ever control me again. You will pay for what you did, to my mom, to Vik, and to me. This forest will make you pay. God, I'm starting to really love this place." She smiled at the silhouettes slowly engulfing them. The ethereal beings were closing in, all those shadows she'd seen *that* night, with Vik, they weren't human. Maybe they once had been, but they weren't now. They were vengeance personified. Phil followed her stare. Yes, he could see them too. He knew what was coming. For him, and him alone. He'd started this. It was his plan. His tea. He'd used these creatures. "What happens to you, here, tonight, it's exactly what you deserve, bestie."

"Mariella Morse! Drop your weapon!" a female voice shouted with heavy authority.

Mariella turned and spied a woman standing a few yards back. She had a gun, and it was pointed directly at Mariella's head.

CHAPTER TWENTY-THREE

TESSA

Omigod, omigod, omigod! Mariella Morse is in the woods and wielding an actual axe!

Of course, moments ago, Tessa was also drowning Phil Barker in a swamp. But this was different. Mariella wasn't just murderous right now, she had sort of confessed to actual homicides—of her parents.

"Wait, that's Vik's girlfriend?" Oscar whispered in her ear, his tone full of disbelief. Tessa didn't know what to say.

"Physically, yes, that's her," Tessa answered.

Mariella's blond hair was greasier, her skin was sallower, but that was the dull shell of Vik's girlfriend. Whatever was happening inside her, though, that was completely unfamiliar.

"Seems sweet," Oscar muttered, his sarcasm rich, as they watched blood swim down Phil's face.

Was it Tessa's eyes, or had the scene gotten darker? She glanced up at the tree canopy, dense as a fortress, yet somehow shadows were looming. Obstructing. Her eyes formed an impossibly tight squint as she struggled to make out Phil's shape in the blackness. Nearby, branches seemed to be gliding. Shifting. With almost human movements.

No, those weren't the trees.

Tessa gripped Oscar tighter.

"Mariella Morse! Drop your weapon!" A female voice boomed from the trail behind them.

Tessa immediately knew who it was. She spun around. "Detective Ertz!" she screeched before anyone could stop her.

Her text had gone through!

Mariella was confessing.

The detective would hear her.

Vik would be free.

"We're over here!" Tessa waved her cell phone light like a flare.

The detective emerged through a tangle of bushes, with no backup behind her. Her arms were straight, and she gripped the gun in her hands. It was pointed at Mariella's head.

"Don't shoot!" Tessa cried. There was no way they were going to get this close to exonerating her brother only to have a gun go off and kill the one person who could set him free.

"Tessa, what is going on here?" The detective's voice was low and measured.

"I'm not exactly sure," Tessa said.

"Mariella Morse, I'm not gonna say this again. Drop. Your. Axe," the detective ordered.

Mariella lowered her arm, releasing the bloody hatchet into the swamp. "You're too late."

"For what?" Ertz asked, stealing the words from the tip of Tessa's tongue.

"To stop this. Can't you feel it? They're coming." Mariella lifted her arms toward the heavens. Then her blue eyes caught the moonlight, and her gaze looked . . . vacant. Tessa gasped at the lack of life left inside this girl, who up until a week ago she would have described as having the bubbly shine of Miss Fall River.

"Mariella, I'm gonna need you to step away from Mr. Barker," Ertz instructed.

"Gladly." Mariella sloshed forward, her boots—huh, Mariella did own hiking boots—gurgling in the noxious swamp, twigs and vines seemingly shifting to make way.

"Mariella, don't! Help me," Phil squeaked, his arm struggling to lift and reach as his shoulders jerked back. His torso writhed. Something was constraining his body. But what? Tessa could barely make out his silhouette, his figure obscured in a shadow so massive, no moonlight touched his skin.

"You're on your own now, *brother.*" Mariella said the last word like a curse.

"Mariella, what happened that night? With your parents? With Vik?" Tessa pointed her cell phone light at the girl she'd eaten lunch with almost every day for a year, and then she hit record.

Mariella looked between Tessa and Ertz, then shrugged with an *Oh well* gesture. She seemed so blasé. So content. "Phil thought

I wouldn't have any options. That he'd be able to control me for the rest of my life." She angled back to look at him. He was struggling to free his foot from where it was caught in a branch. Or was the branch squeezing him tighter? The night was playing tricks. "But I *do* have choices. I can confess."

"Confess to what?" Ertz asked.

Mariella turned directly toward Tessa's phone and she—swear to God—smiled for the camera. "Phillip Barker created a poison made out of plants found in *these* woods." She swung her hands around the crop of trees. "He said it was a potion, some recipe he found in an old book belonging to one of my ancestors. I freakin' believed every word he told me. I was so desperate, I would have tried anything. I drank it."

"What did it do?" Ertz prodded.

"It was supposed to solve all my problems, grant me some superpowers that could stop my dickhead father. But really, it just messed with my head. It made me hear voices." She arched her brow at the camera as if she were oversimplifying. "It made me want to not just stop my dad but kill him."

"Mariella Morse, did you kill your parents?" the cop asked with deliberate language.

A rumble rose in the air, the sound of a train emerging once more, barreling too fast to stop at the station. It came with the wind.

No. Not now. Tessa gnashed her teeth.

But Mariella continued, her voice elevated, ensuring she was heard above the wailing winds. "Even with how much I hated my father, I couldn't do it. Not myself. Then, one day, an idea just whispered inside my brain—that Vik could do it for me."

"What?" Tessa spat, nearly dropping her phone as she reflexively lunged toward Mariella. Oscar grabbed her elbow, tugging her back. A vine caught her ankle.

"Stay where you are," Ertz ordered, gun still drawn, eyes flicking to Tessa before shifting right back to Mariella. "Go on," Ertz shouted over a gust of wind.

"The poison . . . Vik drank it, only it had a different effect on him." Mariella's words seemed to echo, lifting with the gales. Her hair fluttered, and pressure built, the wind intensifying, whistling through the branches.

Tessa rocked back a step, struggling in the sudden storm.

"Your brother became catatonic," Mariella bellowed.

"Don't!" Phil howled, then his head snapped back as if someone had gripped his hair and violently tugged. Only no one was there. Tessa scanned the swamp water, the cracks between the trees, but all she saw were shadows.

The gusts thundered harder, leaves and twigs spinning and smashing. Tessa kept her phone pointed.

"To say Vik was drugged would be an understatement." Mariella looked directly at Tessa, not the camera, as she said this. "He was a robot, lacking any control. It was like he wasn't inside himself anymore. That's why he has no memories."

"Did Victor Gomez kill your parents?" asked Detective Ertz.

"You're not hearing me," Mariella snapped.

A gale blew so forcefully then, Tessa slammed into Oscar, and he bear-hugged a nearby tree trunk to keep them upright. Ertz lowered her weapon, her elbow bent in front of her face to block the particles careening their way.

"Victor Gomez was drugged by Phillip Barker. Vik was set up. It was *Phil* who killed my mother. It was *all* him. Phil's idea. His plan. *Phil* is the one responsible for my mother's death."

Wind sent the strands of Mariella's long golden hair splaying out like arms beckoning the forest to take her, welcome her. She looked almost gleeful.

"Mariella," the detective shouted above the commotion. "If Phil killed your mother, who killed your father?"

Mariella's head jerked toward the detective with otherworldly speed. And the gusts quieted so abruptly, Tessa jolted, slipping in the muck.

Leaves fell to the blackened soil.

Branches stopped shifting.

The air grew weighty.

Then a crack sounded from the maddening stillness. Somewhere sticks were breaking, crunching under feet, but all Tessa saw was darkness. Shadows.

"I did," Mariella confessed.

Phil let out a squeal. Pain. An animal caught in a bear trap. Tessa couldn't see him, not with the shadows seeping from the tall trunks and the grit in her eyes. But she felt the horror in Phil's cries. Another scream ripped hideously from his chest.

"I was infected by Phil's poison. Still am," Mariella continued. "So I'm not even sure if it was me, or what happened exactly, but my body swung the axe. Just once. I killed my father. And he deserved it."

The orbs of light returned, splashing haunting colors through the sky once more. Oily lime green and turquoise strobes pulsed above the towering tree line that separated the cursed forest from the never-ending expanse of stars. For the first time in what felt like a long time, Tessa saw Phil clearly. Only she couldn't keep her arm, her camera, extended against a sudden burst of wind. Her hands dropped to her sides, and she stumbled back. She watched as vines wrapped around Phil's wrists and ankles, his body flung back and drawn tight, a medieval victim about to be quartered and beheaded.

The shadows waved and skittered, bleeding with a burning, sinister awareness. This was a darkness that held shape, density, and intelligence, and it was clawing at the boy Tessa used to consider more than a friend.

Phil's chest was hoisted upright by the fabric of his shirt, suspended only by air. Or spirits. Phil looked ahead, directly at something, at whatever controlled him. Then Phil's head jerked back, neck taut, face angled toward the piercing half-light of the moon as his scream devoured the forest. Detective Ertz fired her weapon, not at Phil, but at the vines that held him prisoner. She was trying to hit the plants that tangled with Phil's body, writhing in pain. She was trying to free him. But from what?

Tessa's mouth was dry with fear. She couldn't speak. She couldn't spit. She didn't even think she could cry.

"I'm sorry! I'm sorry for what I did! To you! To your parents. To Vik!" Phil wailed. "Stop! Please stop!"

A breeze lifted Mariella's hair in a way that almost seemed pleasant. She grinned. "What's the matter, Phil? Hearing voices?"

The agonizing sound that rose from his chest was not human. Then he released another and another.

"I wonder what's inside you." Mariella's voice cut through the whipping wind. "Looks like it hurts."

Detective Ertz discharged her weapon once more, and the bullet hit the vine wrapped around Phil's left wrist, but it bounced off. The bullet didn't make a dent, let alone break the spiny plant. The bondage seemed only to tighten.

Detective Ertz fired again. At nothing. She knew the legends. She had suspected *something* from that very first day at the station. But now she was aimlessly firing a gun at supernatural shadows, because this couldn't be real.

Oscar squeezed Tessa's hand, pulling her closer. She dropped her phone in her pocket, afraid to lose it. Then she hugged Oscar as though she were gripping on to her own sanity.

"I'm one of you!" Phil shouted, with what sounded like his last breaths. "The Morses were horrible people. I thought you'd want them dead! I want to show the world you exist. Stop, please, stop!"

"Did you really think *you* could control all these forces?" Mariella's voice was flippant.

"I did what you wanted," he cried into the face of *something*. Nothing.

But it was Mariella who replied. "No, Phil, you did what *you* wanted."

The wind spiraled into a tornado of twigs and leaves, Phil

thrashing at its center. Shrubs ripped from their roots. Bits of dry grit pelted Tessa's face, and the stench of decaying death slid down her barren throat.

But Tessa didn't look away. She needed to see. She squinted through almost-closed lashes, as neon strobes danced, lighting Phil's lanky body enough to catch the vines that confined him. His limbs were cranked way too far. Then a singular shadow stretched halfway up the nearest oak, feeding off the forest, the moon, the air. Its massive form blocked out every star that speckled the sky. The world was black. Black, black, black. Phil's cry lifted high in the air, floating above the trees, until it whistled down like a bomb hitting its mark. It was a long drawn-out hiss, far too long, and it cut off with a splash and a wet, pounding thud.

Tessa flinched, covering her head, expecting debris, tree branches, and spraying water to hit her cowering figure. Only there was nothing.

Just stillness. A grave silence throbbed with her heart.

It's done, a voice whispered in her ear. The same voice.

Tessa pried open her eyes.

The moon gleamed, its light glittering into the eerie hush of the swamp.

Phil was gone.

Tessa could see the swamp clearly in the moonlight. There was no body. Anywhere. The surface of the muck didn't ripple or bubble.

Whatever had crashed down into that mire, into that final darkness, took Phil with it.

The shadows were gone.
The wind had ceased.
The vines were just vines.
The branches were branches.
And once again, they were alone in the woods.

CHAPTER TWENTY-FOUR

MARIELLA

It was so quiet. For a moment, Mariella swore she could hear seeds exploding beneath the soil and vines creeping toward the moon. The wind idled, dry leaves plummeting back to earth. But Mariella wasn't shocked merely by the still night air. No, she was rocked by the silence *inside her mind*.

No voices were present.

No whispers. No scratching. No bugs beneath her skin. No hot, blistery feel of someone, something, worming parasitically into her organs.

Mariella was alone. She could *feel* it.

And Tessa Gomez, her random ex-boyfriend, and a cop Mariella kind of remembered from the night of the murders were all staring at her.

"What the hell just happened?" the boy asked.

"I have no idea," Tessa replied.

"What are we gonna tell people?" he pressed.

"That Vik is innocent!" Tessa blurted, excitement in her eyes. It was nice someone was happy. "Screw the rest of it. Vik was set up! He didn't kill anyone!"

Mariella smiled, her shoulders relaxing blissfully away from her ears. Let them believe that. It was the least she could do for Vik.

Mariella gazed at the starlight; the orbs of neon were extinguished. She didn't see a single shadow hunting or tree oddly shifting. Phil was gone.

And Mariella's chest was so much lighter. She could breathe.

Forget everything Phil said about these woods and the Bridgewater Triangle infecting the local air with sinister energy. Because right now, when Mariella inhaled deeply, she simply felt . . . at peace.

"W-where is he?" Bewilderment clogged the cop's voice as she eyed Mariella. "Those were just stories, legends. They're not real. What . . . what was all that?"

"Do you really wanna know?" Mariella may have sounded flippant, but she meant it sincerely.

A pause hung, then the cop marched forward, firmly clearing her throat.

"Mariella Morse, you're under arrest." She was trying to regain control with an authoritative tone. *Good luck with that.* The woman didn't wear a police uniform nor show a badge, but Mariella wasn't going to fight her on it. She had confessed for a reason. Mariella had secretly weighed her options and determined the legal system was better than Phil. At least in court, Mariella had a chance at life.

Her eyes stretched, and her vision sharpened as she took in the midnight sky above the wilderness, the air crisp with the winds of autumn. So cool and fresh.

She turned to Tessa. "It's over." Mariella sighed with relief.

"Looks like it is." Tessa cocked her head, her gaze edgy as she tried to comprehend Mariella's expression.

Of course, she couldn't understand. No one could.

Actually, there might be one person.

"You have to go see Vik." Mariella tried to move closer to Tessa, but the cop tugged her back by her wrists, now locked in silver cuffs. Another leash. Always a leash. "You have to ask him if it's quieter."

"If what's quieter?" Confusion marred Tessa's face.

"His mind. The whispers. The taste in his mouth. All of it." Mariella grinned even wider, then licked her teeth, which felt fresh-from-the-dentist. "He's gone."

"W-we're gonna need a search party," the cop stammered, barking into a walkie-talkie or a cell phone; Mariella couldn't see behind her. "Phillip Barker, senior at Fall River High School, he . . . he confessed to murder. So has Mariella Morse. I have her in custody now, but Barker has . . . disappeared. Possible drowning. I'm . . . I'm not sure. We're at Hockomock Swamp. I'll send a pin."

Phil hadn't drowned, but he *was* dead. Mariella knew that, because the whispers had died with him. The shadow that crept into her nightmares, those slitted crimson eyes, those talons raking her body—it was over.

"Tell Vik I'm sorry." Mariella's voice was as light as the fall-scented air. Did it always smell like apples? Honeycrisp or maybe

Gala. "He's a really good guy, and it'll be okay. I promise. I won't stick around."

Tessa blinked. "No shit. You're going to jail. Then probably hell."

Mariella shrugged. "I was already there."

The cop yanked Mariella's wrists, and they slurp-shuffled from the swamp waters until they reached the hiking trail and whatever came next. Mariella wiggled her wrists in the cuffs.

She felt free.

⌒⊙

TESSA

Tessa had never run up the staircase to her apartment so fast in her life. By the time the police let them go, it was so late, there weren't even any reporters on the sidewalk. Tessa *needed* to deliver the news first.

Her soaked sneakers slid, pounding on the metal treads. There was no yellow light under the seam of her apartment door. Everyone was sleeping.

She fumbled for the key—the hall light had been out for weeks—and she heard Oscar's footsteps hobbling up the staircase behind her, his knee in a temporary brace fitted by the paramedics. He refused the ambulance, insisting Tessa could take him to the hospital tomorrow. An MRI could wait. He wanted to be here for this moment. He wanted to see.

Tessa slid her key into the lock and hauled open the door so quickly, she was surprised the hinges stayed screwed.

"Mom!" she shouted, her voice on the verge of laughter.

She spied her tío Ricardo spread out on the faded blue recliner in the living room, a yellow crocheted afghan sprawled across his legs. Oscar's mom startled upright on the sofa, tossing the fuzzy red blanket from her hips. Frankie groaned, rolling over on her pillow on the floor. She and Tía Dolores had given up their bed to Tessa's abuela, and Tía Dolores was now cuddled with Tessa's mom.

"Mom! Everyone! Wake up! Wake! *Up!*" Tessa clapped her hands in time with the words.

Her fingers reached for the nearby wall, searching for a switch and finally flicking on the recessed bulbs. Amber brightness blasted through the nighttime space. Bleary eyes squinted and voices moaned.

"What? What happened?" Tío Ricardo jumped to his feet, abruptly alert and ready to run.

"It's over!" Tessa hollered, arms spread wide with excitement. Oscar stumbled into the entryway behind her.

Bedroom doors cracked. Tessa's mother, her tía Dolores, and her abuela slowly wobbled out.

Tessa darted to them, her disgustingly wet sneakers thwacking on the parquet wood floors. She grabbed both of her mother's hands, clasping them tightly between her own. "Mom, she confessed. Mariella Morse confessed!" Tessa twisted, trying to look at all of her relatives at the same time, her entire family gathered in a football huddle.

"Mariella killed her father!" Tessa yelped. "Phillip Barker, my . . . some guy I know, drugged Vik. And Mariella! With something, I dunno. But Vik was out of his mind, that's why he doesn't remember anything! Phil did it. He set up Vik, and he didn't deny it. Now he's missing, probably dead, but whatever. We still have Mariella's testimony saying *she and Phil* did it. Not Vik!"

"Dios mío." Mom put her hand on her chest, slumping back, but Tía Dolores caught her before she fainted.

"Teresa, are you sure?" Tío Ricardo clamped her shoulder, then spun her his way. "Can you prove this?"

Tessa's smile was ready to burst off her face. "I have it all on video. I gave it to the police. Mariella confessed! And that detective was there! She heard *everything*!"

"Detective Ertz?" Frankie already had her phone pressed to her ear, no doubt calling the police station, her colleagues, and a judge all at once. "What about her partner? Fitzgerald?"

"Just her." Tessa shrugged, realizing how differently this might have turned out if a different cop were assigned, one who didn't know the local history or wouldn't show up when Tessa called. The world wasn't always quick to believe teenage girls, especially one with a name like Gomez.

"Man, her captain's gonna be pissed . . ." Frankie hummed.

Tessa turned to her mother, grabbing her shoulders. "Ma, it's over. Vik's gonna be free."

Tessa didn't fail him or run away. Tragedy struck, and she dealt with it.

A peace came over Tessa that she hadn't felt in a long time, as her mom threw her arms around her and whispered in her ear.

EPILOGUE

One year later . . .

VIK

Vik sniffed his rumpled jeans, then grimaced from the stench. He tossed them into the mesh laundry bag that held his entire wardrobe, which he'd just cleaned from his dorm room floor. His sister was visiting.

He checked his closet's tiny mirror, which was tacked on with puffy white double-sided tape. He'd gotten a haircut for this. And he'd changed not only his own bedsheets but also his room-mate's. Jon was staying at his girlfriend's off-campus apartment all weekend, so Vik could give Tessa his extra-long twin bed. Vik would be sleeping in Jon's bed, and he'd be trying hard not to think about what Jon and Ashley did whenever Vik got a text that read: *Don't come back for an hour.*

He snatched a box of Cinnamon Toast Crunch off the window-sill and grabbed a plastic bowl that was cleanish, then took a whiff of the milk in the mini-fridge. The sell-by date was yesterday. It was fine. He poured himself breakfast, then sat at his desk, knee bouncing anxiously, a fidgety habit that drove his roommate crazy.

He hadn't been able to sit still for a long time.

Mariella's face flashed in his brain; she was wearing that smile that was only for him, her blue eyes extra twinkly. He shoved it down. Again.

Mariella was always there, waiting to spring from his subconscious. Why couldn't he forget her? That look on her face the last day in the courtroom, it had been so remorseful, and even worse, tender. Mariella and Detective Ertz had told the judge that Vik had been poisoned. The organic toxin caused amnesia that allowed Mariella and her longtime friend Phillip Barker to "frame" Vik for the murders of her parents. Mariella said they did it for money, and because her dad was an abusive dick.

The whole truth was never mentioned in any legal filings— the whispers, the rank tastes on their tongues, or the cursed Freetown–Fall River State Forest. That couldn't be admitted into evidence. What Detective Ertz had, solidly, was Mariella's confession, an ironclad video from Tessa, a lab-tested organic poison from two thermoses located near the Ledge, and a boy (mastermind) whose body had yet to be found and whose family had financial reason to want the Morses dead. The cops had drained the swamp and searched the woods, but there was no trace of Phil. He was technically still "wanted," but everyone who was present was positive he'd died.

Mariella had been charged with manslaughter; that was it.

She was fully cooperating, promising to testify against Phil (if he was ever captured), and insisting she had acted under duress, given the poison Phil had administered to her. She was also using the battered woman's defense. Vik had no idea. He knew her dad had been a jerk who refused to meet him, but he'd assumed the man was racist or classist. It wasn't until Vik had spied the bruise on Mariella's wrist that night that he suspected something more. If he had known sooner, Vik would have loaded Mariella into his car and not stopped driving until her father was miles and miles behind them. But Vik hadn't been given that option.

Now Mariella was at least attempting to take responsibility, in a white, rich-girl, privileged sort of way. She'd confessed, releasing Vik from prison, then hired a legal team larger and more prestigious than O.J.'s. She'd been out on bail for a year. The press treated her like a Hollywood headline: "Socialite Slays Parents Optioned for Film" and "Murderer Chic—Steal Mariella's Look" and "Abuse Victim? Or Murderer? You Decide." She was also currently plastered on a billboard in Massachusetts for an axe-throwing bar.

Meanwhile, "Axe Killer of Fall River" and "The Male Lizzie Borden" still came up first when you googled "Victor Gomez."

It would be so much easier if he hated her. Vik wanted to; damn, did he want to. He just couldn't stop seeing Mariella's face, smiling sweetly. All the time.

That last day in the courtroom, when Mariella had been guided off the witness stand, her slender wrists in handcuffs, she turned to Vik with azure eyes full of such piercing emotion (he refused to say love). "I'm so sorry. I never meant for any of this to happen. You're the greatest guy I've ever known, and I can't stop thinking about you. I promise, it'll be okay. No whispers." She smiled so wide. "I miss you."

She looked like she wanted him to say it back, and he would have thought she'd lost her sanity if she hadn't seemed so . . . at peace.

Vik shoved his spoon into his mouth and crunched his cereal. He tapped his finger on his phone, anxiously checking it again, waiting for the buzz. Oscar was picking up Tessa from 30th Street Station and dropping her off on Temple's campus. She was spending tonight with Vik and then the next night with Oscar's family. It was fall break.

His knee bopped, rattling his desk and shaking the pens and pencils gathered in his Temple coffee mug. He shoved in more cereal. Then he checked his phone once more.

He needed music. It was too quiet.

He swiped his finger on his screen, then started a playlist, something loud, thumping—Meek Mill.

Vik closed his eyes, nodding to the beat. Mariella's face flashed again.

This time, she was in his car, lounging in the back seat. Her smile was warm and inviting, her hands stretching for his neck, her lips parted.

No. He forced away the memory, and the tingles that went with it.

She had done this to him. She'd sent him to jail. She'd made him drink—his stomach sloshed—her blood. That had come up in the toxicology report.

Vik didn't want to believe it, but blood was in the poison.

The thermoses located at the Ledge, the ones given to Tessa and Oscar, held traces of Phil's DNA. Then Mariella admitted the truth in court: Vik. Drank. Mariella's. Blood.

A vision of her lips on his chest flickered behind his eyelids, and he abruptly stood. He bounced on his toes, shaking his head, trying to force her out. He had to get out of here. He could wait downstairs, outside his dorm, earbuds in, traffic whizzing. That usually worked.

Vik had taken up running. A lot. He was going to do the ten-mile Broad Street Run in May. He found that the more exhausted his body was, the less he thought about unwanted distractions. So he jogged for miles, pumping music in his ears to clear his head; it helped him study, and it helped him forget.

Vik pushed his feet into his sneakers, then slammed the door to his dorm room shut. He didn't bother to lock it. He pounded down the steps—he never took the elevator. He might not have spent much time behind bars—it was two weeks before Frankie could get all the paperwork approved—but it had been enough to convince him to avoid confined spaces. Vik was lucky. There were people locked up all around the country for crimes they didn't commit, but they didn't have the resources to fight or to even cover their bail. Vik had had Francisca Abreu defend him for free. He'd had friends and family risk their lives to confront the real perpetrators (in some freaky-ass woods!).

Fourteen days behind bars. That was it.

But he still broke into a cold sweat any time a door was

shut (or worse, locked) by someone who wasn't him. He needed to maintain control, and he wondered if he would always be like this.

Vik burst through the vestibule doors, the bustling city street welcoming him with smog and horns. Music blasted in his earbuds as he danced back and forth on his toes, shaking his arms like a boxer.

He just needed to wait. He could do that.

He clutched his phone and checked the screen again. No texts. Tessa's train should have arrived, like, thirty minutes ago.

He continued bopping.

It was the longest he had gone without seeing his sister since, well, jail. His family had practically suffocated him this past year. He returned to his classmates and graduated from Fall River High with more than a few sideways glances. But not too many students made snide remarks, at least not to Vik directly. Most acted scared of him, for a night he didn't even remember and for which all charges had been dropped.

Vik had no choice but to take Mariella at her word. He had to believe her version of events, because why would she lie? In court? She said Vik hadn't done it; it was her and Phil.

But sometimes, when his mind was racing or overly tired, he'd glance down at his hands and swear he could see burgundy-black blood splashing toward his face. He could feel the weight of the axe strain his shoulder. He could hear the sounds of slurping and hacking, his muscles twitching. In the darkest part of his mind, the ugliest part of his soul, Vik worried that he really *had* done it, that he'd swung that axe, and that he *was* a murderer. He tried to force his brain to remember, to prove to himself that he was innocent. He *had* to be innocent. Because if he wasn't, it meant someone had been able to poison him and turn him into a violent predator. And if they could do that once, then . . . could they make him do it again?

No, stop it. Vik turned the volume up on his phone, blaring beats in his ears to force out his thoughts.

A black SUV slowed alongside the curb, greeting Vik with a quick beep-beep of its horn and blissfully pulling him from his thought spiral. Tessa and Oscar sat inside, grinning through the windshield. Relief erupted in his heart.

"You made it!" Vik charged toward the passenger door, a smile tugging toward his ears.

As soon as she stepped out, he wrapped his arms around his sister. Tessa smelled like home, dryer sheets from the laundromat mixing with the shampoo from his mom's salon.

He'd considered going to school in Massachusetts, some-where closer to them, but then he'd also be closer to the story. The Morse name, the crime, it was bigger news in New England than it was in Philly. Vik's roommate had never even heard of him before. He was just another anonymous freshman on a huge city campus. Vik got to start over. And he knew that here, he wouldn't risk seeing *her.*

"Look at you in your Temple T-shirt." Tessa pulled away and eyed the giant red T he was sporting. "I want one!"

"Already waiting for you upstairs." He pointed, then took her duffel bag from her hands. "Hey, Oscar!" He waved through the car window. Cars honked and swerved around his SUV, which was idling and blocking traffic. "We're meeting you later, right?"

"Yeah, I'll see you tonight." Oscar waved, then turned his eyes back toward the road. Another honk.

"Bye, babe." Tessa flicked her wrist, and the look she gave Oscar was so sweet.

Just being near his sister lifted the barbells from Vik's shoulders. She was here. It was okay. Everything was fine.

They trudged through the vestibule doors of his dormitory, and Vik waved a keycard at the guard. City school. Lots of security. Just the way Vik liked it. He was never stepping into a wooded area ever again.

They climbed up the stairs, Tessa's bag on his shoulder; it felt like his sister had packed for a week, not a weekend. That made him smile, the familiarity. "So have you and Oscar talked about next year? You gonna try to go to school together?"

Tessa didn't ask why they skipped the elevator. She knew. "I dunno. I love Oscar *so* much. But we both gotta pick the school that's right for us." She sounded so logical, so responsible, yet so in love. Vik smiled.

"Hey, you guys already have the long-distance thing down pat." He nudged her. "You still thinking journalism?"

"Well, the world could use a few good ones." She gave a knowing look.

If Vik had never dated Mariella Morse, if the murders hadn't put him on the cover of magazines and newspapers, maybe Tessa would be going to school to become an artist, or a kindergarten teacher, or an oceanographer. Sure, she was on the school newspaper before all this happened, but Vik's trauma changed his sister's outlook on the world. It changed his as well.

Vik was currently prelaw. He wanted to work with Frankie one day—pay her back and pay it forward. It seemed an impossible debt to settle, but he wanted to try.

"You okay?" Tessa studied his face.

He nodded, maybe a bit too fast. She could always see beneath the surface, and she was constantly looking for signs that he wasn't broken. Or maybe she was just looking for signs that whatever Mariella and Phil had done to him wasn't permanent.

He didn't hear whispers anymore. There was no more buzzing in his ears or itching below his skin. He was fine, really, he was.

His mind flicked to Mariella lifting the hem of his shirt, yanking it up, and biting her lip.

No. He shook his head, running his fingers through his black hair and forcing himself into the present. He was with his sister. Tessa was here. "I'm good." He shrugged. "Even cleaned for you."

"Well, aren't I lucky?" she said, poking fun. She grabbed his arm, and they moved down the dimly lit hallway. A kid tossed a Nerf football Vik's way. He caught it, then chucked it back.

"Don't hit my sister!" Vik warned.

"Ah, the famous Tessa!" The guy waved. "You coming here next year?"

She shrugged, playing coy, then turned back to Vik. "You all right if I don't follow through with our plan?"

Tessa had already decided Temple wasn't in the cards for her, after all. She thought it was Vik's place and his people. Instead, she was looking at BU, Columbia, Northwestern, and NYU.

"I'd be mad if you did come," he said sweetly. "You gotta be *you*."

He swung open the door of his room, and Tessa dropped her backpack, glancing about. The walls were decorated with sports posters, and the windows offered a view of the city streets. "Wow, Vik." She waved her hands around. "You made it. Dad would be proud."

"Are you kidding? He'd be so proud of *you*."

"You think?" She gave him an uncertain look. "I hope so."

Vik lifted his arms to hug her, but his phone buzzed in his pocket. He stopped and pulled it out. Tessa moved toward the Temple T-shirt folded on his bed, for her, and offered him some privacy. His screen displayed a Google Alert for the name "Mariella Morse." Vik fought to keep his face expressionless. Mariella had attended the opening of a new bar in Boston last night. "Slasher Socialite Spotting," the headline read.

Her blond hair was swept off her long neck, and her expression was mysterious, nearly winking. She wore a silver dress so tiny, you could see every inch of her long legs, toned and lifted in sky-high heels.

Vik flicked off the image before Tessa could see. But it was too late. The picture of Mariella—that seductive gaze, that dress—would linger in his mind for a while. It always did.

I'll see you soon, he thought.

Abruptly, Vik's spine jolted, his eyes narrowing. Where had that idea come from? He wouldn't see Mariella anytime soon. There was no way. Why would he think that?

Then his sister grabbed his arm and pulled him toward the window, wanting to take in the view of the city skyline they both knew so well, where they'd begun the first chapter of their lives.

The next chapter, however, was still just a whisper.

THE TRUTH

Lizzie Borden (1860–1927) was accused of killing her father, Andrew, and her stepmother, Abby, with a hatchet on August 4, 1892, in Fall River, Massachusetts. Her murder trial was a national news sensation, and the rhyme it inspired was sung during Lizzie's lifetime. Lizzie was found not guilty, and the case remains unsolved.

Lizzie's father was a prominent local businessman known for being stingy. Lizzie and her sister, Emma, had an antagonistic relationship with their stepmother.

The morning of the murders, Lizzie's father returned home for a nap. Around 11:15 a.m., Lizzie discovered her father dead in the sitting room, his head struck about ten times with a hatchet. When the police arrived, they discovered that Abby Borden was also dead, upstairs, having been struck eighteen times. Lizzie was thirty-two years old. Her alibi was that she was eating pears in her backyard. Both she and the maid, Bridget Sullivan, claim to have heard nothing.

Lizzie's sister, Emma, was out of town the day of the slayings.

Lizzie's uncle John Morse, her biological mother's brother, had a firm alibi—he could name the horses, the driver, and all the passengers in the horsecar he was riding. He returned to the Borden house while the police were still there, and like Lizzie, John ate pears in the backyard before entering. Abby Borden was murdered in the guest room where John was staying.

It is rumored that Lizzie kept pigeons as pets, and that her father slaughtered them, possibly for food. After the trial, Lizzie and Emma inherited their father's wealth. Lizzie bought a high-end home in the Highlands of Fall River that still stands today, called Maplecroft. Lizzie also became an animal rights activist. To this day, the Animal Rights League of Fall River operates partially from funds bequeathed by Lizzie and Emma. Portraits of the sisters hang in the animal shelter.

The Lizzie Borden Bed & Breakfast is currently operating in the real Borden murder house at 230 2nd Street (lizzie-borden.com).

Despite accusations in various ghost-hunting YouTube and television shows, there is no evidence that Sarah [Morse] Borden, Lizzie's biological mother, or her brother, John Morse, were connected to black magic.

The Bridgewater Triangle comprises two hundred square miles in southeastern Massachusetts, including Fall River and the Freetown–Fall River State Forest. The nickname was coined in 1983 by cryptozoologist Loren Coleman in his book *Mysterious America* due to the area's abnormally high levels of alleged paranormal, demonic, and deadly activity. For centuries, there have been reports of ghosts, UFOs, glowing light orbs, and satanic rituals. In addition, people have claimed sightings of Bigfoot, thunderbirds, and pukwudgies (creatures of Wampanoag folklore that look like furry, three-foot-tall monsters).

The Freetown–Fall River State Forest is a five-thousand-acre forest, with twenty-five miles of hiking trails. *Condé Nast Traveler* named it one of the most haunted forests in the world. The land was originally home to the Wampanoag tribe, and some researchers believe the transfer of land from the Wampanoag to the colonists cursed the area.

The Assonet Ledge is located in the Freetown–Fall River State Forest. The Wampanoag word *assonet* means "place of stones." The ledge stands ninety feet above a former quarry now filled with water. The ghost of a lady in white has frequently been seen jumping to her death at the site. To this day, there are reports of people falling or jumping from the precipice, resulting in death or critical injury. There are no signs warning visitors not to jump.

Dighton Rock is located in Dighton Rock State Park and features etchings, or petroglyphs, of unknown origin. There are carvings of people, symbols, geometric shapes, and animals. Suggestions about who inscribed the drawings include the ancient Phoenicians, Vikings, Native Americans, colonial Portuguese, and even medieval Chinese sailors. The rock was first written about in 1680.

Hockomock Swamp is a 17,000-acre freshwater swamp. It is the largest swamp in Massachusetts and includes a Native American burial ground that dates back thousands of years. The Wampanoag people gave the swamp its name, which means "the place where spirits dwell." The English colonists called it the Devil's Swamp. Some consider the swamp the heart of the Bridgewater Triangle. The swamp was a fortress for Wampanoag chief Metacom (known by colonists as King Philip) and his tribe during their bloody war with the English settlers.

King Philip's War was a rebellion led by Wampanoag chief Metacom (King Philip) against the British colonists in southeastern Massachusetts from 1675 to 1678. It is considered to be the bloodiest war per capita in US history—surpassing the Civil War—and took place primarily in the Bridgewater Triangle. The war ended when Chief Metacom was captured, beheaded, and quartered. His head was displayed on a pike for twenty-five years at the Plymouth Colony. Surviving non-Christian Native Americans were sold into slavery, including Metacom's wife and son. Many historians attribute the dark energy of the Bridgewater Triangle to the Wampanoag massacre.

The Author's Experience: As research for this novel, my husband, Jordan, and I stayed overnight at the Lizzie Borden House, sleeping in the Bridget Sullivan room—the maid's quarters in the attic. We took a very informative murder house tour and listened in on a spooky ghost hunt. I also interviewed the staff, which included a father and son who worked there. In the middle of the night, I shot video of our guestroom in complete darkness. The footage includes an oddly moving and very distinct circular light—was it a ghost orb or dust? You decide.

Additionally, we hiked the Freetown–Fall River State Forest for five miles, venturing to the Assonet Ledge, the pond below, and the deep dirt-bike trenches. We explored the woods for hours, from sunset to nightfall, and during that time, we did not see one bird or hear one tweet. We also did not spot a single squirrel, rabbit, deer, or any other form of wildlife. At all. The air was completely still and disturbingly silent.

Additionally, we hiked through the Hockomock Swamp. While we didn't see any ghosts, we did experience strange activity when we returned home. My Ring Doorbell began sending a barrage of alerts to my phone with no one present at my front entry; there would just be a shift of light on the video. Similarly, the cursor connected to my computer mouse began frequently darting around my screen. I changed the mouse's batteries and I blew on it, but nothing worked. Finally, I said aloud, "If this is a ghost, can you please stop?" It did. Coincidence or a paranormal experience?

There are photos and video of our trip to Fall River, the Lizzie Borden House, and the Freetown–Fall River Forest on my website, dianarodriguezwallach.com.

Please note that I took artistic liberty with the geographic locations depicted in this novel. While the Assonet Ledge, the Hockomock Swamp, and Dighton Rock are all located within the Bridgewater Triangle, they are not as close together as described in this story.

ACKNOWLEDGMENTS

I'd like to start by thanking Lizzie Borden for letting me stay in her childhood home. I hope that wasn't your ghost orb I saw. I'd also like to acknowledge the entire Borden household—Lizzie; her sister, Emma; her father, Andrew; her stepmother, Abby; their maid, Bridget; her biological mother, Sarah; and her uncle John Morse. If they hadn't lived—and died—so tragically, this book would not exist. These were real people whose lives were more than just one horrific day, but the inspiration from those notorious events led to *Hatchet Girls*.

Before writing this novel, I traveled to Fall River and I spoke to many historians. I tried to include as many theories and factual tidbits as I could throughout the book. I'd specifically like to thank Caroline Aubin and Michael Martins of the Fall River Historical Society for opening the museum and offering me a personal tour during its off-season. Mariella's mansion is based on the estate the historical society now occupies, which (just like in the novel) is located in the Highlands and was once owned by the Brayton family. Caroline, your information about the town's revitalized textile mills was particularly useful.

Also, a special thanks to my tour guides at the Lizzie Borden Bed & Breakfast, Jack Sheridan and his son Caleb. I never imagined I'd find a real-life father-son duo working at the B&B to interview! Your insights on what locals think of the Bridgewater Triangle and how blood would splatter if a person was axed to death were incredibly helpful. Jack, your stories as a prior EMT were so applicable, and I love your accent.

The *Fall River Reporter* covered the news of my *Hatchet Girls* book deal as soon as it was announced, and I'd like to thank journalist Ken Paiva for providing me with local information, particularly on the town's Portuguese community, before my trip.

I did my best to represent the criminal justice system, and any mistakes made are my own. But I'd like to thank criminal defense attorney Arik Benari for answering my many legal questions. Vik's first meeting with his family is much more realistic now.

Thank you to my literary agent, Lane Heymont, for your enthusiasm for this project from my very first email. We sold this book with just the first two chapters, and you helped fulfil my dream of publishing a hardcover novel with a Big 5. Thanks for all you continue to do for my career.

We submitted our proposal to Underlined, the imprint that published *Small Town Monsters,* and we were happily surprised to get an offer for a hardcover novel from Delacorte Press as a response. Thank you to the entire team that made that happen, but especially my editor, Ali Romig. This is our second book together, and I love your thoughtful changes. Fans of the Tessa-Oscar-Phil love triangle can thank Ali. I'd also like to thank Wendy Loggia, Beverly Horowitz, Liz Dresner, Cathy Bobak, Tamar Schwartz, Colleen Fellingham, and Tracy Heydweiller.

I'd like to acknowledge my film agents at William Morris Endeavor, Carolina Beltran and Nicole Weinroth. Do you know how cool it is to say I'm repped by WME? You make me feel very Hollywood.

Thank you to author Cynthia Pelayo for reading early pages of *Hatchet Girls* and offering encouragement. A special thanks to Chris Klock for taking all my author photos. You knocked it out of the park with this one; I'm so glad you married my college roommate.

A loving thanks to the friends who have stood by me for decades—the Ridley Girls, my BU roommates, my Spain friends, and everyone who makes my book launch parties so much fun.

Thank you to my in-laws, Larry and Paula Wallach, for volunteering your careful eyes as copyeditors on all of my manuscripts. You excel at catching typos. And thank you to all the Wallachs for your enthusiastic support.

To my Rodriguez family—Lou, Natalie, Mom, and Dad—I appreciate you always cheering me on. When my dad was a patient at the hospital at the University of Pennsylvania, he talked about my books so much, I brought a nurse a copy of *Small Town Monsters*. I know my writing about demons and axe murders creeps you all out (Mom, I don't think you'll want to read this one), but I appreciate your constant belief in me during my publishing journey.

I wrote *Hatchet Girls* during the pandemic, while overwhelmed by obstacles beyond my control. If my husband didn't have so many MGM points, enough to send me on writing retreats to the Borgata Hotel in Atlantic City (twice!), this book would never have been written. Jordan, thank you for watching the kids while I locked myself in a hotel room and got this novel done. (I'd also like to apologize to the Borgata for never leaving my room during that time or placing a single bet in the casino.) Jordan and I met when we were sixteen years old, so in a sense my entire life is an epilogue to a YA novel. Thank you for the happily-ever-after.

I normally thank my kids, Juliet and Lincoln, by saying they are too young to read my books—but that is not the case anymore! A special thanks to my tween, Juliet, for teaching me TikTok dances to promote my novels. I can't wait for you to read this. (Linc, you're still too young.)

This book is dedicated to my sister-in-law Esther Clinton. Esther was married to my husband's oldest brother, Jeremy Wallach, and she died suddenly and far too young. Esther was a professor in the Department of Popular Culture at Bowling Green State University with a PhD in Folklore. I always wished I could have taken her course on heroes, villains, and tricksters in popular culture. Esther was a lover of dragons and heavy metal music, and she married a PhD professor who is a lover of dinosaurs and heavy metal music—a perfect pair. It was said at her funeral that no one is forgotten until their name is said for the last time, so if you are reading this, please google Esther Clinton. Read her scholarly papers and peruse her art and needlework; then say her name and remember that Esther Clinton lived and was very, very loved.

THE TRUTH SOURCES

Aubin, Caroline, assistant site manager at the Fall River Historical Society. In-person interview with the author, March 11, 2022.

Bridgewater Triangle, The. Cadieux, Aaron, and Manny Famolare, directors. 2013.

"The Bridgewater Triangle, Massachusetts's Paranormal Vortex," roadtrippers.com, September 19, 2016.

Encyclopedia Britannica. "Lizzie Borden," britannica.com/biography/Lizzie-Borden-American-murder-suspect.

Fall River. Day, James Buddy, director. Epix. 2021.

Froyd, Madeline. "195 Things: Freetown Ledge Will Take Your Breath Away." *The Herald News,* January 22, 2016.

The Hatchet: A Journal of Lizzie Borden & Victorian Studies, lizzieandrewborden.com.

Martins, Michael, curator at the Fall River Historical Society. Phone interview with the author, March 9, 2022.

Morton, Caitlin. "These Haunted Forests Are As Eerie As It Gets." *Condé Nast Traveler,* October 19, 2021.

"Paranormal Activity Reported in Massachusetts' Bridgewater Triangle," 94.9 WHOM, March 2022.

Robertson, Jake. "How Massachusetts Came to Have Its Own Bermuda Triangle." *Atlas Obscura,* June 13, 2016.

Sheridan, Jack. Sheridan, Caleb, tour guides at the Lizzie Borden Bed & Breakfast. In-person interview with the author, March 12, 2022.

Sudborough, Susannah. "What Is the Bridgewater Triangle Anyway?" *Taunton Daily Gazette,* October 10, 2020.

ABOUT THE AUTHOR

DIANA RODRIGUEZ WALLACH has hopefully never been cursed by a supernatural forest, but she has hiked through one. She is a lover of ghosts, historical murders, and all things spooky. She is also the author of eight YA novels, including her previous YA horror novel *Small Town Monsters*. Additionally, Diana spent four years living in Massachusetts as an undergrad at Boston University, where she gained an appreciation for New England's accent and its many haunted stories. She lives in the Philadelphia area with her husband and two children.

dianarodriguezwallach.com